THE SERVICE OF WOLVES

A VINCE CARVER THRILLER

MATT SLOANE

BLOOD &
TREASURE

Copyright © 2022 by Matt Sloane. All rights reserved.

Published by Blood & Treasure, Los Angeles
First Edition

This is a work of fiction. Any resemblance to reality is coincidental.

No part of this work may be reproduced or distributed without prior written consent by the publisher. This book represents the hard work of the author; please read responsibly.

Cover by James T. Egan of Bookfly Design LLC.

Print ISBN: 978-1-946-00853-4

Matt-Sloane.com

Preface

I'm Matt Sloane, I like great stories, and I hope you do too.

The cool thing about stories is they come in all kinds. Everyone has their opinions and nobody's wrong. (Which must mean I'm right.)

So here's what I like in a story: Smart dialog between characters that feel real. Spurts of action, moments to breathe, and plenty to think about. Complex plots that aren't easy to predict, with realistic twists that don't make your eyes roll. And most of all, a satisfying ending, because you can't cheap out on those.

The Vince Carver books are high action, high intrigue spycraft on the world stage, and I hope they're your kind of story.

If you'd like to get in touch to say hi, offer a correction, talk shop, or otherwise gab, feel free to drop me a line:

matt@matt-sloane.com

Or you can get an email from me every time a book is released at: Matt-Sloane.com

Happy reading,

-Matt

★★★★★ "**Sensational**. A taut thriller that has a great deal more to offer than bullets and brawn."

★★★★★ "The fight scenes are the **best you'll find** in crime fiction."

★★★★★ "Very real and **very very good**."

THE SERVICE OF WOLVES

"If you go out with wolves, they'll teach you to howl."

- *Mexican warning against associating with narcos*

1

A rare and fortunate isolation followed Carver on his run along Coyote Creek Trail. The morning air invigorated his lungs while the cloud cover kept the sun from doing its worst. The scenic beauty of the water was so inviting that he extended his usual distance of five miles, content to exercise in a peaceful trance interrupted only by the occasional errant cyclist and ornery duck.

Carver caught himself twenty minutes past his mark. He slowed but didn't stop, took a gulp from his water bottle, and turned around to resume his pace. By the time he made it back to the bridge over the creek, a pleasant burn sapped every muscle in his body. He had a few ideas for how to cap off such a perfect morning, but meeting CIA Officer Lanelle Williams was not among them.

Under the enclosed metal frame of the pedestrian bridge, Carver slowed to a stop beside the woman and reopened his water bottle. It was a shame, he thought as he watched the creek through the links of the fence. His private paradise had become routine to the point of predictable. He would need to change his habits.

"I'm still mad at you," said Lanelle curtly.

Carver's heavy hand hung on his hip. "Mad-mad or mad-ha-ha?"

"You're not making it better."

He killed off the remaining water in the plastic bottle, crushed it, and screwed the cap shut. He hadn't seen the case officer since his debrief some months ago. It was in her nature to only be around when she needed something, which suited Carver just fine. Theirs was a working relationship.

At least it had been until Carver veered off-script.

"Are you trying to tell me I'm in the doghouse, Laney? Because months of neglect clued me in."

"It can't be helped. A few of my colleagues suspect your indiscretions."

"Only a few? Isn't that a saying, a few can keep a secret?"

"I'm pretty sure that's not right."

Carver crossed his arms and leaned on the fence. "I can't believe anyone's crying over a corrupt Russian oligarch."

"It's not about crying, Vince, it's about exposure, and there's not enough deniability in the world to pretend you didn't cross a red line. What you did was reckless. It could have come back on us."

"Between exploding oil pipelines and misdirected car bombs, there are too many black ops in that corner of the world to keep track of."

"Superyachts going down in the Black Sea don't go unnoticed."

He tried not to shrug his shoulder. "Lucky for us, bigger boats have since joined it at the bottom." The Moskva may have been a military casualty, but the point was Russia had plenty on its plate to worry about already. Settling a private score wouldn't make the cut.

"There's the greater good to think about," offered Lanelle, somewhat opaquely.

"I noticed. From where I sit, Ukraine is still under the gun, and Russian citizens are suffering for their government's greed."

She shook her head like humanity was a lost cause. "The world has gone crazy. Who would have thought Malkin's death would end up little more than a footnote?"

Carver grinned at the characterization. He had said as much to the smug bastard himself. As far as the lack of CIA contact, Carver understood what he had signed up for. Besides, they were quite busy these days. Every intelligence agency in the world was now focused on analyzing ground combat in the modern era. It was wild to see old artillery units paired with new drone technology. The NSA was working overtime for Kyiv as well as keeping tabs on similar prospects in Taipei, both cities Carver had recently visited. He wasn't sure if that made him good or bad luck.

"Long story short," continued Lanelle, "I'm not even supposed to be talking to you right now. Hence this... clandestine ambush in the boonies."

"And I always took you for the outdoorsy type. Although I doubt those flats would make it half a mile."

Her expression withered. "Vince, if you see me running, it's only because I've lost my gun and there's a homicidal clown after me. Are you done being cute or do you need to go a few more laps to burn off the testosterone? I'm here as a courtesy."

This time Carver kept his mouth shut and waved an invitation for her to continue.

"You're a good guy, when you get over yourself," she said, which might have been the most magnanimous thing to ever come out of her mouth. "I know you've got mouths to feed. The problem is no one can touch you with a ten-foot pole right now. So I found you some work outside the Agency."

"I can find private security work on my own. Hollywood's been hounding me for a consulting gig, but I'd rather not pander."

That prospect earned an amused chuckle. "I would love to see that, but it's nothing like that. This is for a three-letter agency—just not the CIA. See, you may be persona non grata right now, but the DEA has it worse in Mexico."

Carver groaned. "The War on Drugs, Laney? Really?"

His pain had the opposite effect of lightening her expression. "I'm aware Mexico isn't as splashy as your last two destinations, but it's real work with genuine national security ramifications. We can't fix the cartels and we can't stop the drugs, but we can shield the government and police from corruption. As you know, it's a dangerous time to be a reporter or politician in Mexico."

"Only if you're honest," he interjected.

"So here I am, keeping my distance from you like a respectable intelligence officer, and a contact in the DEA throws out a feeler. He's a field guy, a real grit and grindstone type who sees rules as suggestions. You'd like him."

Carver ignored the implicit jab. "I get private enterprise in Mexico is booming these days, but my understanding was the DEA kept out of that."

"Your understanding might be outdated, just like the Merida Initiative. Heard of it?"

He nodded. "Financial support by the United States to take on the cartels."

"More than a billion dollars worth over a decade, for aircraft and materiel to engage transnational criminal organizations, to retrain police forces, and to revamp the justice system. And what do we have to show for it? Spiking levels of violence, trafficking, and drug abuse. Kidnappings and homicides are at an all-time high. It turns out American defense contractors received the brunt of that money. The Merida Initiative is dead in the water, with politicians now placing their hopes in the new Bicentennial Framework for Security."

Carver conclusively clapped his hands together. "Problem solved then."

"The problem's not too big with the right allies, but those are few and far between. In 2018, Mexico elected a populist president on promises to combat corruption. This guy threw the three previous presidents under the bus. He overrode the power of local corrupt police forces by creating a National Guard that answers to him."

"Meanwhile we've taken a hard line at the border."

Lanelle nodded. "If this ever was a marriage, there sure

wasn't a honeymoon. The US recently arrested their former secretary of national defense in Los Angeles for drug trafficking. Mexico responded by limiting our federal powers in the country. And when we released their general, they leaked US intelligence anyway, effectively warning the cartels about everything we knew. It was an operational disaster."

"Were agents compromised?"

"No casualties to speak of unless you count their balls being snipped. The DEA's operational capacity in Mexico has been vastly reduced."

"And, due to your recommendation, the Drug Enforcement Agency believes I can be an asset?"

She returned a sly smile. "Testosterone is something the DEA can never have too much of. Unless you're not interested... ?"

Carver showed his teeth. Case officers were expertly trained to wiggle the line just enough to ensure a bite, and Carver was, if nothing else, a shark. "Cut the crap, Williams. What's the job?"

She handed over a business card. "I'll let you hear it from the horse's mouth. I'm not talking to you, remember?"

Special Agent Albert Pineda was printed beside the official DEA seal on cheap card stock. There was handwriting on the reverse side with a time and location.

"Get out of town," urged Williams. "Sit down with him. If you like what you hear, take the job. No need to run it by me. I won't be in San Jose for a while."

She retreated from the bridge and he pocketed the card

without further examination, instead focusing his attention on one final longing glimpse of the fading tranquility of Coyote Creek.

2

It had been a while since Carver visited San Diego, and he was always surprised how nice the weather was. The sky was a field of crystalline azure unmarred by a single cloud. Seagulls fluttered between high palms as the sun beamed energetic warmth onto girls in short shorts and guys trying to lure them with patio cocktails and games of cornhole.

Juliette Morgan sat in a bikini with her legs dipped into the rooftop pool. The patio doubled as a public bar with its own curbside elevator. While far from fancy, the hotel was centrally located in the touristy Gaslamp district. The busy foot traffic of the neighborhood made for the perfect spot for a public rendezvous.

The rooftop vantage served as overwatch on the seafood restaurant across the street where he was set to meet Pineda. It wasn't that Carver didn't trust the DEA, it was that trust was a privilege that first needed to be earned.

As he returned poolside and cast a shadow over his teammate, Morgan said, "If you push me in, I'm striking below the belt the next time we do drills."

He grinned. "Are you really going to accuse me of being so basic while drinking a Long Island Iced Tea?"

"We can't all be as cosmopolitan as you, Vince."

He sat next to her without plunking his boots into the pool. "I don't think there's anything to worry about down there."

"Of course there's not. But we run security. It's what we do."

He absently nodded and repeated his mantra. "If you're not thorough, you're careless."

Within the pool splashed a gaggle of women who were either part of a bridal shower or finalists in the Ms. Silicone USA competition. They weren't much for sport but they sure bounced a lot.

"Last chance," offered Morgan when she noticed his gaze. "You can always get a Long Island yourself and relax in the sun. Perks of being the boss."

"Being the boss means I need to worry about the money. Demand is the engine of private enterprise."

She agreed with a conciliatory nod. "It can't all be globe-spanning spy games, you know."

And there it was, a knife to the heart of the niggle that had been bothering him. A drug cartel hardly qualified as a hard target service, and Carver wasn't entirely convinced the cocaine trade was a national priority. Still, he was open-minded by philosophy. It didn't hurt to hear the special agent out.

"We've taken a long enough vacation, Jules. Might as well get to it."

She sighed as he stood, took her hand, and hefted her lightly to her feet. He headed to the outdoor elevator while she assumed her post on the overhang, watching the San Diego skyline. He was in her view as he stepped onto the sidewalk, crossed the street, and entered the restaurant.

The large bar top didn't have many patrons this afternoon, but quite a few tables were occupied for lunch. The darkened recesses reinforced a nautical theme featuring wood and brass, more classy than kitsch. Instead of venturing too deeply, he sat in a bright booth facing the door, beside an airy window so large he may as well have been on a patio. He ordered a rye old fashioned and relaxed in the sun, breeze on his face, confident without looking that his team had eyes on him.

Carver watched a man pass on the sidewalk and veer into the restaurant. He had a dark tan, was clean shaven and clipped bald, and wore black sunglasses and lightly colored clothes that might have been described as San Diego chic. He was built like an Army grunt and flashed a confident smile at Carver as he approached.

"*Jefe!*" he exclaimed, giving Carver's hand a boisterous shake. He pointed at the approaching waiter. "A mojito for me." The waiter detoured to the bar and the DEA agent slid into the window-side booth. "Albert Pineda. I don't know your name."

Carver arched an eyebrow. "She didn't tell you?"

He returned a bombastic snort. "People in her position don't volunteer information unless they absolutely need to. She passed on your bona fides and that was it. You were part of that hostage thing in Addis Ababa? They say it would have fallen apart without you."

"It almost did anyway."

"Not your fault. I've been in the shit enough times to know that no operation can account for all circumstances."

A nod. "Vince Carver."

"A pleasure, bro. I think this is gonna be fun." When Carver didn't share in the excitement, his smile nearly faltered. "Sorry, is that not professional to say? We do things a little differently south of the border."

"It's not that. If I'm honest, I'm not sure weed and coke are worth the effort."

He removed his dark glasses. "Hey, I hear that, but we're talking *cristal* these days. No agriculture, no coca plant, no poppy seeds—meth is made in an indoor lab in a blender the size of a professional coffee machine. They're giving our domestic producers a run for their money, too. For the first time, the Mexican stuff is higher purity and a lower price. Just two bucks a dose for a little colored balloon of product."

The agent sighed. "Real talk. Lots of people crap on the War on Drugs, but there's good to be done when, for the first time, more Americans are dying by OD than car accidents. San Ysidro is the busiest land border crossing in the Western Hemisphere, the largest drug smuggling corridor in the nation."

Carver sipped his cocktail. "I hear Mexico's hit hard times too."

"An understatement if there was one. Baja California has the highest homicide rate in the country. Double the national average. Tijuana is its deadliest city."

"What broke down?"

"What didn't?" He grunted. "Look, cartels derive their power from access to the US border. A little over ten years ago, El Chapo and Sinaloa went to war with Tijuana. There were a lot of public deaths and kidnappings, even targeting police and upper-class residents. The Kingpin strategy took out the cartel leaders to mitigate that collateral damage. By 2012, homicides fell and TJ had a blossoming arts and music scene, craft breweries, the works. Let me tell you, things were nice. But then Jalisco moved in, El Chapo was finally extradited to the US, and homicides have doubled every couple years since. The state's ground zero for a full-on drug war."

"How can I help?"

Pineda's smile widened. "This is where Baja California congressman, Ignacio Espinoza, comes in. He's a rancher who lives halfway between Tijuana and the capital seat of Mexicali. He's a populist, like the president, and a rising star in the party. He could be the next mayor of Tijuana."

"Aren't they the anti-corruption party?"

"They are, and it paints a target on his back. He's promised to clean up the state."

"How's that going over?"

"Apparently the sentiment isn't unanimous. Congressman Espinoza's youngest son was just kidnapped. It's a common narco tactic."

Carver suddenly understood why his Delta experience was relevant, and why he was asked for. Before he could say anything, the waiter returned and set a sparkling drink of muddled mint leaves on the table.

"Thanks," said Pineda, reaching for his wallet. He nodded at the old fashioned. "You want another?"

Carver shook his head and Pineda handed a pair of twenties to the waiter.

"That's all for us. Keep it."

The waiter thanked them and retreated.

Pineda tasted his cocktail as Carver spun his glass on the table, watching the central ice cube remain motionless. "There are companies who specialize in cartel kidnappings."

The DEA agent smacked his lips and set his glass down with a shake of his head. "Ignacio Espinoza can hire security companies. What he wants is US government support. Maneuvering in politics is about having the right friends, especially in Mexico. The congressman has made it clear that he is an ally, and he wants our help."

"Close protection?"

Another head shake. "Ignacio has his own bodyguards. Private security is all the rage in Mexico these days."

"I'm getting that sense."

"The Espinozas have done well for themselves. Ignacio has the means to hire whatever team he wants, but he doesn't want a team. He wants one guy, an expert, with the unofficial backing of the US government. Normally this is where the DEA trades favors, but the presidents of our respective countries are still locked in a pissing match, only it's decades of cooperation that are being flushed down the toilet. We've officially been classified as foreign agents."

Carver frowned. "What does the designation entail?"

"It means we have no immunity, no unilateral arrest power. We have limits on government contact and intelligence gathering, and are burdened with new reporting obligations. We can't even get authorization for our firearms without their okay."

Carver took a sip as he digested that. "In other words, as a private security contractor, I'd encounter a lot less red tape than you would."

"That's one way to put it. Another is that the DEA, at this time, is flat-out unable to conduct further operations in Mexico. We have incoming guys who have been waiting six months for entry visas."

"That's no way to run an op."

"No it isn't. Which is why I'm outsourcing this one. I reached out to the Agency, looking for a more discreet solution, and you came gift wrapped. Your experience on hostage teams makes you the ideal candidate for search and rescue."

"So no drugs," concluded Carver. "No protection details. You just need me to recover the son of a congressman."

Pineda chuckled. "If you want to pretend things are that simple." He took an extended gulp of his mojito and made it look like the most refreshing thing under the sun. "So do you trust me yet?"

Carver responded without hesitation. "It's not a question of if I do, it's how much."

The DEA agent hiked a shoulder. "Let's say enough to call off your boy chugging expensive espresso. I'm a federal agent and I don't intend on being followed."

The Service of Wolves

For the first time since sitting down, Carver's gaze locked on Nick Shaw loitering across the street at a coffee cart. He was Kinetic National Security's third and newest employee, fresh off recovery from a graze with a Spetsnaz bullet, though Carver had a longer history with him than Morgan. Shaw was a more-than-capable operator. Even without an overzealous eye on the meet, the DEA agent had spotted the lookout. Pineda was good.

"He's that obvious?" asked a deflated Carver.

"Not bad, but the special ops beard gave him away. He doesn't look like your average Padres fan. And I assumed you'd bring backup."

"You didn't," noted Carver, sweeping the street one last time to make sure.

"No need, my friend. We're just two guys sharing war stories."

They both took a sip this time. Pineda may have been overly gregarious, but he seemed genuine enough. More importantly, beneath his congeniality was a pragmatic streak. The two of them probably had a good deal in common.

"So who took the kid?" asked Carver, getting back down to business.

Pineda wagged a finger in the air. "That's the thing. The pull happened in TJ. The Tijuana cartel's a shell of what it once was. Sinaloa moved in and dominated for a time. They just might be the most powerful transnational criminal organization in the Western Hemisphere. But with El Chapo going away, they've had some difficulties too."

"Difficulties?"

"There's a new alliance between Tijuana, Jalisco, and a few others, built for the express purpose of challenging Sinaloa. They call it *Nueva Generación*. New Generation. But don't assume because there's a common goal that there's no infighting. No honor amongst thieves, right? On top of that, with everybody and their mother being able to manufacture meth themselves, the local dealer map is fractured into a hundred pieces. A lot of the action is independent of the cartels."

"This is starting to sound like the various tribes and factions in Afghanistan."

"I'll take your word on that, bro. I live and breathe a different desert, and this one's right in our backyard so it hits closer to home. We've been trying to track the upswing of methamphetamines crossing the border. Years of infighting and border restrictions have disrupted the trade, but this new operation is sophisticated. There's a lot of gross making it across and things are getting bad everywhere."

Carver killed his glass and slammed it to the table hard. "And the truth comes out. You want me to save the kidnapped kid *and* track down a new cartel."

Pineda's grin never faltered. "Hey, you seem like the extra-credit type. But I'm just asking you to keep an eye out. Ignacio Espinoza's son is a dangerous escalation. It could be related to a regional power grab, and it could point to the new players. But don't get the wrong idea. The kid's the priority. I just want you to understand what you're walking into."

"Understood." Carver did appreciate the background and the heads up. Maybe Pineda was onto something about Williams not being forthcoming with information. "What about your opinion then?"

Pineda studied the bare tabletop. "If you're asking me who in Mexico could be terrorizing a state politician, it could be Tijuana, Sinaloa, Jalisco, a new group muscling in, or a random constituent with a grudge. Take your pick."

"Sounds like a party."

Pineda laughed and leaned back in the booth with an arm along the back. "You private guys have all the fun. But no judgment from me. As long as you don't abuse your position, have all the fun you want. I'm just jealous you get to see some action."

That caught Carver off guard. "You won't be there?"

"Eh, I pop in and out of TJ, just not in any official capacity aside from intelligence gathering. I'd be useless to you, anyway. I can't even hook up local favors because talking to law enforcement needs to be rubber stamped. No joke, the local agencies need permission from a high-level security panel before even meeting with a 'foreign agent' like me. Lucky for you, you're working for a congressman, so someone high up already has your back."

"Just not Uncle Sam."

"Ain't that always the way?" He reached for the last of his drink.

"I work with a team," asserted Carver, just to be clear.

"I can see that. Support from an arm's length is fine.

When it comes to meeting the congressman, it's gotta be only you. This is a delicate family matter. Besides, I was told you excelled at going it alone."

Carver could vividly imagine Lanelle Williams wearing a smirk as she conveyed that particular aspect of his personality.

3

They were in Tijuana the same day. *Zona Centro* is the traditional downtown area and perhaps the most widely known by American residents. Palm trees lined the busy parkway of *Avenida Revolución*, where hotels, shops, and restaurants catering to tourists were plentiful. Most of the buildings were a few stories high and opened to wide pink sidewalks. In the distance, the Tijuana Arch looped over the street. It reminded Carver of the one in St. Louis and, more recently, the one in Kyiv, except this one had suspension cables supporting a giant TV playing a perpetual Samsung commercial.

They booked a few rooms in a cheap hotel on the strip. The tacky accommodations were a feature, not a bug. As a bustling tourist destination, nobody would look twice at a few gringos unless it was to sell them a photo op with a donkey painted like a zebra. Carver and Shaw remained stoic in the face of such adversity, but Morgan broke down and posed with the zonkey.

The instructions from the DEA were to reach out in the morning, so their crew had some time to kill. They patronized a local joint that served giant salted margaritas with sidecars of imitation Grand Marnier.

"*Zona Norte's* the red-light district," explained Shaw over a still-sizzling combination of peppers and carne asada. "The strip clubs are wild. They build them right into the hotels. It's down to a science here."

Morgan rolled her eyes. "I thought Navy men were banned from visiting TJ."

"You can't ban talk."

"Like I'm going to believe this is just talk," she countered.

Shaw was undeterred and unabashed. "You know there'll always be a place in my heart for you, Jules, but don't make me choose between you and the *paraditas*."

"Poor ladies," she muttered. "Having to stand on the street all day to attract attention."

"That's nothing," snorted Carver. "You should see what they do to the donkeys."

Night fell and they called it an early one since they were due for business. In the morning Carver kept his exercises to his room before showering and gearing up. Since he was meeting a client, he only packed a pistol and a ballistic vest for now.

Firearm ownership in Mexico was strictly regulated and mostly limited to home defense. Armed travel was not permitted, and even the firing range was off-limits without separate authorization and membership in a shooting club. A carry license was nearly impossible to get. With a fraction of a hundredth of a percent of the population enjoying the benefit, it was a rounding error.

The Service of Wolves

That said, gun control was fast and loose in the sense that, if he didn't get caught doing something stupid, there likely wouldn't be a problem.

The rest of his assumptions weren't so nonchalant. Rather than have anyone know about his team or where he was staying, they made arrangements and then split up. Carver called his contact from his cell phone while at a coffee shop down the street. He skipped breakfast so he wouldn't be bogged down and waited.

It was just before 9 am when the black Lincoln Aviator pulled to the sidewalk behind an already thickening line of passenger cars. Despite the seven-seat capacity, there was only one guy inside, and he didn't pose much of a threat since he was driving. That fact did not alleviate the need for other precautions. Carver opened the back door and took the captain's chair opposite the driver so he could keep an eye on him.

"You Vince?" asked the man. He had a thin mustache and slicked-back hair.

"I am."

He returned a not unwelcoming nod. "Gonzalo. Ready?"

These situations were sketchy even when dealing with the good guys. Carver had read about a kidnapping specialist who was picked up in a truck and never heard from again. A quick calculation of his environs convinced him he was safe enough. Carver shut the door. "Always."

Gonzalo silently resumed cruising down the *avenida*. He took the first turn off the busy strip and looped east.

"How far are we going?"

"Into the country," answered Gonzalo. "Mr. Espinoza lives outside Tecate. It's an hour away so you should make yourself comfortable."

Carver wondered what beer had to do with anything but kept that to himself. They continued through a sprawling city that was vibrant in parts and muted in others. It was a sunny day with minimal cloud cover. Beautiful by any standard. The streets were animated with people going about their daily routines. He spotted an abundance of construction workers, buses, food stands, and *abuelos* sweeping storefronts.

But Carver also noticed dealers working every corner. The residents were practiced at keeping their eyes down, actively heading off trouble and desperately keeping to themselves. Like they were prisoners in the public. A paradox, like the city itself: full of life and zeal while being suffocated by the black market and the constant threat of extreme violence.

Carver paid only passing attention to the landmarks, occasionally catching glimpses of Shaw following in a silver Ford Ranger. He also unassumingly watched Gonzalo, who likewise made constant checks in the rearview mirror at his passenger. The curiosity on both their parts was normal.

"You're security, right?" asked Carver to break the ice.

Gonzalo nodded. "Former Colombian military. I did a lot of jungle work."

"I can imagine." That tracked with Carver's assessment. He couldn't tell from here, but he was sure the man was armed and confident of handling himself in a fight. "What

The Service of Wolves

made you come to Mexico?" he asked.

A shrug. "Same as you. I followed the money."

"Just you?"

"*Sólido Seguridad.* We're still small for a protection company—just a few teams working for Mr. Espinoza to start out—but we're the best of the best."

"Solid," said Carver, echoing the company name. Then, "I thought the cartels got the best guys?"

"Not a chance. Their armies are mostly kids and degenerates."

"Makes you wonder how they're so successful."

Gonzalo scoffed dismissively. "They get by with numbers, taking big risks, and paying people to look the other way."

Carver nodded. One thing you couldn't say about the cartels was that they weren't creative. Gonzalo likely had homegrown stories from growing up in the aftermath of Pablo Escobar.

"You said you guys are a few teams?" probed Carver.

"To start out. We plan to expand across Tijuana."

"You sound pretty big already for a single politician."

"Mr. Espinoza has a few properties and runs several businesses. He'll tell you everything himself. I doubt I can answer your questions."

The answer indicated a concern for possibly being unhelpful, but his expression was more cagey than apologetic.

"How many men is that?" Carver pressed.

Gonzalo was quiet a second. "You know, I never

counted."

The man wasn't interested in revealing the operational details of his security company. Fair enough. Maybe it came from a place of defensiveness. Here he was, supposedly among the best of the best, yet his principal's son had been kidnapped under his nose. Then, to add insult to injury, Espinoza hired an outside contractor to run the recovery. The testosterone alone would negate any sympathy among the *Sólido* team.

Silence consumed most of the drive as they exited the city and the terrain grew rural. Rolling hills gave way to a backdrop of rocky mountains, and staggered buildings surrendered to farmland. The sheer beauty of it forced Carver to wonder why he hadn't visited before. Maybe there was something to be found out here.

Instead of entering the town of Tecate, they continued their trajectory along the US-Mexican border a little further. Carver knew they were close when the Aviator pulled off the paved road onto dirt where a pair of police cars had erected a checkpoint. He tensed at the prospect of trouble. The stern faces of the officers held on the SUV as their hands hovered over the weapons on their hips.

Gonzalo buzzed down the window and waved two fingers in casual greeting. The police backed away with barely a glance at the back seat. It wasn't clear what purpose the process had served.

As they drove down the dirt road, Carver leaned forward. "What are they looking for?" he asked.

"Mr. Espinoza is understandably concerned with his

safety," explained Gonzalo. "With the danger to his family, he wouldn't want us followed."

The ex-military man's eyes practically smiled in the rearview mirror. Carver nodded nonchalantly and unassumingly leaned into his seat. It appeared Ignacio Espinoza had more than private security on his payroll. Carver pulled out his phone as if to check their arrival time. In a quick text message, he warned Shaw away from the checkpoint. That was as close as his friend was going to get.

The SUV rounded the hillside and the brown backdrop transformed into a curated lush green. Rows of grapevines, looking like soldiers mustered for war, lined the terraced mountain. They drove past smaller farmhouses and stables where an identical black Lincoln Aviator was parked. It stood out for lacking the coat of dust everything else had out here.

Farther down, in a gated grass enclosure, a black stallion galloped by, its rider a thin man with a long frame accented all the more by the large white cowboy hat. The arriving SUV warranted no attention from him, but the stable hand leaning on a fence post watched like a hawk as they passed.

Another bend of the dirt road took them through a grove of trees that opened to a long valley. Nestled in a bed of manicured grass was an extravagant ranch house surrounded by textured stone walkways, shade trees, and even a stone bridge over a stream with multiple levels for bubbling white water to cascade down into a private lake.

Gonzalo pulled around the water feature onto the driveway and parked. No other vehicles were visible but that wasn't odd since the house had four individual garages and the expansive property had other buildings to park beside. Carver exited before waiting to see if Gonzalo meant to get his door. He was ready for business, and the driver led him toward the home.

Despite the size and abundance of wood and stone, the overall architectural expression of the ranch house was decidedly understated. It was Rustic Nouveau, rich in material but simple in taste, evocative of countless Texas barns. A little less evocative was the gray-haired Mexican with a shotgun slung over one shoulder. He was posted by the front door and watched with hard eyes while otherwise remaining motionless, not unlike a reptile gathering sun.

They stepped between the timber columns of the porch where they were greeted by wide steel-framed windows meant to showcase the idyllic countryside from within the spanning central living area. The front door was inset between planks of weathered reclaimed wood.

Before Gonzalo could knock, a young woman in a maid outfit opened up. She said something in Spanish that was too quick for Carver to parse, and Gonzalo nodded. He stopped outside the door, dug into his pocket for a cigarette and a lighter, and eyed the far-off mountain as if Carver was already a distant memory.

The maid said, "Come with me, please."

Carver scuffed his boots on the rugged door mats, both inside and out, before following on the wide wooden floorboards. The interior of the house was modeled much as the exterior, which was to say unfinished stone and wood,

The Service of Wolves

lines leading the eye up to grand overhangs and iron fixtures. Either the maid was a good hustler or she had a whole team backing her up because the house was spotless.

They strolled past a cherrywood table that was large enough to accommodate extended family, a Mexican-styled rug with patchwork adobo colors, and a gourmet kitchen with jumbo appliances. The first doorway in the rear hall led inside a modest office where the maid announced Carver's arrival. A man in his late fifties thanked her in Spanish and stood from his desk.

"Vince, my friend, come here."

They met halfway around his desk and locked in a solid handshake. "I'm sorry to meet under these circumstances, Congressman Espinoza."

"Ignacio, please. When it comes to real business, I cut the bullshit as a butcher cuts the fat. Quick, and with a big cleaver. I want you to know, I take care of my family. Every father in the world wants what's best for their children."

The disclaimer seemed strangely out of place for some reason so Carver simply nodded.

Ignacio Espinoza was perhaps exactly what Carver had expected. Average height, which was noticeably short beside the Delta operative, with dyed black hair that was showing gray at the roots, more above the ears than anywhere else. He had a healthy but unobtrusive mustache that was taken over by silver. His suit was basic but tailored. A large paunch revealed a man who had lived a plentiful life, yet the calluses on his hands proved he had earned it through hard work. Despite sagging eyes and wrinkles on his forehead and chin, Ignacio retained a youthful vigor.

"I rode in with your man from *Sólido Seguridad*," said Carver. "I was curious if they were tapped to assist on this job."

Ignacio shook his head. "They have their own duties. They're mostly ex policemen and soldiers. Good fighters but not trained for hostage situations. I don't need to tell you this takes a delicate hand."

Carver nodded. "There are companies that deal exclusively with cartel kidnappings."

The congressman chortled. "In the last six months alone, experienced men from the two largest of these companies went to a location to arrange safe delivery for their client. They both disappeared. Both within the Tijuana metro area."

So the rumors Carver heard were true, and things were getting worse.

"It is my opinion," Ignacio continued, "that there is some bad blood with these organizations. They are tainted and are no longer as effective as they once were."

He took a few steps away. Carver thought he was going behind his desk, but Ignacio put his hands in his pockets and moved toward a window that showed off an impressive sycamore beside the private lake. "If I could get the DEA, I would, but that would go against *el presidente* and the founder of my party. They tell me you are the next best thing, if not better."

It seemed strange to let politics interfere with a critical family matter, but then the congressman probably viewed

The Service of Wolves

everything through such a lens. Besides, Carver couldn't fault the DEA recommendation.

"You realize I can't go around the city advertising my government affiliation," he explained.

"That is understood, Vince, and it won't be necessary. Word gets around Mexico easily enough, especially in the unofficial circles you'll be snooping in. You'll hear things, and the people you talk to will hear things too."

Ignacio waited for debate over the possibly touchy subject, but Carver didn't object. Agent Pineda had more or less implied as much. As Ignacio waited, something on his desk caught his eye, and he walked over and picked up a framed picture.

"This is my family," he said, handing it over.

The photograph might have been taken five years ago. Ignacio was less gray and a little thinner. He stood in front of his vineyard flanked by a man, a young woman, and a boy. The family looked happy together, with more genuine joy than usually seen in posed photographs, though the absence of a mother drew it short of the fairy-tale ideal.

"They are the heart of my life," he explained. "This is Christian, my eldest son."

"I think I saw him riding on the way in."

Ignacio nodded proudly. "He loves that horse. Broke the stallion himself. He's here often."

"He doesn't live here?"

"He's a grown man, Vince. A few years older than you, I imagine. Christian lives in Tijuana but comes and goes a lot. He runs the day-to-day company interests on the commercial side. Sales, shipping, that kind of thing."

"You're talking wine?"

"Yes."

"But it's your business?"

"Yes. I started it. Tilled that soil with my own hands. I enjoy the cultivation of the wine, the supply side of the business. Of course I have workers that do that these days. I'm a public figure now. A politician, if you can believe it. The Congress of the State of Baja California convenes in Mexicali."

"Do you stay there?"

"I have an apartment for busy periods, but it's not home. Besides, my daughter's here."

Ignacio placed a stubby finger back on the photograph, as if that was necessary. His daughter was the only woman in the picture and was quite striking.

"Alma has been my rock. Like the mountain outside, if she were not here, the winery would collapse. There would be no foundation, no roots, and no angle at the light."

"And this is Manuel?" prodded Carver, referencing the pictured teenager. "Does he live here too?"

"He has a room, but he was spending more and more time at a girlfriend's house in Tijuana."

Carver angled the photo to minimize the glass pane's glare and snapped a picture of the family. "Do you have a better portrait of him? Something close up and more recent?"

Ignacio sighed as if it was a shame that he didn't. "I don't know. It's better to ask Alma about that. She has lots of pictures."

Carver nodded and handed the frame back to the worried father. "That's fine. So what exactly do you want me to do?"

The congressman set the frame back on the desk. "You're the expert. I expect you to tell me."

"I'm only checking if you have special instructions."

Ignacio shook his head. "Nothing special. Just find my son."

4

"Let's get down to it then," said Carver. "Manuel was taken in Tijuana?"

"In the middle of the day. His girlfriend was the one who first notified us."

"It's been three days. Has there been any contact?"

Ignacio shook his head, but the expression lacked conviction. "This is what worries me. It's normal for these people to reach out immediately. To let people know they want something. These things are almost always about money, which I would gladly pay for my son's safety. You need to understand, I would do anything to get him back. *Anything*. That is your job, Vince. Get Manuel back as safely as possible. If I need to pay, I pay."

"Except no one's asked for money."

"No. I've heard nothing."

Carver frowned. "No contact means no deal. We need to at least consider that this is about something else. Could it be revenge?"

The wrinkles on his brow furrowed into deep grooves. "What for?"

"With respect, Ignacio, I need you to tell me. You're a

politician, rising in prominence from what I've been told. You've supported anti-corruption legislation, haven't you?"

"I have, but only what's in line with the MORENA party. These initiatives are spearheaded by the president of Mexico. Removing power from the local police, empowering the National Guard to focus on the cartels. This is trouble for them, but it's not specific to me."

"Then leverage for the future. Is there a notable vote coming up?"

"Nothing like that. To be honest, I wasn't planning to shake any more trees while I explored becoming a mayoral candidate in Tijuana. But this isn't about politics, Vince. It's about terror. This is *Nueva Generación*, no doubt in my mind. They're a plague and they're taking over my state with gutless attacks on a helpless population. Coming after me signals that no one is untouchable."

"Okay, let's say that's the right read. Aside from hiring me, what have you done so far?"

He shrugged, waffling between decisive politician and heart-struck father. "There's nothing to do but wait."

"That's not an option, sir. You claim this is the cartel. Is there a way I can reach them?"

"Who knows these things?"

"Someone has to. Let's face it, these guys aren't subtle. They walk around like they own the city and should be easy to find. In the absence of a ransom demand, we need to inquire with possible suspects."

He stammered and seemed to have lost his power.

"Ignacio, it's likely they want a deal and are keeping you

in the dark to make you sweat a bit. It works in our favor to initiate contact if they don't. The longer your son is in their hands, the greater the chances of something going sideways."

"Okay," he snapped, shutting the possibility from his mind. "I... I can't personally call them, but my daughter is a bit of a socialite. She knows all the hot spots in the city and can point you to their... hangouts." He lifted an adamant finger. "But I don't want you taking her anywhere near those places, you understand me? These guys are inhuman. Literally, animals. Keep Alma out of it otherwise she may be targeted next."

Carver nodded agreement. "That's helpful. What about the spot Manuel was grabbed? Where was it?"

"His health clinic on *Calle Riviera*."

"Did anybody see anything?"

"Nobody in Mexico who wants to keep their eyeballs sees anything. But to answer your question, he was apparently alone when it happened."

It was what he'd expected. Regardless, without anything substantial to go on, it was worth a visit. "We're almost at seventy-two hours. Given the logistics of living so far from the city, it's still a possibility you'll be contacted. Are you working?"

"Not for couple more days," he said. "I'll be at the house waiting for anyone to reach out."

"Good. I'll shake up what I can in TJ. If you don't mind, I'd like to have a word with your family first. Ask around a little."

"Of course. Whatever you need. I have some petty cash for you." He walked to the desk, opened a drawer, and withdrew an envelope thick with bills. "You'll need this if you're asking questions. I'll pay whatever daily rate you want, plus a bonus for bringing him home within the week and another for bringing him home in one piece. Guadalupe is making a room for you here."

"That's very generous. I hope it's not a problem if I stay in the city as necessary."

"Not at all. Gonzalo will drive you anywhere you need."

"I'd prefer my own car," said Carver.

"That's out of the question." Some of Ignacio's business mentality resurfaced. "As my employee I need you in my circumference at all times."

"I was under the impression your security was being run by *Sólido*."

"It's not for my protection, it's for yours." His hand waved off the oncoming objection. "I know you are capable of protecting yourself, but it's never good to be alone around the cartels. They're vicious dogs. My people know the ins and outs of the city. You also don't want to find yourself at odds with the police forces."

"Sir, I can navigate a few local—"

"The matter is settled, Vince. You don't know the history here. If it helps, think of it as me protecting my investment. Gonzalo will back you up whenever you need, and he won't interfere when you don't. He answers to me on this."

Carver took in and released a long breath. He didn't like

being babysat but this appeared to be a sticking point with the congressman. On the plus side, there was value in having a local show him around. He begrudgingly agreed.

They hashed out a few more details, pay and contact numbers, as well as useful close contacts and locations related to Manuel. Ignacio was a little light on details, only knowing the broad strokes of his son's circles. It was, unfortunately, a well-worn family narrative.

Carver left Ignacio longingly staring out the window. He stepped into the hall and wandered back past the kitchen, surprised to find the house empty. After lingering in the common area to study family pictures and decorations, he heard movement down the front hallway, opposite the one where Ignacio was. He wondered if his bedroom was being prepared and peeked just as a beautiful woman emerged into the living room.

She was tall like a model, with deep brown eyes, large lashes, and expressive eyebrows. Long brown hair swooped over her head in elegant waves, and her thin pointed nose jutted over thick, full lips. She stood tall on heels, white gown showing off a voluptuous bust and hips cinching at the waist in an impossible hourglass. Carver couldn't tell if she was on her way to a gala or fabulous by default.

"Alma Espinoza, I presume."

The woman smiled and offered her hand in a way that would immediately disarm any red-blooded man. "Are you the one finding Manolito?"

"I'll do my best. Your father said you had a recent picture of him?"

The Service of Wolves

"Of course I do."

She floated to the fireplace on light toes and retrieved her phone from the mantel. It didn't take many swipes to locate a perfect close-up of a twenty-one-year-old with happy eyes and an infectious smile. Manuel was darker than his brother and sister, more like his father.

"How recent is this?"

"That's last week at lunch."

"Send it to my phone?"

She smirked and took his number. She held her phone low, at her waist, and gave Carver's idle eyes time to explore her attentive posture and full cleavage. It really was too early in the day to be wearing a strapless gown.

"Are you going somewhere, Alma?"

"No. Why do you ask?"

"Just the makeup and the dress."

"I like to cultivate a powerful image. What do you think?" She twirled in a full circle.

"You're a knockout."

She smiled. "If I didn't know any better I'd think this was a ploy to get my phone number."

She sent the text and Carver's phone buzzed. "Nothing wrong with killing two birds with one stone." He checked the picture. "You eat lunch with your brother a lot?"

"All the time. Is that not normal?"

"I just didn't get the sense your father knew that much about what Manuel was up to."

She tsked the comment. "Your sense would be right. *Papá* will tell you he's all about family, but he's not good with emotions. His love comes through in how hard he works to give us a good future."

"And *your* love?"

Her lips pressed together mischievously. "You mean my relationship with Manolito?"

"Sure."

"I love him more than the world, and I openly share that fact with him and anyone who listens. You won't understand until you meet him. He's good—truly good—from the inside out. He's not poison like the rest of this family."

Carver blinked coolly. "Define poison."

Her naked shoulders shrugged. "Shrewd. Calculating. I admit it freely. We're a family of cutthroat business people and politicians. That success doesn't come out of kindness."

There was something about the way Alma spoke so openly that was refreshing. Her father was a congressman. He claimed to cut through the crap but probably focus tested every word that came out of his mouth. Alma was coy and cunning and unafraid to say it like it was.

Of course, that in itself was a form of play acting. Her statements were a little too forced to be completely natural. More likely shock was a tool she used to blunt people into acquiescence. She played up her remarkable beauty by contrasting it with the ugly truth. Rehearsed or not, it left a strong impression.

"You don't strike me as a politician," Carver said, somewhat generously.

"No. We support *Papá's* campaigns and give him advice, but I'm a businesswoman at heart."

The Service of Wolves

"What do you do?"

"The finances. I don't have a degree but I'm good with numbers and learned on the job. *Papá* is wary about outsiders."

"In the wine business?"

She chuckled. "The wine is a passion project, stemming from his younger dreams with *Mamá*." Alma paused and made the sign of the cross in deference to the deceased. "The wine business isn't as profitable as it looks."

"Is it in the red?"

"Nothing like that. It pays its own way, but it's slow going. The real profits are in real estate."

"Another company?"

"A series of companies. Commercial properties and private, not just selling but building. We employ contractors and distributors that supply everything from steel and lumber to household paint."

Carver was unironically impressed. It seemed that the politics came later in life. "That's quite the empire. Which part is Manuel involved in?"

Her eyes lit up dramatically. "The best part. He's not involved in the family businesses at all. Manolito's different from the rest of us. He's a bleeding heart. Where my father tries to help people through law and order, and Christian snags them with the tactics of a salesman, Manolito holds their hands and picks them off the ground."

Carver wondered what Alma's tactic was but didn't interrupt her.

"He's studying medicine," she went on. "He interns at a

clinic in Tijuana and wants to open his own when he graduates."

"That sounds expensive."

She scoffed. "Look around, out the windows as far as you can see. That's *Papá's* land. Money is no object."

"Mm-hmm. And how does the family feel about his career path?"

"It doesn't cause problems. It makes *Papá* look good on the campaign trail."

"And your opinion?"

"It's important our family does something to help. Manolito's path is a breath of fresh air." Her lips parted in concern. "Of course, being a man of the people means he spends a lot of time with them. It was too easy to grab him."

Carver's face was stoic but respectably sympathetic. "Is it your opinion that the cartels grabbed him?"

She rubbed her neck absently. "Who else?"

"What about motive?"

The same distracted tone. "What else? To get at our family. Even if he's the only one who doesn't deserve it."

"Come on, Alma. You keep making yourself out to be a bad person. Why is that?"

As if ready for her next line, her smile turned sly. "You might look at me and think I'm a harmless flower, but I'm a Venus flytrap."

"Are you saying you're carnivorous?"

Her eyes sparkled at the instant comeback, and her response took a moment longer than probably intended. "You'd better be careful. I've broken a lot of hearts in my time."

"It's surprising to hear such a self-assured woman dooming herself to failure."

Alma pressed her lips together to consider the comment. Then she took a step back to look him up and down. "I'm about your age, I think. A little younger even. Tell me, do you see yourself changing anytime soon?"

"Touché."

She brandished a satisfied set of white teeth. For the first time in the conversation, they both stopped to take a breath at the same time. The pause encouraged them to study one another, and made them intimately aware that they were doing so. The vein in Alma's neck tensed with a slight intake of air. Carver decided to let her off the hook.

"That's one hell of a dress, Alma."

She flashed a pleasant smile that didn't look at all interested. "Thank you for the compliment. Now, mister... Is there anything else I can get you?"

"Carver."

"Carver?"

"The part that comes after mister."

She regained her composure. "And your first name?"

"I'm sure I told you."

She chuckled lightly. "I'm good with numbers, great with faces, but embarrassingly bad with names. One of my many failings."

"You're breaking my heart already."

"I did warn you."

He laughed. "When you're right, you're right." He

stepped closer to her so she would remember this time. "Call me Vince, or call me Carver, or call me whatever you want."

She lifted her chin slowly, bringing her face closer to his. "I'll have to think of something original. For now, Vince, is there anything else that can help Manolito?"

"Actually, yes. I'm going to be looking around in Tijuana. Your dad called you a socialite."

"What." The blood in her face drained, though she recovered quick. Alma puffed her chest out and narrowed her eyes alluringly.

He smiled. When she was backed into a corner, she used her sexuality for power. "I'm asking because you might know where some New Generation lieutenants hang out."

Her eyes fluttered. "This is *Papá's* way of shaming me. He believes I should be a good woman. Settle down with a husband and crap babies. Tell me, what do you think?"

"I think that's not how babies are made."

She chuckled. After watching him a moment, she shook her head and dove back into her phone. "*La Cascada* is a seedy nightclub. *Nueva Generación* owns it and the surrounding hills. It's safe for them."

Carver's phone buzzed with the name of the club and the cross street. "How do you know this?"

"I get around, and so does word about who to avoid. The club is safe as long as you don't cause trouble. It might be a tall order with that mouth of yours."

Rather than make empty promises, Carver remained silent.

"If someone's in the VIP section," she explained, "they're probably VIPs. You get my drift?"

"I got it a long time ago," he said.

"Be careful of the girls too. They wear skimpy outfits and are maybe even more dangerous than the narcos. They would fall all over you, I imagine."

"Is that what you imagine?"

Her eyes narrowed. "Trust me, Vincent. You don't want to get mixed up with me."

"Because you're bad."

"The whole family is rotten. Every single one of us besides my baby brother." She grabbed Carver's hand and squeezed with a little too much desperation to be an act. "Find Manolito. No one else in this family cares for him the way I do. I want him back without a hair on his head removed. Will you do that for me?"

He dipped his head. "Yes ma'am."

5

Alma retired into the hallway, leaving him alone once again. Carver gazed out the large steel-framed windows. Gonzalo leaned on a tree with another member of the security team, enjoying the shade and what was likely his third cigarette. Old Gray Hair was still statuesque on the porch with the shotgun. Rather than look around the rest of the house, Carver joined them outside.

As the front door shut behind him, a burnt orange Jaguar rumbled from the driveway, garage door closing in its wake. Christian Espinoza sans cowboy hat drove toward the grove of trees and the main road.

Carver marched toward Gonzalo. "Where's he going? I haven't talked to him yet."

The security driver gave a noncommittal shrug. "He works in the city. Real estate keeps him busy most of the time."

"He didn't look busy a few minutes ago."

Gonzalo didn't offer a countering perspective.

Carver bit down. "Has he said anything about his missing brother?"

"I don't know."

The Service of Wolves

"Yeah."

Given the current dire circumstances, there was no doubt Christian Espinoza was aware of Carver's purpose here. He had been on the ranch, riding, as Gonzalo pulled in. For Christian to cut and run without so much as a hello didn't sit right, no matter how busy he was. Unless there was some legitimate emergency, one would think he'd be very interested in talking to the man looking for his little brother.

"Was Manuel around the house the last few nights before he went missing?" Carver asked.

Gonzalo flicked his cigarette to the ground and twisted a boot on it. "He has a room, but I'm not sure when he was last here."

"Don't you pay attention to the comings and goings at the ranch house?"

"Not usually. I worked at Christian's house in Tijuana until today."

That was an interesting snippet, but not what Carver wanted at the moment. He turned to Gonzalo's friend in the shade. "What about you?"

The man stared blankly.

"He doesn't speak English," explained Gonzalo.

"Then can you ask him?" Carver grated.

Gonzalo raised his eyebrows defensively, like how was he supposed to know what to do. After a short exchange in Spanish, he answered. "He says Manuel was here five or six days ago. But usually he slept in Tijuana with a girl."

All signs kept pointing that direction. Carver's boot

twisted in the dirt as he took in a panoramic view of the countryside. It was pretty out here, but it was also vast in its emptiness. Without expensive irrigation the mountain and valley wouldn't be nearly as green. He wondered if this was the superior state of the land, twisted and terraformed beyond its natural limitations.

The bodyguard on the front porch watched Carver with a detached expression, not tired or apathetic so much as calm. They were the eyes of a man who'd seen it all and lived to talk about it, in the face of a man who refused to talk about it. Carver knew better than to underestimate capable old dogs like him. There was a reason they had reached that age after all.

Carver's initial assessment was playing out in real time. The security staff was not eager to assist him. He saw no point in taking out his frustration on them. There were better uses of his time.

"Let's go," announced Carver, marching to the Aviator.

Gonzalo chatted with his friend another lackadaisical minute before getting behind the wheel. "Where to?"

"Back to the city."

The Lincoln wound through the grove and past the now-empty riding enclosure. Beside the stables, the man who had watched them from the fence on the way in was untacking the now-saddleless stallion. Christian had left the grunt work to the stable hand, which didn't jive with the image of someone who loved their horse, though it did support the possibility that he was busy. Then again, it was likely all meaningless. With this class of money, there was help for everything.

As they curved past the farmhouses, Carver noted the parked Aviator was now gone. Two got you twenty the *Sólido Seguridad* escort had followed Christian out.

Gonzalo waved through the police checkpoint without bothering to put down his window. The officers were less concerned with checking people leaving the ranch than those coming in. The tires hit pavement and the Aviator picked up speed as they headed west. A few minutes later they passed Shaw's car on the side of the road with the hood open. He would wait till they were out of sight before going after them.

"You want to go see Christian?" asked Gonzalo.

Carver chewed his lip. "Not yet. If he has work to do, I don't want to keep him. What about the clinic Manuel works at? You know it?"

"Sure."

"Take me there."

The drive didn't feel as long on the way back. Maybe it was because Carver knew what to expect now, or maybe it was that musing on family politics kept him adequately distracted.

The high-rises of *Zona Río*, Tijuana's business district, came into view soon enough. Surprisingly, before they reached the hub of hotels, restaurants, and hospitals, the Aviator detoured toward a residential hillside. It was fortunate Gonzalo was behind the wheel because *Zona Este* wasn't in any tourism brochure. Many of the alleys and backstreets lacked asphalt. Only a portion of the houses were structurally sound. Most others were ramshackle and almost definitely lacked proper plumbing. Gang markings and members were everywhere.

Per GDP, Mexico spends less on security than most countries in Latin America. Tijuana is often in contention for deadliest city in the world, where nine out of ten killings go unsolved. That dynamic was at play everywhere Carver looked. People worked the streets, some shady, some legitimate. The ones that cared enough to notice the shiny Aviator watched it pass with nothing in their eyes. No jealousy or hatred, just the emptiness of despair.

Their shortcut led them to a wider road at the base of the hill where apartment buildings and small family homes tightly packed the slope, mostly beige but interspersed with vivid splashes of red, blue, and yellow. The commercial corridor they drove along did not constitute a great part of town, but neither was it a slum. They seemed to be at the intersection of high society and impoverished vagrants, where working-class locals labored hard for what they had far away from the campy glitz of *Avenida Revolución*.

This was a swath of Tijuana abandoned by its government. Not rich enough to drive beneficial policy, but unwilling to cater to the violence in their backyard. By all appearances, better times were just a few years ago. With a little elbow grease they might even return. Life was a constant push and pull that way, a squeezing from both sides as honest everyday citizens tried their best to navigate a loaded game.

Unfortunately, they were unable to sequester themselves

from the plague of drugs and violence. If there was a solution to that problem, Carver wouldn't be here.

Gonzalo pulled into a parking spot at the mouth of a cross street adjoining a single-story health clinic. He shifted into park and leaned back as if he was on break. Carver didn't want to strain the driver by pressing him further. He left him in the Lincoln and hit the sidewalk, rounding to the front of the building on the main strip.

The clinic's orange paint was faded in the sun except for fresh patches where graffiti had been dutifully covered. A few men and women waited outdoors. As Carver entered, he realized it was because there was no air conditioning. Several open windows did little to reduce the stuffiness of a cramped waiting room that was two-thirds full.

Carver approached the woman at the desk. "Do you speak English?"

"Yes," she said, though her curious look revealed it wasn't often. "Sign in please." She politely slid over a clipboard.

"Actually, I'm not a patient. I'm here on behalf of Manuel Espinoza's family. I was hoping I could ask some questions."

She averted her eyes to the counter. "I don't see Manuel."

He nodded reassuringly. "That's all right. Is there someone I can talk to about the day he disappeared?"

Her posture was rigid as she weighed her answer. "We are very busy, please. We only have time for patients."

The poor woman was obviously afraid of saying

anything, and visibly terrified of Carver. He leaned into that a little bit.

"Ma'am," he said, tone sharp and unwavering, "I only need a few minutes. If you give me that, I'll be out of your hair. Were you working when Manuel disappeared, or is there someone else I should talk to?"

The woman didn't have it in her to obstruct anymore. She turned to another woman and said something in Spanish. Carver caught the name Jasmine and was hoping he hit pay dirt. The other lady went to fetch her. When she returned with a young nurse in tow, he knew he had his woman.

"I'm Jasmine," she said, ending the statement as if it were a question.

She was young, maybe still a teenager, and understandably nervous. Jasmine was short, with wide hips and legs. She had thick lips and eyebrows, both dramatically enhanced with cosmetics. Fingers twirled curls of black hair so long you could get lost in them.

"I'm a friend," he assured. "My name is Vince Carver. I was hired by Manuel's father."

At the mention of her boyfriend's name, she relaxed and flashed an incessantly cute smile that dimpled her cheeks. She was the type of girl that Mom would love, if there was a mom in the picture anyway.

"Is he okay?" she asked, eyes hopeful.

"I'm sure he is. I was hoping I could—"

She waved off his question with animated hands. "We're very busy in here. I'll walk you outside." Jasmine consulted with the woman at the desk, went to the back, and emerged with a purse. "It's my lunch break anyway."

She went out the front door. When Carver followed, he found her fifteen paces down the block already. He increased his pace to keep up.

"Walk with me?" she asked.

He did, conscious of his surroundings and not saying anything for a minute so they could get situated away from prying eyes. Jasmine led him across and down a side street, up to the back of a pickup truck where a man slaved over a cooktop with two pots of meat, warming tortillas, and a slew of fixings.

"Have you eaten yet, Mr. Carver?"

He shook his head. "I'll have what you're having. My treat."

She ordered and then dug into her purse. "I don't want money. I can pay."

Carver handed the pesos over before she could complete the transaction. "It's just lunch."

She clicked her tongue but didn't argue. The street vendor prepared two tacos for her, one carnitas and one chorizo. The tortillas were small but buried in greasy meat, as well as cilantro, onions, and salsa.

"Dos más para mi," requested Carver once it was clear that Jasmine had only ordered two for him. The man obliged and Carver waved off the change.

They stepped away from the truck. Groups of workers were scattered in the alley, sitting on the curb or the bed of their truck as they enjoyed a quick lunch. A young kid loitered half a block down at the far corner.

Lots of glances noted Jasmine as they approached an empty spot of wall. The gazes immediately snapped to Carver. He saw them all without watching, passively taking in his surroundings. Jasmine took a bite of food and Carver decided he would let her work up to it. He scarfed down three tacos in the time that she ate one. The juicy meat was delectable. It made him think about his friend, Mike Davis, who had always been a fan of street food.

"I don't know anything," said Jasmine as she finally broached the reason for his visit. "This, what you see right now, is routine. Every lunch we do this, getting tacos here, or *pupusas* there. On a tough day we might share a *cerveza*. They keep them ice cold."

She hooked her thumb behind her. Besides two other food stands, the kid on the far corner stood outside the overhang of a bar. It was small but well-attended, even at lunchtime.

"Last week Manuel came out to pick up lunch for both of us." She shrugged her shoulders and wagged her head absently. "Normal day, normal lunch. Only he never returned."

"No one was with him?"

"Usually I would be, but I had to finish cleaning a *cinco bravo*."

"What's that?"

"Oh." She smiled in embarrassment. "It's code for a gunshot wound."

Carver wrinkled his brow and glanced back to where

they had come from, even though the small clinic was out of sight. "Are you equipped to treat those here?"

"Not really, but what choice do we have? The man had a non-vital wound in his arm. It had been stitched up before, but it tore open and was getting infected. He wasn't a narco, just someone who happened to be at the market during a gang hit."

"Wrong place, wrong time."

She nodded. "It's a common story around here. We do what we can." She sighed. "Manuel wanted to do so much for the community. He's one of the few privileged people who hasn't forgotten about Mexico—the *real* Mexico. That's why I fell in love with him..."

Carver finished his last taco while she silently enjoyed a memory. Jasmine ate too, and they dumped the foil and napkins into a nearby trash can.

"So the *cinco bravo*..." prodded Carver.

"We were short-staffed that day, like most days," she went on. "So I stayed behind to wrap the wound and Manuel went on without me. I came out and asked around, but nobody had seen anything. He just disappeared."

"What about the street vendors?"

"They all knew him. They joked with him sometimes. Egged him on when he complained about the corner kids. But they swear they didn't see him that day. They say he never bought food."

Carver surveilled the street vendors as he listened. Nobody watched them back or was otherwise concerned with his presence. Given a brisk lunch rush, it was plausible that Manuel walked down this street without being noticed. If he had ordered food or joked with them, they would have definitely remembered. Either he never got that far or someone was lying.

As he scanned the surrounding activity, the adolescent on the corner outside the bar locked hands with an older man. They discreetly exchanged items between palms before the man went on his way.

Carver grunted. "You said Manuel complained about the corner kids. Like that one?"

Jasmine rolled her eyes. "Yeah. He always got into it with them. This block used to be pleasant. Grab a bite for lunch, have a beer after work... It seems like every month, the dealers move closer."

"Are we talking fights?"

"No," she chortled. "Manuel wouldn't hurt the kids. That would defeat the purpose of helping them." She pouted in contemplation. "He always said I was too accepting, but I like to describe myself as a hopeful person. Manuel couldn't understand a world where dealing was an attractive option." She shrugged. "I can, even if I disagree with it. But he came from a good place. He wanted to help."

"I'm guessing his help didn't go over too well."

"Sometimes they argued. He would tell them to go home, but he would hand them a burrito at the same time, you know? I always tried to convince him to live and let live."

Carver latched onto the obvious scenario. "Jasmine, do you think Manuel could have gotten into an argument last week? He came out here without you to talk him down, something he saw set him off, and the narcos decided to teach him a lesson?"

"Those kids are harmless."

"I'm talking about the people giving the kids their marching orders."

The dimples disappeared from her cheeks. "I don't know, Mr. Carver. Manuel was careful not to push too hard. He grew up far away from *Zona Este*, but he isn't stupid."

Carver nodded instead of telling her good intentions often were.

"What about this kid specifically?" he asked, pointing to the dealer currently outside the bar. "Do you remember if he was on the street the day Manuel disappeared?"

"No. I actually don't remember seeing anyone on the corner that afternoon."

"No one was there?"

She laughed nervously. "It's not that. I was panicking at the time. I just can't remember what I saw. Someone might have been there. I mean, I assume someone was. Someone always is."

Carver bit down and stared at the kid. Jasmine must have noticed his ire.

"Carver is a vicious name," she said.

He looked at her oddly.

"I'm sorry. I don't mean to be rude. It's just that, if you're going to look for Manuel, you're going to need to be vicious."

He simply nodded.

"Do you think you'll be able to find him?" she asked. "Alive?"

He took a drawn-out breath. The girl was smart and hopeful and maybe a little naive. She was a pretty thing in an ugly situation, and he didn't know what to tell her.

"It's okay," she said. "You don't need to answer that. Manuel's family has influence, so if they hired you, I'll keep my hopes up. Just please do your best, okay?" Lines of worry creased her forehead. "I was going to marry him."

Her hand shot to her mouth. She cleared her throat and blinked wet eyes. "I need to get back. I wish I knew something that could help, but I don't. What I can do is pray for your success. I've been praying so much for Manuel it will be nothing to add you to the list." She wiped an eye and swallowed. "If you need anything, anything at all, I'm here every day."

She rushed away in such disarray that Carver decided against reeling her back to collect her contact info. He followed to the corner as she weaved between passersby, and watched as she crossed the street and went back into the clinic. Just in case.

6

There was still plenty of daylight so Carver took Jasmine's recommendation and went to the corner bar for a cold one. Gonzalo could wait in the car. Carver ordered chips and a *cerveza* and took a table well within the dingy interior, away from the window but with a good view of it and the kid selling drugs on the sidewalk.

The chips tasted like something fried in a vat of oil in the back, which was to say they were good. The guac wasn't fresh so Carver stuck with the *pico de gallo*. It's difficult to mess up chopped tomatoes and onions.

He watched the dealer and nursed the beer, knowing he might be in for some time. Being in a locals bar off the beaten path, Carver was keenly aware that he didn't fit in. This was a working-class Mexican joint far removed from the tourism industry and American eyes. Luckily, the kid on the corner was clueless and didn't put two and two together.

Customers came and went every five minutes. No one was making a killing on this one corner alone, but if the business was spread around and didn't incur too many operational costs, there was definite money to be had. Especially in a place where money didn't come easy.

Carver was three quarters done with his bottle and just about ready to order a new one when a tatted-up gang member swung by. Instead of welling with the anticipation of a junkie making his next score, this guy was abrasive and demanding. He nodded the kid toward the bar entrance. Carver turned his back to the window and deeply studied his beer label.

The rest of the eyes in the establishment did likewise as first the kid and then the gang member passed through on the way to the bathroom. They closed and latched the door. It was a full minute before they opened up. The two brusquely walked out, and the kid once again took his post on the corner.

The gang member must have been in his mid twenties and had something else on his mind. He marched down the street, away from the clinic and deeper into a worsening neighborhood.

Carver's chair scraped the concrete as he stood and took his unfinished beer out the door.

Sunlight cascaded harshly from above. Carver could imagine the patrons of the bar in a similar position, after a few beers, the lure of the dark interior calling for them to stay. The corner kid turned to him, a new prospective customer. Carver avoided eye contact and slid on his brown aviators. He patted his pockets like he was looking for a cigarette and had forgotten he had smoked them all. In the face of his disinterest, the kid turned back to the road, just in time to greet a woman who was something next to homeless. Carver pulled brown leather gloves over his hands.

In a place like this, the dealers had no reservations about conducting business in the public eye. It was actually beneficial to do so. A corner presence was free advertising as well as a territorial claim. Beside him, not five feet away, the kid traded a few bills for a little red balloon of meth.

Carver's gaze transferred to the older gang member half a block away and moving fast. For an operation so brazen, it had definitely stuck out that the two had conducted their business in private. The only reason to go into the bathroom was for a bulk transfer, either dropping off more product or collecting the running sum of cash or both. Carver figured the tattooed gang member was a bagman. And if he was suddenly flush with pesos, he would have to secure them somewhere.

Carver crossed the street and started after the bagman from the opposite side. There was no sidewalk from here on and the asphalt looked like it was ready to give up after a couple of blocks. Carver breezed along the dirt, careful not to be spotted in a neighborhood that even expats would avoid.

On two occasions the bagman actually scanned his six. His situational awareness didn't live up to his doctrine. Carver was able to duck behind a parked vehicle both times, confident he wasn't seen.

Around a corner and down some ways, the bagman strolled up to the porch of a sky-blue casita. The surrounding homes were single story and run-down, and this drug den was no exception. The notable difference was the presence of three deadbolts on the reinforced front door. The bagman glanced around one last time before digging into his pocket for a ring of keys. When he faced the door, Carver closed the distance to his target.

The three locks clicked sequentially. The bagman reached for the doorknob and Carver sprinted the remaining fifteen feet, timing his rush so that as soon as the door popped, he had him. Carver planted a shoulder into the man's back and they tumbled inside so hard the door bounced off the interior wall and closed.

The bagman rolled on the floor to look up at Carver. "What the hell, you stupid mother—"

Carver had already clocked that the bagman didn't have a weapon. He was concerned about anyone or anything else already in the house. Sure enough, a big guy labored out of a recliner in the living room. A nasty scar ran up his cheek to an eye that darted from Carver to the shotgun resting against the wall.

The big man went for it and Carver beamed his beer bottle. It socked the man in the cheek and he tripped. Carver got to the shotgun first. As the enforcer pushed to his hands and knees, the butt of the gun came down on the back of his head and put him out.

The room was empty, quiet except for the exaggerated dub of the cartoon on the television. Carver spun the weapon on the bagman.

"Wait!" he cried. "Okay! Okay, just wait!"

Carver accommodated the request.

The bagman huffed frantically as he appraised a man

who was very obviously not your garden-variety drug thief. "Shit. Did *El Vaquero* send you?"

Rather than disabuse him of the notion, Carver said, "Empty your pockets."

"Sure. Whatever. Just don't shoot me."

He pulled out two wadded rolls of cash and a stack of loose bills.

"That's it?" Carver quickly patted him down. "What do you know about a kid who was kidnapped from your corner last week?"

"What?"

"Don't screw with me. This kid works at the health clinic. He disappeared over lunch three days ago."

"I didn't see anything."

Carver kicked him in the stomach and he doubled over. "That's not what I asked."

The bagman was coughing and gasping for air, being melodramatic about the whole thing.

Carver sighed. "Don't move."

He wandered to the dining room, where little red balloons were organized into freezer bags. A ledger had a record of daily tallies in handwritten black ink. The money was steady but not excessive.

The kitchen had used appliances and cracked tile and, for some reason, a brand-new and expensive juicer. The only bathroom hadn't been cleaned in months. The first bedroom was empty except for a beat-up metal blender and paraphernalia for cooking meth. Boxes of supplies with Chinese labels were stacked against the wall.

This was a small operation. Local, for sure. The bagman wasn't a bagman, he was a boss, and he couldn't have had more than a few kids on his payroll.

Carver checked the last bedroom. A topless woman lay over the bedsheets wearing boxer shorts. She was lethargic and slow to respond to his presence. Even so, she didn't cover up or fight. Poor thing was too young to be so used up.

"Where's the gun?" he asked, opening the top drawer of the nightstand and finding some underwear and a battery-powered massager.

She blinked as if dreaming and pointed to the pillow where he found a revolver. Carver emptied it and tossed it in the trash before returning to the dealer who was just getting to his feet. Carver grabbed his shirt collar, dragged him across the room, and threw him on the cigarette-stained sofa. He found the remote and clicked off the TV. A pillow on the floor indicated one of them, probably the bodyguard, slept here.

"Take everything," said the dealer. "It's yours."

"The only thing I want from you is information."

The big man stirred on the floor. Carver walked over and kicked him once in the ribs. Then he dropped the remote on his back.

"Stay down."

The big man nodded.

Carver returned to the couch. "If you tell me everything you know, I'll walk out of here and you'll never see me again. Trust me when I say that's a good deal."

The dealer watched him evenly. He had no reason to believe him but no other option presented itself.

For Carver's part, he had to begrudgingly agree with Jasmine's assessment. This operation had nothing to do with Manuel's disappearance. They were two guys with old guns cooking meth where they slept.

"Are you tied up with New Generation?"

The dealer shook his head. "No, man. No one owns this hill. There aren't a lot of junkies, and the locals still give us trouble."

It was like Pineda had said. The ease of cooking meth had fractured the trade. With the big cartel bosses going down and product springing up on every other street, small gangs had formed everywhere. The cartels were still king, but they were no longer the only game in town. This was the cause of Tijuana's explosion of violence. Less coordination meant more turf wars. And, far from being the export business, this was good old-fashioned homegrown capitalism.

"If the New Generation cartel did swing by," posed Carver, "would you know about it?"

The dealer huffed with the frustration of not knowing what was going on. "Look, man, I don't want any trouble. I tell my boys, if they see *Nueva Generación* or any other narco cats, I tell them to disappear, okay? I'm not looking to get shot up over this. I'm just here to provide a service."

"What about three days ago? Did your boys spot narcos at lunchtime? Did they see anyone being kidnapped?"

He shrugged. "I don't know, dawg. You'd need to ask

them. They don't talk about it, they just do what they're told. The whole point of keeping away from the narcos is so you can't be a witness to anything. Possible deniability."

Carver rolled his eyes and took him at his word. This operation was far from organized. He bet a good deal slipped beneath this guy's notice. Carver checked the ledger on the dining table. The daily numbers on the day Manuel went missing were in line with the others, indicating neither a payoff nor a significant drop in business. It was just another day.

He strolled back to the living room and cracked open the double-barreled shotgun. He removed the only cartridge and dropped the gun in the corner.

This wasn't getting him anywhere. Even worse, there wasn't a good way to uncover what had happened that day without beating up every pedestrian who claimed they hadn't seen anything. Even that was unlikely to turn up anything. This area was lawless. Absolutely anything could have happened.

A sinking feeling grew in Carver's gut. What if Manuel hadn't been kidnapped at all? What if he had pushed one low-level dealer or strung-out junkie too far and got himself killed in spontaneous retaliation? His body could have been hidden or maybe even recovered in a police station as a John Doe. That scenario would certainly explain the lack of a ransom note.

"Why did you ask if *El Vaquero* sent me?" Carver asked.

The dealer blinked. "Didn't he?"

Carver stared hard without answering.

"Uh, it's just that he's been making a lot of moves lately. Consolidating territory. He doesn't like dealers cutting with fentanyl. Not that I do that. Not always."

"Could he have taken the boy?"

"No way, man. *El Vaquero* doesn't do kidnappings. He has a code."

"A code?"

"Yeah. Like, sort of. They say he's not like the other narcos. You know the stories of *Nueva Generación*, right? They kill kids and do satanic rituals and shit. *El Vaquero* is the opposite of that. They say he's cleaning up the streets."

Carver frowned as he watched the run-down houses through the iron security bars of the window. "They don't look so clean to me."

7

Carver knocked on Gonzalo's window to wake him up. The driver opened his eyes and looked around but didn't locate the source of the sound until Carver rounded the Aviator and opened the opposite back door.

"Morning, sunshine."

Gonzalo checked the dash clock. "You took your time."

"I got lunch."

"Why didn't I think of that?" He strapped on his seat belt. "What now?"

"I was thinking it's time to talk to Christian. Can we make that happen?"

Not one to emphatically express himself with words, Gonzalo shifted into gear.

It was amazing what a ten-minute drive could do in some places. Heading south and away from downtown, they summited a series of hills with nice houses. The rich in Tijuana don't have showy front yards with strong curb appeal. Instead they wall off the streets with high spans of concrete and solid metal gates in a one-two punch of privacy and security. Christian Espinoza's house was at the end of a cul-de-sac. Its three stories rose from behind the white ten-foot wall as it followed the slope to the crest of the hill.

Gonzalo leaned out his window to address the intercom. After a short exchange, he shrugged and said, "He's not here."

Carver frowned. "What do you mean he's not here? You said he was home."

"He was. He just left."

"Where did he go?"

"They didn't say."

"Let's call him."

Gonzalo sighed at the mere thought of the effort involved. Instead he buzzed the intercom again. After a few words, the motorized gate sprang open. It slowly panned out of view, revealing a modest front yard that was fully paved. It was really just a driveway leading to the double garage. A *Sólido* guard strolled to the window and gave Gonzalo a fist bump. Some type of submachine gun with a folded stock was slung over his shoulder, maybe a Mendoza HM-3. The other guy in the yard held the same weapon.

They chatted in Spanish a few minutes. From what Carver could gather, at least some of the conversation concerned Christian's whereabouts. The rest sounded like Happy Hour plans. Carver was relieved when they finally waved each other off. The guard returned to the house and activated the gate closure.

"He said Christian went to the warehouse to coordinate shipping," explained Gonzalo.

"Great. Let's go."

Gonzalo frowned. "He'll be busy the rest of the

afternoon."

"I'm sure he can spare a few minutes. Just take me to the warehouse."

Carver tapped the back of the passenger head restraint twice and leaned back, as if their course of action was settled. Gonzalo seemed less certain.

"What's the matter?" asked Carver.

The driver shook his head. "I don't think we should bother him."

"Gonzalo, what's the problem I'm missing? It's still early and I need to talk to Christian."

"He'll just..." Gonzalo hissed. "I'm the one that works with him, okay? He gets upset when people interrupt his routine. You throw your weight around and he'll get angry. Only it won't be you he takes it out on. This time next week, you'll be long gone and I'll be the one stuck with him."

Unbelievable. "I think Manuel being kidnapped takes precedence, don't you?"

Gonzalo deflated at the prospect of making a difficult decision.

"I'll tell you what," offered Carver. "I'll make this simple and take it out of your hands. I'll call Ignacio and have him tell Christian I want access. Then father and son can be mad at each other, the way it was meant to be. Deal?"

"You don't need to do that," Gonzalo ruefully decided. "Let's go."

The Aviator retraced its route north and to the outskirts of downtown Tijuana. Their destination was a bustling industrial complex lined with small and mid-sized warehouses.

Carver whistled. "The Espinoza family owns all of these?"

"Nah, just some of the lots. A ton of different businesses are packed in here."

Many of the warehouse doors were open, revealing workers in forklifts moving pallets between trucks. They stopped in front of one such warehouse. An empty truck waited with open doors as a few gruff figures huddled in the sun. None of them were Christian.

Gonzalo parked and they headed toward the office.

"What are they shipping here?"

"Wine," he answered. "The bottles are shipped all over Mexico. A significant volume goes north of the border and to the airport."

Carver expected wine barrels but only found boxes. It made more sense that the bottling would happen elsewhere. They entered the office and Gonzalo inquired with the woman at the entry desk. He thanked her and turned back to Carver.

"She says Christian left."

"He's not here?"

A shrug. "He was. I have an idea. Come on."

Instead of returning to the SUV, Gonzalo led him on foot along the string of warehouses.

"The Espinozas export steel," he explained. "They stock parts from China and sell them to builders all over Baja and the United States."

Carver silently wondered if the process skirted tariffs. Either way it looked like there was a lot of money moving around.

Several warehouses down they found workers enjoying a snack of fresh fruit. No trucks were on the lot but the warehouse was open. Fully stocked shelves supported boxes of all sizes. To the side was a line of pallets loaded and wrapped in plastic. As Gonzalo spoke with the workers, Carver inspected the labels. Zinc-plated fasteners. Hot-dipped galvanized beam clamps. It was like a Home Depot. A shipping label on one pallet had a Shanghai source address.

"He's not here either," reported Gonzalo. "They own a lumberyard close to here."

They returned to the Aviator and went through the motions. Carver didn't get his hopes up. In fact, he was getting the distinct impression they were giving him the run around.

The lumberyard was a few streets down in a rattier area. The fenced lot was larger and private. They pulled in and asked around. As with the other locations, it was business as usual but there was no sign of Christian.

As they returned to the SUV, Carver reached for the door before spinning to Gonzalo.

"Just call him up."

"But—"

"I don't care if he doesn't like it. Either you call him or I call Ignacio and get it done myself." Carver pulled his phone from his pocket to make his point.

"Okay, hold up." Gonzalo sighed and made the phone call.

Carver wasn't entirely surprised when Christian didn't pick up. At this point it was glaringly obvious the elder brother didn't want to talk. For once, though, Gonzalo showed some initiative and called his friends on the security detail. They talked a bit before making him wait and finally getting back to him.

"Okay," said Gonzalo, slipping his phone into his pocket. "This is the deal. Christian said he's sorry but he's buried with work. He would love to help but today's impossible. He promises he'll make time for you tomorrow morning. How does that sound?"

Carver checked his watch. After wasting a couple of hours with a tour through Tijuana's industrial sector, it was a compelling compromise. "It's something, at least."

Rather than push Gonzalo past his limit of helpfulness, Carver had him return to the glitz of *Avenida Revolución*. They parked outside Central Bar & Restaurant.

"You can just drop me off," instructed Carver.

"You're not done for the day," said Gonzalo, like a statement.

Carver eyed the sun stubbornly holding out in the sky. "Far from it. I figured we could take a break, refuel and recharge, and you can pick me up same place at ten. The real investigation starts tonight."

Gonzalo mulled over the unexpected change in plans, and then shrugged. "Works for me."

Carver nodded and exited the car. Two steps later he was

surprised by the sound of Gonzalo's door shutting. He turned to find him following.

"Don't worry," he said. "I won't stay in your hair. I just need to take a leak."

They pushed into the building with large white floor tiles and cream-colored brick walls brimming with minimalist artwork. It wasn't quite dinnertime but that hadn't stopped the tables in the well-trafficked area from filling up. Morgan and Shaw sat at the bar in richly leathered dark-red stools with high backs. They clocked him as soon as he entered.

As he converged Shaw said, "Had a bit of a field trip, did you?"

Carver strutted past without acknowledgment or eye contact, a few stools down around the bend in the bar, and grabbed a seat by himself. Shaw eyed him with curiosity as Gonzalo slowed on his way to the bathroom.

Everyone was watching everyone for a moment, and Shaw opened his mouth to say something. Carver widened his eyes in sudden recognition and leaned forward, hands on the zebra-marbled counter. "Dave, is that you?" he boomed with boisterous energy. "What the hell are you doing here?"

Shaw pulled his head back and blinked, whatever he'd been about to say lost in confusion.

"That *is* you, you old dog, isn't it?" Carver wagged a showy finger at him. "You were demonstrating at the gun show in Dallas last year..."

"Holographic sights," blurted Morgan, quicker on the uptake than Shaw. "Yup, that was my hubby, all right!" She clutched Shaw's arm like she was fiercely proud of her beau.

Carver leaned back with a satisfied smile. "I *knew* that was you. I never forget a good shooter. What brings you to TJ?"

By this point, Gonzalo's curiosity was bordering on intrusive. Rather than appear nosy, he went about his business and disappeared into the men's room.

Shaw leaned forward, brow still furrowed, and spoke under his breath. "You okay, boss?"

Carver gave his head a single small shake, and Morgan whispered into her new hubby's ear. He finally got it and stopped trying to chat. Carver grinned at the bartender and asked for a menu. There were only a handful of entrees to choose from. It was always a good sign when a restaurant focused on a specialty and ditched everything extraneous. He ordered as Gonzalo exited the restroom. The driver, seeing him busy, didn't interrupt and left the establishment with only a sideways glance at the couple from Dallas. A minute later the Aviator continued down the avenue and they were clear.

Thus far Carver had made an effort to keep certain aspects of his operation compartmentalized. Ignacio Espinoza didn't want a team of people sniffing into his business, which was fair enough. Just as fair was not having *Sólido* Security poking into Carver's. Given Tijuana's lawless reputation, he rested easier knowing locals didn't have a bead on his hotel room or his friends. OPSEC would proceed on a need-to-know basis.

After the bartender entered their food orders and served

a fresh set of cocktails, he made himself scarce. Morgan and Shaw slid over a couple of stools to share the corner with him. Shaw had a bourbon on the rocks, Carver a rye old fashioned, and Morgan a giant blended piña colada with assorted fruit and two umbrellas.

"What's the deal with the driver?" prodded Shaw.

Carver shook his head. "Still trying to work that out. Gonzalo isn't exactly a go-getter, but I'm not sure if his lack of initiative is his true nature or an act."

"You think he's holding out on you?" asked Morgan.

"Could be. At the very least he's babysitting."

"That don't make sense," said Shaw.

"Not unless he knows something about Manuel," suggested Morgan.

Carver swirled his drink. "That's a little presumptive. I'm working for a politician. The man has to have walk-in closets full of skeletons. They might just want to make sure I'm coloring between the lines."

"Do they even know you?" she guffawed.

"Such are the parameters of my mission." He sighed and finally enjoyed a sip.

"Ol' Iggy Espinoza's definitely locked down," mentioned Shaw. "Police on his payroll watching the ranch. Security teams escorting the kids."

Morgan clicked her tongue. "Can you blame him after what happened?"

He dipped his head and turned to Carver. "What do you make of the PSC?"

"*Sólido*?" he asked. "Ex military and police. Gonzalo

doesn't give me a lot of confidence, but maybe he's the B Team. They're bound to have some real hitters on the payroll. Christian's residential security team was armed with automatic submachine guns."

Shaw stroked his beard. "Maybe I should have followed this Gonzalo cat. What do you suppose your driver's up to now that you cut him loose?"

A shrug. "Could be he's waiting around the corner to see if I do something unexpected. Could be he's calling Ignacio and reporting on me. Or maybe he's getting dinner and a beer."

The discussion shifted to the specifics of the investigation, and soon enough they were enjoying their meals. Carver ate an herb-butter rib eye with a cognac sauce reduction because it sounded fancy and a plate of Parmesan garlic fries because it didn't. Morgan ordered lamb wherever she could find it, and Shaw tackled a tomahawk chop that Carver suspected was intended for two.

"The way I see it," Carver concluded after a long-winded recap, "I could play this two ways. One, I can be the nice guy and inquire around and get a bunch of non-answers while I wait for news to come to me... Or I could kick in some heads."

"Gotta speak the language of the land," interjected Shaw while chewing a hunk of fat.

"Exactly my thinking. Except why waste the day knocking around low-level dealers who don't know anything when we can cut right to the heart of the matter?"

He looked up the nightclub Alma Espinoza had given

him, *La Cascada*, and slid his phone over so they knew the place.

"You hoping New Generation's just waiting around for you?" asked Shaw.

"They own the place and the surrounding hill. I have a better chance at scoring a hit there than anywhere else."

Morgan pouted. "Into the belly of the beast..."

"Some things can't be helped, Jules. Besides, I won't go without backup." He pointed at Shaw.

"That's what I'm talking about," replied his friend.

"I want you to recon early, get there before Gonzalo and I show up. Scope out the place. Maybe find a way to sneak weapons in."

He scratched his furry cheek. "We planning on shooting?"

"I'm planning to avoid it, but you know how plans go."

"You'll be outgunned," Morgan warned.

"Which is why we won't hesitate if things get violent. But we'll be on their turf, going as emissaries. Respect where it's due. We can even pay them for their time."

Carver produced the envelope with Ignacio's petty cash, split the total into three stacks, and passed them around. "That's look-the-other-way money. Maybe get-out-of-jail money too. It might warrant an audience with the cartel, but it's not enough to buy them off. They may have weak links among their ranks, but we don't have the time or the intelligence to cultivate assets. We are, at the end of the day, outsiders, and we must assume they'll form a united front against us."

Morgan's eyebrows went up as she silently counted. "The congressman is serious about finding his son. That's a plus. What am I doing with my cut?"

"I want you touring the police stations tomorrow. There's a chance Manuel Espinoza is rotting in a half-refrigerated morgue somewhere. The family is too invested in the idea of his kidnapping to have checked this eventuality, and Mexican police procedure is not renowned for its efficiency. If there's a body, I want you to find it. Start in *Zona Este*, in concentric circles around his clinic, but don't be afraid to venture further out. It would make sense to dump the body in another neighborhood."

"Easy enough," she said. "Should I present as a DEA liaison?"

"Just the opposite, actually. The police aren't motivated to work with the US government these days, but they have no qualms about partnering with private enterprise."

She rolled up the money and slipped it into her bag. "Especially enterprises that are willing to grease the wheels a little."

"Cost of doing business. If you need more, dip into our own funds. I'll expense Ignacio."

"Just be careful tonight," she warned. "It's bad enough I'm looking for one body. I don't want to add two more troublemakers to my list."

"Shaw and I?" asked Carver innocently as he took a chunk of beef into his mouth. "How much trouble can a couple of tourists get into in Mexico?"

8

It was eleven by the time the black Aviator pulled up to the nightclub. The parking lot was moderately crowded, with dressed-up patrons lined at the metal gate beside the entrance. Carver quietly exchanged text messages in the back seat.

"You really going in there?" asked Gonzalo, voice skeptical.

"You think it's a dumb move?"

"It's poking the bear."

"This is a bear that needs poking."

Gonzalo dipped his head, not agreeing or disagreeing so much as showing a measure of respect. "I don't think I can cross this line."

"I don't expect you to."

The statement didn't set Gonzalo at ease. He huffed. "Look, if you get into it in the street, my job is to protect you and anyone else in the car. But this club... these people... I'm not authorized to go in there."

Carver was surprised to see the security contractor taking pride in his work, even if it was just to let him down. Frankly, this scenario worked better for him. An extra gun is only as valuable as your trust in the man holding it, and Gonzalo was a big question mark. Besides, his jungle experience wasn't suited to the mission. This kind of work called for a special type of personality.

"Don't worry about it," said Carver in earnest. "I shouldn't be more than an hour or so. Then you can take me home and we can call it a night."

The driver nodded. Carver exited the car and shut the door. He wore black slacks and a light-blue button-up that hugged his chest and shoulders. The shirt hung loose over his leather belt, and his boots were freshly polished.

La Cascada wasn't in the touristy part of town, and it wasn't in the fast-developing sleek business center either. The neighborhood, if it could be called that, verged on industrial, with auto shops and construction companies dominating the block. Right beside a locked-up air-conditioning supply depot ran a high metal gate and the parking lot for the club.

The building itself was two stories, converted from an old warehouse. The front facade was redone with neon signs and velvet ropes, but it was a paper-thin sheen over industrial grit. Carver approached as the door to a stretch limo opened and a man with a wild mahogany beard disembarked.

"This is the spot, ladies!" exclaimed Shaw with a subtle wink at Carver.

His friend wore a suit with a casual jacket, unbuttoned, no tie. He assisted from the car a woman wearing a tight black number that was at once cut too low and too high. A clump of colorful balloons escaped with her, and Carver could already see this was too much. Shaw dipped in and helped a second woman out, this one wearing bright red and somehow less of it. She cradled a bakery box. Carver sighed as his friend repeated the action with two more ladies until finally the limo was empty. The last girl carried a piñata.

"You've got to be kidding me," Carver muttered under his breath.

"Girls," announced Shaw, "I'd like to introduce you to my brother from another mother, Vince. Give him a warm welcome now."

No matter how grumpy you are, there's something magical about a gaggle of beautiful women decked to the nines zeroing in for a kiss. They hugged him, pecked his cheeks and lips, and were handsy with his arms and stomach. They were warm all right.

As Shaw herded them toward the front of the line, Carver sidled up to him. "What is it with you and *paraditas*?"

"When in Rome, Vince. When in Rome." He handed Carver one of the gift bags and approached the security staff.

As a man, there are two universal ways to guarantee entry into even the most exclusive of nightclubs: spend a lot of money and bring a lot of girls. If you do it right you won't even need to wait in line.

But this wasn't Ibiza and it wasn't Spring Break. The truth was competition was light, and Shaw had pressed the easy button by paying for a VIP table. It was flashy but it was smart. Their troupe of six was immediately ushered toward the door.

Carver waited at the metal detector as the ladies stepped through and recovered their purses on the other side. One of them wore shoes with giant metal buckles that set the scanner off. Even though the thin straps over naked feet and tight dress left little to hide, the security guard waved a wand and confirmed she was clear.

As Carver set his phone and money clip into the basket, another guard commenced a brisk search of the gift bags full of trivial items like paper party hats, plastic glasses, and LED blinkers. Along with the balloons and the girls, they were obvious distractions to keep the security team busy. Unfortunately, they balked at the soccer-ball piñata.

The checker hefted its weight and gave it a shake as Shaw stepped through the scanner. "I'm sorry, sir. We can't allow this."

Shaw dropped his jaw. "Aw, come on now. It's for Carla's birthday party."

The girl gave Shaw the stink eye. It took Carver a second to notice the cake through the box's plastic window. The letters in red icing clearly read, *"¡Feliz cumpleaños Carmen!"* He supposed getting the girl's name wrong could be part of the act.

"I'm sorry," asserted the security guard. "It's not allowed."

"But the limo's already parked. Can't you make an exception for Carla?"

Carmen made just about the droopiest puppy eyes

Carver had ever seen, but her target's heart was made of ice.

"The best I can do is leave it with the coat check. You can pick it up on the way out."

Carver frowned. The coat check was right next to the security team, in the immediate area exterior to the club. They would have no access to it without drawing a lot of attention.

Shaw huffed in disappointment. "Fine. Sorry for the trouble."

"It's no trouble, sir. We'll keep the cake refrigerated for you."

"That would be nice."

Carver stepped through the scanner. The alarm beeped and the wand identified the culprit as his belt buckle. A quick pat down confirmed he had no weapons, not even his folding everyday carry. The security team handed the bags and balloons back, and a hostess greeted them with a smile and a request to follow.

The club was a modest space that was more obnoxious than it had a right to be. Electric red light permeated packs of men and women sweating on a central dance floor that buzzed with loud Mexican trap music. Lounge tables and booths lined the walls, many staffed by drinkers and smokers and users of various other substances. The end of the large room featured the main bar and cordoned-off VIP sections with elegant couches and long tables.

It was only once they reached the center of the building that Carver could see the mezzanine behind them. It was built above the entrance overlooking the dance floor and enclosed in glass. He wordlessly met Shaw's eyes and glanced that way. A bouncer was posted at the bottom of each stairway leading up, one on the right wall and one on the left. They had no visible weapons.

Once they were brought to their seating area circling a long table, the hostess referred to her phone, holding it so close that her face glowed with blue light. "You have two bottles of Don Julio on the way. What juices or mixers would you like?"

Shaw corralled the girls into a giggly huddle before they could sit. "Whatever the ladies want." His finger motioned back and forth indicating they communicate. One asked for margarita mix. Another said all she needed were limes and salt.

Carver and Shaw sat next to each other with their backs at the wall so they faced the full house. The nearby bar was clumped with eager patrons, many of whom watched them with hard eyes. It was probably an effort to look tough for the girls who laughed and traded seats and danced in place as the VIP bottles and glasses arrived. It took a few more minutes for the juices and garnish to hit the table, but the staff was quick and well prepared. It wasn't good business to keep your high rollers waiting.

Carver leaned into his friend. "You spent your share of the cash quick."

"You're not wrong, brother. Speaking of, I'm gonna need your share too. These ladies aren't as cheap as they look, which is a win on both counts. Inflation, am I right?"

"It probably has more to do with keeping them off their

street corners most of the night. That's a lot of lost business."

"Sure, but how often do they get to be VIPs like this? Don't worry, I told them what to expect."

He poured a bottle as the women crowded around. One sat in Shaw's lap and balanced a shot glass in her barely contained cleavage. As he poured, she sprinkled salt on her thigh and fit a slice of lime between her teeth. Using only his mouth, Shaw licked the salt, upturned the cup, dropped the empty on the floor, and locked lips that squeezed every last drop from that poor lime. The watching girls applauded.

Carver could see the two of them were in more danger than he'd thought.

The group lounged for twenty minutes to settle in and get the lay of the land. They chatted and Carver got the names of the girls. Carmen, Meredita, Isa, and something that sounded like Mabel but different. Meredita insisted she could make killer margaritas. She took two glasses and fervently shook them in what was more a show of wagging hips than competent cocktail execution. The resulting drinks were mostly juice, which gave Carver and Shaw the perfect opportunity to partake without overdrinking. Another win for the *paraditas*.

Eventually, Shaw caught a passing barback and whispered in his ear. Then he suggested the ladies work up a sweat while he and Carver talked business. After topped-off drinks and a parade of blown kisses, the girls departed to the dance floor as Carver and Shaw admired the view.

"It wouldn't be a bad life," commented Shaw wistfully. "If I ever get burned and need to disappear, this might be a good spot." He watched the shapely troupe of women dancing in pairs. "The girls are something else."

"This whole place is something else."

"You're not wrong." Shaw made a subtle nod to the mezzanine. "You see that?"

Past the ladies and the dance floor and directly above the gesticulating DJ, a cozy pair of lounge tables hosted the ultra-VIP on a private balcony. Two narco soldiers in their early twenties kept a keen eye on the crowd, a few friends permanently inhabited a circular couch, and a pair of men in their forties shared beers at the central table beside the window.

"New Generation," stated Carver, who had clocked the players some time ago. "I'm willing to bet they're the stakeholders here. The guy with the glasses handles the business, and the bald gym rat handles the trouble."

Shaw nodded. "That was my take too. They also look like brothers. Outsiders like us aren't going to be able to play them against each other."

They sipped the overly sour margaritas as they watched for ways in. While they drank, the barback returned with Carmen's cake.

"It's really her birthday," said Shaw, "if you can believe that."

Carver grunted. "I'm not sure you can believe anything they say, especially while they're on the clock." He surveyed the party favors. It was a bunch of plastic crap from the dollar store. "It's too bad about that piñata."

Shaw dumped a plastic bag full of LED lights onto the table. "Why? If you want something sweet, Isa could help you out. She's half unwrapped already."

"Naked is the problem," returned Carver. "It's how I'm gonna feel going to that mezzanine without hardware."

"Well why didn't you say so, boss?" Shaw stuffed a hand into the plastic bag he'd emptied, spread his fingers wide, and mashed them into the cake. Carmen's birthday message mushed through layers of white frosting and vanilla cake. The makeshift glove found purchase on a plastic object within the baked good. Shaw pulled it out and to the floor behind the table, so that they were the only two people in *La Cascada* who could see the large freezer bag that contained a Beretta M9 and a Sig Sauer P320.

"Nick, you beautiful bastard."

"I have my ways."

He opened the bag, distributed the hardware, and stuffed the frosted-covered trash under the table. Both men slipped the pistols into the smalls of their back.

Carver stood. "I say we get this over with before Carmen sees what we did to her cake."

They stepped onto the main floor. "You going left or right?" asked Shaw.

"The guy on the right's been pissed off and checking his phone all night. Looks like a spat with the girlfriend. I'm betting the guy on the left will be more hospitable. I'm thinking we go together."

"Copy that. Let me take a walk, get a close-up on the

opposite guy, and then join you."

They split up, each approaching the mezzanine from opposite sides of the dance floor. Shaw had more ground to cover so Carver slowed as he passed the girls. Isa grabbed him and pulled him close, pressing her soft body into his. Margarita Meredita put a hand around Carver's waist, brushing against his steel. He grabbed her wrist and pulled it away.

"No."

Isa drew away from his sharp reaction. If Meredita had caught on that he was packing, she didn't show it. Along the far wall, Shaw strolled past the distant guard and rounded the corner toward him. He was just doing recon, making sure the guy wasn't armed. These wouldn't be. They were normal bouncers who dealt with normal douchebags. The same wouldn't hold true once they were upstairs.

"Sorry," said Carver as succinctly as he could before moving on.

At the bottom step, the bouncer watched Carver approach. He was above average height but not much more than that so had to look up at his visitor.

"Sorry," said the man sternly. "Invitation only."

"I have one," replied Carver. He pulled a folded envelope from his pocket and spread it open to reveal the cash contents.

"Who's that for?" The man's eyes grew suddenly suspicious as Shaw converged on them.

"It's not for you," explained Carver. "It's for the *jefe*. And there's more where that came from."

"I wasn't told to expect anyone."

"That's because he's not expecting us."

"Then you're not allowed."

Carver bit down and shook his head in concern. "That's a bad decision, man. Just because he doesn't know us doesn't mean he doesn't *want* to know us, know what I mean?"

The bouncer's face blanked for a second as he processed that. He recovered his cool, appraised both of them, and then glanced to the second floor. "Okay," he concluded after a drawn-out breath. "I'll let them know. But no promises. And you stay right here while I check. Anyone who comes up these steps without permission is in for a world of hurt."

"We read you loud and clear."

He nodded, satisfied. He went up one step, paused, and turned back to them. "Who should I say you are?"

"A concerned party with mutual enforcement interests."

The bouncer's lips silently practiced the phrase a couple of times, like he was prepping for a test. He seemed unhappy with the non-answer, but he let it slide. He went up another step, stopped, and turned back again, this time with a hand out. He stared in wordless expectation.

Carver sighed and placed the envelope of cash in his waiting palm.

The bouncer nodded, mumbled "mutual enforcement interests" again, and went up the stairs.

"You know we might never see that envelope again," muttered Shaw.

"Isn't that the point?"

"Only if we get visitation rights."

They waited below the enclosed balcony an extended minute. The music was loud, and their steep angle right below the mezzanine blocked any view through its windows. When one of the bodyguards planted a face in the glass to peek down, they at least knew the message had been delivered. He disappeared and they waited another minute. Then the original bouncer opened the door at the top and slowly descended. His expression didn't reveal the outcome of the conversation. It was only once he reached the bottom of the stairs that he circled past them and held up a hand, inviting them to proceed.

9

At the top of the steps, Carver and Shaw were greeted by a pair of narco soldiers. One had a semiautomatic Five-seveN pistol tucked into his belt. The other carried a Galil ACE carbine. The bodyguards wore sneers as general warnings. It was a simple intimidation tactic, and likely the weapon they were most proficient at. Neither appeared especially strong or smart. They came to within a careless distance of him and left their guns exposed. They were amateurs without military training.

As the door closed behind them, the sealed glass room grew surprisingly quiet. The mezzanine reverberated with the banging beat below, but the music was now faded white noise. Two men and a woman laughed around a couch, lost in their drunken world and giving the newcomers little notice. The main players watched them from the central table at the window overlooking the dance floor.

Both men were in their forties, a little weathered and past their prime but still fighting for the top of that mountain. Their faces were alternately curious and bored. The unannounced appearance of two Americans had at least earned their attention. The envelope fat with cash rested on

The Service of Wolves

the table.

"Who are you?" demanded the thinner man. He had sweaty black hair, round glasses, and a five o'clock shadow.

"I'm Vince. This is my associate, Nick."

Shaw dipped his head. "Don't believe we've had the pleasure."

"We're assuming you run things here?" prodded Carver.

The thin man looked at his partner, bemused. "They come to us and they don't know who we are?"

The second guy scoffed. "What I want to know is who the hell are Vince and Nick?"

Shaw shrugged. Carver said, "No disrespect intended. We're familiar with your organization, just not any individuals. We're from north of the border and don't usually have cause to cross it."

The second guy, the gym rat, held his expression of disdain. He was bald, perhaps the slightly older of the two, and had a ridiculous long gray mustache over a bare chin. It was hard to be sure while he was sitting, but he didn't appear especially tall or foreboding. Well muscled, sure, but with a habit of capping off his workouts with a few too many *cervezas*.

The thin man clapped his hands together. "Whatever, fine. You come to us with respect. My ego doesn't require you to have known my name. It's Esteban Gallo, by the way. This is my brother Pancho, and you would do well to remember that."

Carver knew a lot about Esteban already. Since it was what the cartel boss was looking for, he simply nodded.

Esteban flashed his teeth and splayed a hand to the set of chairs opposite. "Please, sit."

Carver checked the two narcos. He'd been hoping for a position that didn't have two guns behind him. At the very least, Shaw could stand and watch his back. But Esteban had invited them both to join the table, and there were two empty seats waiting. It was a daunting position, no matter how little training the narcos had.

Carver was here to be friendly, to make a deal, and that required confidence. Unfortunately, his hesitation betrayed that confidence.

Pancho leaned forward, rammed a finger on the table, and growled. "He said *sit down*."

The bodyguard with the carbine jammed the barrel into Carver's back. It took a major force of will not to yank the weapon from his hands and beat him over the head with it. Instead, Carver coolly turned as if he'd barely noticed the force.

"Israel Weapon Industries Galil ACE. Not the best piece of hardware around these parts but serviceable enough. Manufactured in Columbia. You get your supply from the guerrilla forces out that way, or do you just tap the local police for an under-the-counter arms deal here and there?"

Carver's unruffled reaction earned a curious look from Esteban. You couldn't show fear with these guys. It was the only way they would respect you. That said, talking tough was far from an olive branch, and Pancho grew more upset.

"You think this is a joke?" he fumed.

Carver spread his hands. "We're not here for trouble, if

you'll hear us out." He motioned forward, and he and Shaw took a seat.

A situation like this, two unknowns meeting face-to-face, came with a lot of maneuvering. Both parties worked to be the bigger dog: more mysterious, more connected, more capable. Keeping up that pretense was often the difference between walking away with a deal and being dumped in the back alley beaten to within an inch of your life.

They let Esteban take the lead so he would feel in control. "You know a lot about weapons," mused the boss. "That's what you want me to understand. Are you arms dealers? Do you come to us with a business proposition?"

"A proposition, but one that has nothing to do with your business. I won't intrude on that. My intention is for both of us to shake hands and walk away happy. We'll pay for your time, and you'll never see us again."

After watching them a moment, Esteban patted the envelope. "This money, you have to understand, it is nothing. It got you an introduction. Five minutes of my time."

"That's just a taste."

Pancho's eyebrow twitched but Esteban retained his poker face. He casually leaned back in his chair and crossed one leg over the other. "Let's hear it then. What is it you want?"

"A kid was kidnapped by the cartels. We were pointed in your direction."

Pancho scoffed. "You're a hostage negotiator."

"That's one way to put it."

"We don't do ransoms, gringo."

Esteban put up a hand to calm his brother. "You should know better, Vince and Nick. Which company are you with?"

"We're not," said Shaw. His eyes bore holes into Pancho.

Esteban frowned for a moment as he looked them over. "If someone was kidnapped, I advise you to pay what they ask. It's how business is done here. But my brother is right, it's not our business. You've got the wrong people."

"With respect," said Carver, "I'm not sure that we do."

"You calling us liars?" challenged Pancho.

"I didn't say you took him, just that you could help me. You need to appreciate that this isn't a run-of-the-mill hostage situation. There was no ransom demand and we're not your average negotiators. You could say we represent... more *official* channels."

Esteban nodded along tiredly, signifying he was getting the drift but wasn't impressed. "So you're a couple of cowboys is what you're telling me."

"You're a smart man and can come to your own conclusions about which agencies we may or may not be operating under. At the end of the day, we're just looking for a kid."

Esteban smiled, traded a glance with Pancho, and then leaned forward. "And what kid is this?"

"The youngest son of Congressman Ignacio Espinoza. Manuel was working at his clinic three days ago. He went out for lunch and never came back. His father wants him back safe and will pay you more than handsomely if that happens."

The pair of drug bosses had a successful thing going, but they were nowhere near as opaque as they thought they were. Recognition glinted in their eyes as soon as the name was mentioned. The surrounding air grew stale. Carver was sure they knew something. If they hadn't nabbed the kid, they had at least heard about it. In their circles, they might even know why. All things considered, that would be a damn good start.

"Hector," called Esteban without removing his eyes from his guests. "I need the room."

A guy on the couch looked over. "Seriously bro?"

"OUT!"

Hector swallowed his tongue, pulled his friends off their asses, and shuffled them out the door as the music blared. Carver's gaze followed them, taking the opportunity to spot-check the bodyguards who remained.

The music faded as the door closed softly. Pancho was speaking in his brother's ear. The Spanish was blended together and too quick to parse, but Carver distinctly made out "*El Vaquero.*" Esteban shushed him and they straightened, leaving the mezzanine in the awkward silence of muted drum beats.

Eventually that silence was broken with forced laughter.

"The Espinozas?" chuckled Esteban. "That explains your boldness. But what makes you think we know anything about the boy?"

"You're the biggest cartel in Tijuana," said Carver

matter-of-factly. "Are you telling me you don't know what's going on in your own backyard?"

"Flattery will only get you so far, Vince. Yes, we have heard the boy went missing. From a neighborhood devoid of our operations."

"That's not all you know."

"Puta madre," spat Pancho. "How about I wipe that clever grin off your face?"

"How about you try?" replied Shaw.

Pancho swiveled his attention to the boy from Kentucky. They locked into a macho staring contest.

A sigh escaped Esteban's lips. "My brother is easily upset. It's a fault. He experienced a lot, as a boy. Shielded me from most of it, too, so I'm in no position to complain about his temper now. But faults aside, my brother has a keen eye for cons. He's not one to be taken advantage of, believe me."

Pancho leaned forward. "Is this a shakedown? *El Vaquero* flexing his muscles?"

Carver failed to hide his confusion. "I'm here for the boy, that's all. Whatever disputes you have over trade or territory or politics don't concern me."

"And what if the boy is part of that dispute?" challenged Pancho.

"Is he?"

"Culero!" snapped Esteban. "Look around the city, Vince. You walk ten blocks in any direction and you'll find drugs from two separate outfits. Everything—killing, selling, and kidnapping—is about territory. It's all tied

together. You can't get the kid back and pretend to stay out of the drug trade at the same time."

"I don't care what it takes," said Carver. "I intend to get him back."

"Great! Now you're being honest. Pat yourself on the back."

Carver's eyes narrowed.

Esteban signaled one of his men over. The bodyguard with the pistol leaned to his boss and accepted whispered orders. Then he disappeared out the door and down the steps. The two drug bosses looked at each other, leaving Carver worried that something was about to go down.

"This can be profitable for both of us," he assured. "Is Manny still alive? If you give him back you can name your price."

A snicker from Esteban. "You're serious."

"I might surprise you."

The cartel boss sucked his lips and scratched the scruff along his jaw. He had the angles running in his head and took time to turn them over. "Since you're from north of the border, how does one million American dollars sound?"

Carver crossed his arms and bit down, feigning a difficult decision without overdoing the drama. "If the kid's still in one piece and you hand him over tonight, it's a deal."

Pancho's eyebrows went up again. "That's it? You have the cash on you?"

"The money will be traded for the kid. Same time, same place." Everyone stared a moment and Carver added, "It's a good deal."

The door opened and everyone turned as the bodyguard strolled in accompanied by four bombshells: Carmen, Meredita, Isa, and something that sounded like Mabel. The girls giggled and bounced, pleased to be welcome among the ultra-VIPs. Carmen rested delicate fingers on Shaw's shoulder.

"Thank you for coming, ladies," said Esteban. "You made quite the splash when you walked into my club."

They laughed and said humble stuff like "Me?" and "No I didn't." Everyone was really amused except for Carver who wondered where this was going.

Esteban grinned at his apparent control over his guests. "You're right, Vince. It is a good deal. Better than good. There's only one problem... We don't have the boy."

He stood and held out a hand for Meredita. She took it and he spun her around before gently pushing her away. Then he sat on the edge of the table beside Carver.

"It takes balls to walk in here, Vince. Maybe more than balls. Connections, am I right? I don't know who you are or what kind of pull the Espinozas think they have, but, I have to say, as respectful as your tone has been, I'm more than a little insulted."

Carver worked his jaw and casually spot-checked the narcos again. The idiots had let the girls obstruct their line of fire.

Esteban scooped the envelope off the table and rifled through the bills. "You cowboys walk into the territory of *Jalisco Nueva Generación*, throwing your cash around, swinging your *pollas*, and you want us to think you're tough shit?"

As the congenial conversation turned, the smiles of the *paraditas* evaporated. They were more professional than scared or frightened. They'd doubtless seen bad things and catered to bad elements before. They knew they weren't the target of Esteban's ire. As long as they remained calm and pleasant, while not making light of his anger, they should be all right, and they knew it.

But apparently, like his brother, Esteban had a bit of a temper.

"You take your money," he said with spittle on his teeth. "Pay it to your whores!"

He beamed the envelope hard into Meredita's face. It made a wet slapping sound and pesos flew everywhere. Carver's muscles tensed at the unnecessary display, and Meredita shivered in place, fighting back tears.

"I said take it."

Esteban's eyes smoldered, and Meredita squatted and collected the cash.

Pancho leaned half his body over the table and showed off yellow teeth. "Hey gringo, you ever think that since nobody asked for a ransom, nobody wants your stinking money?" He snickered like violence was his only joy in life.

Carver and Shaw traded a resigned glare. So much for the easy way.

"You ever think," continued the boastful enforcer, "that before you shit in our house, you should look closer to home first?"

"Pancho!" warned his brother.

That moment of rebuke gave them the opening they needed.

Shaw grabbed Pancho's neck and heaved him over the table and onto the floor, relieving him of the pistol in his belt. Carver spun out of his chair, slid low between Isa and Meredita, and caught a surprised narco with a fist to the chin. He went woozy and stumbled.

The problem was the still-unfettered narco with the carbine. His slow reaction was gaining pace as the situation dawned on him. Shaw moved to cover him but the *paraditas* were in his line of fire. Carver reached for the weapon under his shirt, but there was too little time. Lightning reflexes kicked in and he barreled into the soldier and kept charging till they hit the plexiglass window. Instead of cracking, an entire rectangular block of plastic dislodged from the frame. It and the bodyguard careened over the railing. The narco's head clipped the edge of the DJ booth before he smacked the dance floor, down for the count.

The crowd started and spun to the mezzanine. A gunshot barked as Shaw warned off the first narco drawing his pistol. Shaw stomped over, cracked him in the head with the butt of Pancho's gun, and relieved him of his weapon. Carver finally pulled the Sig from his back and turned it on Esteban.

Collective screams joined the blaring music that now flooded the mezzanine through the broken window. Shaw cycled the pair of pistols and tossed them aside, opting for his Beretta.

"Go get the car, ladies. Party's over."

They rushed down the stairs toward the panic below.

Esteban clenched his jaw in subdued outrage. "You're dead."

"Say that again," warned Carver. He pressed his gun deep into Esteban's neck. *"Say that again."*

The drug boss worked his lips into an empty swallow.

Carver nodded. "So you're not as dumb as you look. That means by now you can tell we're not like those other hostage negotiators. Where's Manny Espinoza?"

Esteban scowled. "We didn't take the boy. That's the truth."

"But you know who did?"

After a delay he shook his head.

Shaw held a weapon on Pancho, still on his hands and knees. He checked over the wall. "Vince, it's about to get real hot in here. We need to move."

Carver worked his jaw. "Your temperamental brother said we should look closer to home. What did he mean by that?"

The wiry drug boss sneered defiantly. It was a tough act but it was paper thin. Carver cracked the butt of the Sig into his forehead, splitting open the skin above his eyebrow.

"What was Pancho talking about?"

Esteban growled in helpless frustration. "He means the Espinozas are more involved than you think."

"I don't believe you."

"Your funeral."

"I'm not the one with a gun in my face."

The cartel boss grimaced. "Think about it, *pendejo*. Why

else snatch the boy?"

"Politics. Anti-narco laws."

He snorted. "We don't care about the laws, man. The police answer to us."

Carver worked his jaw. Shaw whistled. "Vince, backup's on the way. It's time to go!"

Carver kicked Esteban's chest, sending him to the floor. After a peek downstairs, he followed Shaw out the mezzanine door, holding his weapon ready.

The club was in a state of chaos. Most people were in the process of fleeing, but there was still a good deal of confusion about what had happened. Despite the DJ no longer attending his booth, the music hadn't stopped, and a third of the party crowd were oblivious to the panic. The narco on the dance floor was still sleeping like a baby, his carbine untouched beside him. Carver grabbed it on the way to the exit.

They pushed outside and pointed their guns at security. The bouncers weren't armed and backed away. In the parking lot, the limo peeled right by them, bounced onto the road, and disappeared down the block.

"That's love for you," muttered Carver.

Shaw ruefully shook his head. "I don't believe I'll be tipping that driver."

They backed away as people flooded out of the club. A Ford SUV swerved into the parking lot. Armed narcos threw open the doors.

Carver pointed the Galil ACE and opened fire. The soldiers dove away and cowered behind the vehicle. Instead of aiming at them, Carver ventilated the engine compartment and front wheel. They continued backtracking while covering the club, searching for an exit.

The black Lincoln Aviator screeched on the asphalt behind them. Gonzalo shoved open the passenger door and yelled, "Get in!"

Carver backed inside while Shaw jumped in the rear. The SUV tore into the street before the narcos had a chance to give chase. With their responding vehicle out of commission, it would take them a minute to regroup. That minute would be too long.

Carver checked himself and his team to make sure nobody was injured. Then he realized the enemy had been so imbalanced during the sudden attack that they had never fired a single shot. They had gotten out clean. Carver swiveled his attention to Gonzalo who had come through in the clutch.

"An old acquaintance, huh?" asked the security driver in regards to Shaw.

Carver shrugged. "He freelances."

"Yeah right..." Gonzalo smartly kept an eye on the rearview mirror. "Looks like we're not being followed. What did you get from them?"

"Not much. The Gallo brothers don't like to talk."

Gonzalo nearly spasmed. "You fronted on Esteban and Pancho?"

"Should we not have?"

He gave a futile shake of his head. "You're some crazy gringos, man."

Carver leaned back in the seat and closed his eyes. "Funny, that's what they said."

The lighthearted tone clashed with the dark thoughts swirling around his head. For the second time that day, his search had unearthed the nickname *El Vaquero*. Whether by accident or design, his path was encroaching on the new player the DEA had warned him about.

A competing territorial interest could explain why the congressman was a target. And then there was Pancho's statement about the kidnapper being closer than they thought. One emerging explanation tied everything together: the Espinozas were dealing drugs themselves.

But that didn't answer the question of who had taken Manuel Espinoza. If the motive was territory, the list of suspects was as large as ever. And if New Generation had more inside info than that, they weren't amenable to a deal. They hadn't even bit at his offer of a million US dollars. How could one kid be worth that?

Carver released a tired sigh as the problem wrestled with the drone of the speeding engine.

10

The next morning, Carver paced the wide pedestrian sidewalk beneath the palm trees of *Avenida Revolución* while he thought about real estate. Or, more specifically, he thought about the real estate business.

Ignacio Espinoza's money didn't come from wine. That was according to Alma, the alluring and brutally honest socialite and bookkeeping beauty of the Espinoza empire. Carver had assumed real estate and construction were responsible for filling the shortfall, but what if they were only part of the story?

If Ignacio's political capital was funded with drug money, somebody was staking him. Heck, with his extensive business assets and shipping infrastructure, he might very well be staking himself. Police protection, private security, warehouses, export business... Most of the pieces lined up, but the picture that came together didn't fully explain Manuel's kidnapping.

Every potential answer to the riddle spurred additional questions. It was endless speculation. About all Carver could say for sure was that there was more to the Espinozas than met the eye.

Twice yesterday, in the course of his investigation, Carver had been accused of working for *El Vaquero*. He had never given a second thought as to whether it could be true. Now the possibility gave him pause. *El Vaquero* meant The Cowboy. It could be just another coincidence, but a family of Tecate ranch hands encroaching on Tijuana fit the bill.

So Ignacio might be deep into drugs, but involvement in the kidnapping didn't track. Otherwise he wouldn't have hired Carver to recover Manuel in the first place. In the convoluted plot of a dime-store novel, perhaps—in the real world, that kind of scheming drew too much unnecessary attention to the very thing that was being covered up.

No, Ignacio could have made a show of things by hiring a typical asset recovery company that would have crossed their "t"s and dotted their "i"s but otherwise failed to find Manny. Instead he had chosen to contact the DEA, outside official channels, and hire the real deal.

Likewise, if the Espinoza patriarch knew who was in possession of his youngest son, Carver believed he would have been plain about it. Every day of delay increased the chances of the kid winding up in a morgue, and that was assuming he wasn't already in one. No, there was no indication the father wasn't genuinely worried about the son.

So if Ignacio wasn't the prime suspect, Carver had to consider which other Espinozas might be involved.

Alma was shrewd enough to harbor ulterior motives, or at least she believed herself to be. Her pronouncements of love for little *Manolito* came off a little strong. Then again, she was a passionate person who didn't seem the type to resort to half measures. She was like a wildfire that way.

She also managed the family books, which would give her insight into illicit activities. Her endless assertions that the Espinozas were bad people were more or less a tacit admission of such. The logical conclusion was that she was almost definitely involved in the real family business.

But then, *vaquera* wasn't *vaquero* and cowgirl wasn't cowboy. The gendered language of Spanish ruled Alma out as the mastermind.

That left Christian, the eldest brother and heir to the Espinoza empire, as the obvious conclusion. Carver had first glimpsed him on horseback with a cowboy hat and boots. A *vaquero* encroaching on the big city, he was also coincidentally the only family member who'd been avoiding this investigation. Christian was a rich kid with a privileged upbringing playing with the pieces of Daddy's empire.

Carver's phone lit up. "Long night?" he answered.

Shaw grumbled. After their exit from the club, Carver had posted him on Christian's walled-off three-story mansion. "It's like you said," reported Shaw. "Heavy security that isn't just for looks. Four on the grounds and four inside. These *Sólido* guys have seen action before. They'd put up a capable defense against anyone assaulting the house."

Carver worked his lips together. "The question is whether the security team is the enforcement arm of a drug smuggling operation, or if it's the entirely expected response to his kid brother being kidnapped in broad daylight."

"Your guess is as good as mine. How long has *Sólido* been contracted?"

"They've been around for a while, but it's not unreasonable for them to have taken precautions beforehand given their environment. Have there been visitors?"

"None," said Shaw. "Judging from my peek over the wall, Christian's still inside. At least he is if he was here last night."

"Is there an alternate egress?"

"Negative. The backyard sits on a platform overlooking the bluff."

"Are they in hiding?"

"No need. I haven't been made. There's no reason for subterfuge on their part."

The honk of an approaching SUV caught Carver's attention. Gonzalo pulled the Lincoln Aviator to the curb, ready for a new morning.

"I'm tapping in now," said Carver. "Go home and get some shut-eye."

"You have a plan?" pressed Shaw. "You can't storm that place by yourself, and there's too many guards to sneak past. The downside of there being one way out means there's only one way in. It's well defended unless you know something I don't."

"I *have* something you don't," corrected Carver. "An invitation. Catch you later."

He ended the call and loaded into the SUV.

"Beautiful day," announced his driver. "I don't know about you, but after last night's excitement I slept like a baby. Some *café* and I'm good to go."

Gonzalo handed over one of two steaming Styrofoam cups. Carver nodded in appreciation. The coffee was black, still hot.

"So where to?"

"It's about time I said hi to Christian." Carver decided to test his companion. "If he's at the house... ?"

Gonzalo nodded. "He should be expecting us." They made for the outskirts of the city. "Any thoughts since last night on how *Nueva Generación* is involved in all this?"

Carver wasn't sure what to think of his guide so he remained tight-lipped. If it was true that Christian Espinoza was *El Vaquero*, Gonzalo could be his spy. Though his paycheck was signed by Ignacio, he was a regular on Christian's detail, only reassigned since Carver's arrival. The man's loyalties were a question mark.

Which was why Carver had to play things close to his chest, even with the Espinozas. As long as they weren't onto him, it was in their interest to keep up the pretense of access. Carver would get furthest by playing dumb, asking questions about one thing while actually investigating another. That was his play until he discovered more.

They arrived at the upscale *Cumbres de Juárez* neighborhood where they again drove to the end of the cul-de-sac at the peak of the hill. Gonzalo alerted the residential security team over the intercom and they promptly opened up. One armed guard approached the car, another stood by the opening gate, and another waited at the front door.

The Aviator was waved into a hardscaped concrete

sanctum replete with walled off garden terraces, stepped levels, and a monolithic squared entry arch to the porch proper. Once Gonzalo shifted to park he turned in his seat. "You need to leave your weapon in the car."

Carver shrugged and placed the P320 on the seat beside him. Upon disembarking, the guard that had followed them in instructed him to put his hands up. The guard searched him and uncovered a pair of knives, his BCM Colonel and his ER Police III.

"I'll hold onto these for you," he said.

"Seriously?" Carver pointed to the guard's submachine gun. "Against an HM-3?"

The *Sólido* contractor chortled. "It's an HM-3-S Mendoza Bulldog."

Carver arched an eyebrow. "Is that a .380 pistol cartridge?"

"The largest caliber allowed for PSCs," he beamed.

Carver sighed. Taking away his knives was overkill. "I'd prefer to keep them in the car."

The guard peeked in and eyed the Sig. It was a mistake to have drawn attention to it. "Fine by me," he obliged. He tossed them on the seat next to the pistol and shut the door.

"We good?" asked Gonzalo.

"You mind locking this?" requested Carver.

The driver shrugged and clicked the alarm. Then he led them up the steps to a porch surrounded by high white walls and black double doors with small patchwork windows.

The door guard conversed with Gonzalo in Spanish as the street gate pushed closed. The property was pretty but it felt like a prison and the lock had just clicked. The front door opened and a man in a suit greeted them.

"I'll wait outside," said Gonzalo.

What else was new?

Carver was led through a foyer with handmade terracotta tiles and a central grand piano. He scanned as he walked to get a lay of the land. He had expected an interior security team but there was nobody around except for the man giving him an escort. That didn't jive with Shaw's intelligence. Either the overnight team was more visible or Carver wasn't meant to see the muscle up close.

They arrived in an airy living room at the rear of the house. It featured a double-height ceiling and expansive windows that showed off the distant hills and valleys. The view made you feel like a king.

"Wait please," instructed the man before he disappeared.

Christian may have been busy but, to his credit, he arrived a short minute later and caught Carver nosing at the pool in the backyard.

"It never gets used," announced Christian from across the room. His banter came off professional, businesslike, and lacking any real personality. "I can't tell you the last time I went in. All that square footage, thousands of gallons of water, and it is more or less a painting. But art is art, is it not?"

"I'll take your word for it. I've never understood art."

Christian's skin was rosy, his hair was light-red-brown, and he was trim to the point of bony. His eyebrows rose in mock surprise. "Surely there has to be some form of art you admire. I've always considered it the touchstone of humanity. Without it, we're pretty much animals."

Carver shrugged. "To be honest I don't understand humanity much either."

He chuckled. "Now *that* is a sentiment I can agree with. To a point. After all, there's a little animal in all of us. There's nothing wrong with that."

"To a point."

The yard was spacious for the location, with a square of trimmed green before textured pavers and planters overtook the rear half. The concrete platform was surrounded with high walls on the sides but only low glass in the rear, elevated high enough above the hillside to make it private and secure. A single gunman paced around the expansive pool.

Today Christian wore a tailored suit with a pink tie, looking more like a politician than a cowboy. He converged on Carver and offered his hand. "Christian Espinoza, at your service. I understand you're looking for my brother."

"That's right, and I'd like to ask a few questions if you don't mind."

He signaled to the couches. "Not at all. And I have to apologize for running out on you yesterday. Business doesn't wait for family emergencies, unfortunately. I spent the last three days at the ranch waiting for news. It was time to stop neglecting other aspects of supporting the family."

"Not a problem." Carver took a seat on a long gray number.

"Can I offer you a drink?"

"I'd like to get down to it, if that's okay with you. I can keep it quick and get out of your hair."

His host smiled. "Right down to business. That is the American in you." Christian sat on a pale-green armchair perpendicular to the sofa. "Before we begin, I'm curious if you've made any headway?"

Carver took in a breath as he balanced what he wanted to reveal versus what Gonzalo may have already told Christian. "Honestly, I'm just reaching the end of the information-gathering stage, which is why it was important I speak with you. But I did reach out to the Jalisco New Generation Cartel."

His eyes widened. "You work fast. What did they say?"

Carver glanced over his shoulder at the gunman by the pool. He didn't like leaving his back exposed to the outside, but he had already scoped the yard and wasn't in apparent danger. Keeping an eye on the rest of the house was more promising. Christian noticed his unease so Carver pushed ahead.

"They deny involvement."

"That doesn't surprise me. Business in Mexico is about cultivating relationships, not barging in headfirst."

"With respect, hostage recovery sometimes requires a heavier hand."

"And what does that heavy hand have to show for itself?"

It was already clear that Christian was the type of guy who knew more than everybody else no matter the subject. "As you know," assuaged Carver, "there are a few other players I can reach out to. Today we're also canvassing the police."

"We?" he asked pointedly.

"I have assets at my disposal. There's a significant amount of low-value legwork that is probably a waste of time but nonetheless comprehensive. It would take too long to do it myself."

He nodded. "I understand what delegation is. Do you need assistance with the police?"

"Your father provided contacts and funding so I think we've got that angle covered. I'm more interested in better understanding Manuel's personal life and possibly discovering new avenues of investigation."

Christian matched Carver's professional demeanor. It was somewhat jarring due to his personal involvement, but then Christian seemed well in command of his emotions. "That sounds very logical so far," he said. "Though I have to admit, logic does not translate to optimism."

Carver frowned. "You don't foresee us successfully recovering your brother?"

"It's not that, Mr. Carver. I'm sure you are very capable, and I do hope Manuel's alive, of course, but... well... it doesn't look good. We should have been contacted by now. Every professional I've spoken to has said as much."

"Your father hired others?"

"Not my father. While I respect his wishes to leave my brother's fate in your capable hands, I've made discreet inquiries of my own. All of them have stressed the importance of avoiding escalation."

His words were sharp enough that Carver suspected he

already knew about *La Cascada*. "Perhaps there's a reason your father opted for somebody a little more kinetic."

Christian sighed. "And you are doing admirable legwork but still lack leads. As for this conversation, I'm afraid I don't see how I can provide any insight that will help."

"Then I thank you for humoring me. I—"

They were interrupted by heels clattering into the room. The woman was skinny, like Christian, with the kind of striking face you might expect from a fashion model. Her clothes and jewelry were expensive. When Christian stood to greet her, Carver did as well.

"Honey," said Christian, "this is Mr. Carver."

She kissed her husband and then held out her hand for Carver. "Ines."

Her arm was pointed high toward his chest, so he clasped her hand and kissed it. "A pleasure."

"You're the one looking for Manuel now?" she asked. Her tone implied that she didn't much care about an answer.

"Was there someone else before?"

She snorted. "This isn't the first time that *canijo* has run off. He's a man-child."

Christian chuckled awkwardly. "That was different, dear." He turned to Carver. "Manolo briefly cut contact when he first met his new girlfriend."

"It wasn't briefly," countered his wife. "He disappeared for two weeks."

"He didn't disappear. He was swept up in love."

"I bet that low-class tramp had something to do with this

one way or another."

More nervous laughing. "She would have no reason to lie," asserted Christian.

His wife wasn't convinced. "She's from the streets. Nothing good comes from hanging around those people. You said it yourself." Despite his protests, she addressed Carver. "You need to know, Manuel's always been the black duckling of the family. It's not that he's a bad boy, but he lacks common sense. You never know what he's getting into. Go on," she urged her husband. "Tell him."

Christian equivocated by bobbing his head back and forth. "There is truth to this. Manuel can be a magnet for trouble. He's smart, but he uses his intelligence in the wrong ways."

"He's very judgmental," she said over the top, apparently unaware of the irony. "Maybe it's a generational thing. You know how these university kids are these days, always thinking they have the moral high ground. As if that counts for more than my husband's business acumen."

"The two of you have clashed over the family business?" asked Carver pointedly.

"No," Christian asserted, cutting over his wife's answer and angling his eyebrows at her.

Ines sighed. "Look at me. Who am I to speak ill of the boy at a time like this? I can't keep track of him anymore. I doubt anyone can. Christian, I have my shopping."

"Of course," he said as she made for the front of the house. "Take your security team. I want two of them with you. You can't be too careful."

The Service of Wolves

"Yes, yes. I'll be safe. *Besitos*."

If his concern seemed forced, she lacked any at all. Carver wondered how much was theater for his benefit. They waited till Ines was gone to situate themselves again. Christian appeared slightly off balance after the encounter, which lent credibility to the information.

"Wives," he carped. "You let them get a word in about your family and suddenly it's a book."

Carver nodded along in fraternal camaraderie. "I hear you. But you said there's some truth to what she said?"

"There is, sure, but it's blown out of proportion. Manolo thinks he's in love. He fell off the map when he met what's-her-name. It was irresponsible to ignore us, but he didn't mean harm. It's his nature."

"To be irresponsible?"

Christian frowned at the implication. "To ignore us. He's from a different generation. He's impetuous."

"I have to say," started Carver as gently as possible, "I get the impression his disappearance isn't causing a whole lot of grief in this household."

"Why would you say that?"

Carver shrugged. "It's probably nothing, but he's missing. It seems like the wrong time to be critical of him."

"It's honesty, Mr. Carver. I thought that's what you were here for."

"Sure."

Christian nodded, satisfied. "Manuel has the idealism of youth. He believes he can solve the world's problems, and anyone who doesn't think like him *is* the problem. You understand?"

"He gets on his high horse," prodded Carver.

"Exactly. And his moral superiority often gets him in trouble. He's constantly virtue signaling. He thinks he's better than everyone."

"Even you?"

Christian canted his head. "Are you accusing me of anything, Mr. Carver?"

"I'm trying to get at what's being left unsaid."

He clenched and unclenched his jaw. "Did *Papá* tell you he's illegitimate? While my mother was in the hospital getting radiation pumped into her veins, my father stepped out on her with a woman half his age."

That must have been where the low-class comment came from. "It sounds like there's no love lost between you two."

"With my father? No. I make no secrets about that. He was a dirt farmer who worked his way up, bettered himself. He has my respect for that. He found a good woman, well bred—better than he deserved if you ask me. And what did he do? He squandered it. They say true nature wins in the end."

There he went with nature again. "And what about Manuel?"

Christian hiked a shoulder. "I never held it against him, and that's the honest truth. How can a boy be blamed for the sins of his father? Manolo's no more responsible for that than I or Alma."

"But he's a reminder."

"As if I could forget otherwise. I told you, I don't hold it against him." Christian stared a second. "Move on."

Carver raised his eyebrows like he was surprised by the reception of his comment. "No offense intended, Christian. I'm just trying to get a feel for what your relationship was like."

A curt smile indicated he would play ball, but his face was flushed. "I admit, I could never love him like my sister does. Manolo has always been an outsider. That's something my wife doesn't understand. His path is different. Don't mistake me, I hope he's alive, but he's not fit for the family business."

"The one you inherited from your dad."

Christian smiled defensively. "I've had advantages. I'm not ashamed of that. But so has Manolo. More even." His voice gained an edge. "When it comes down to it, I run things better than *Papá* ever did. And if I was in charge you better believe no one would have dared kidnap my brother."

He realized he was nearly growling and dialed the intensity back. That was the trick with friendly interrogation. A little jab here and there could bring out a person's true colors. It became less about what they said and more about how they said it.

"You know for a fact he's kidnapped then?" asked Carver.

His host shrugged matter-of-factly. "What else? The whole family believes that. It's why we hired you. And why, no offense intended, this conversation is a waste of your time. You won't find Manolo by digging into family secrets."

Carver nodded slowly. The downside to the occasional friendly jab was wearing out a welcome. He stood up. "You might be right, Christian, but let's get something straight here and now. Your father hired me. You had nothing to do with it. And I'm speaking with all family members, everyone close to Manuel, to give him the best chance of coming out of this alive. So I would appreciate you giving me access like everyone else in your family instead of hiding behind your wealth and business responsibilities."

This conversation was at an end. It hadn't been about learning concrete facts so much as getting a feel for who Christian was. And at this point Carver had a pretty good idea.

"You live in the United States," countered Christian with bile, "so you see this extravagance as suspect. These walls, these guards, and these guns—it's what any normal person with money needs in this city." He stood so he could look his guest in the eye. "Mexico doesn't have the luxury of exporting wars to other countries. Here it comes to our doorstep. You'll understand that soon enough if you don't already."

Carver worked his jaw. "Maybe I will."

Christian headed to the staircase and spoke without looking back. "Gonzalo will see you wherever you need to go. Be assured I will be at your future disposal if you need anything at all. Thank you for coming."

Christian's footsteps echoed up to the second floor.

11

As the eldest sibling, presumably bearing the responsibility of caring for the others, Christian wasn't too put out over his missing brother. Returning to his regular routine after a few days proved that much, yet it was a far cry from being directly involved in the kidnapping. Sure, Christian was detached and businesslike and maybe more than a little sociopathic, but those were character traits, not motives. He was hardened and dispassionate and, as he had grandiosely asserted, a reflection of his caustic surroundings.

The only possible motive Christian had admitted to was the animosity he harbored toward his father. It was difficult for Carver to pin the kidnapping on that alone, however. His gut told him it had something to do with the family business.

There remained the strong likelihood that the business in question was trafficking drugs. In order to avoid arousing suspicion, Carver had steered clear of that accusation, but he envisioned an idealistic little brother rebelling against the opportunistic heir. It was entirely possible a fledgling sibling rivalry had escalated into a full-blown battle for the fate of the family. It was very possible for such a war to result in casualties.

As Carver headed toward the door, he was again struck by the eerie lack of staff on the first floor. Being a little opportunistic himself, he wandered through the kitchen to take the long way out.

His weakening theory was that Manuel might be captive in the house somewhere. As unlikely as it was by this point, it was still worth considering. There were no pool houses in the backyard, and Carver didn't think Christian's wife would want the family screwup living upstairs. At any rate, Carver couldn't risk sneaking up there. Not now.

His snooping was rewarded by a basement entrance in the kitchen's pantry area. No noise came from its depths. Carver quietly pried the door open and found intricate wooden steps leading into a wine cellar. The storage area was cool, dark, and small. The only prisoners were overpriced bottles of foreign and local reds. He eyed a label with the Espinoza Ranch logo and could perfectly imagine the tackiness of Christian serving guests his own brand of wine.

Undaunted, he hurried up the steps and moved to a side door with a window that revealed a walkway along the perimeter wall. It was too high to see the neighbor's yard. Carver tried the door. Then he unlocked the deadbolt and tried again. It was still stuck but he budged it with an upward lift as he twisted the handle. A peek up and down the path didn't turn up anything of interest. Carver quietly shut the door.

Next he wandered past the entry area and large staircase

to a hallway. He peeked in an empty den with a TV before the man who had originally greeted him inside turned into the hall from the other end.

"Excuse me," Carver hurried. "I was wondering if there was a bathroom back here before I hit the road."

The man mulled it over for about a second too long. "This door," he said with a very particular tone and accompanying wag of his finger.

Carver spent a minute in the bathroom and ran the water. The trash was empty and there were no toiletries that indicated a guest was staying in the house. He didn't see anything useful and decided he had pressed his luck about as far as it would go.

This wouldn't be so easy. He wasn't going to simply stumble into Manuel. More often than not, uncovering secrets was a long process that required hours of surveillance. He emerged from the bathroom, and the man was waiting for him at the end of the hall. Carver nodded on his way out and found Gonzalo shooting the shit outside.

"Get what you need?" asked the driver.

"Sure. Let's go."

The waiting security team didn't do anything worse than eye him conspicuously on the way out, and Carver's weapons were right where he'd left them. Christian, too, had talked a good game. On the whole, everything about the visit had appeared on the up and up, but Carver still came away feeling slimy.

"Where to?" asked Gonzalo as the Aviator cruised down the hill.

Carver ground his teeth. There were nagging questions he wanted answers to. "Let's check the clinic again."

"Whatever you say."

After the family drama Carver had uncovered, both the *El Vaquero* angle and the brotherly differences, it seemed prudent more than ever to press Jasmine on what she really knew. Family secrets may be buried deeper than bodies, but there was no better shovel than pillow talk. If Manuel would confide in anyone about his ideological struggles, it would be Jasmine.

Which begged the question: if she was aware of the Espinoza's illicit trade, why hadn't she mentioned it? Every detail mattered to have a chance at saving the boy.

On the way, he called Morgan for an update.

"I've checked with several likely destinations," she reported. "Still have a few more. The police have been accommodating so far."

"No legal hang-ups?" he asked.

"The only law is money."

"If only it were that simple. I'm assuming you haven't located any possible John Does yet?"

"None in the various morgues. There are still one or two possibilities to check, but it's not looking like he'll turn up."

Carver grunted. The uncertainty was frustrating, but the alternative to not finding the kid was worse.

"I picked up a curious snippet though," she added with enigmatic flair. "There's a municipal police station on the same street as the clinic but half a mile down. The municipal police in Mexico don't handle serious crimes, but

The Service of Wolves

I figured they might have insight into Manuel since he was a community advocate with overlap in emergency response. I was right."

Carver leaned forward in his seat. "Do they know something about his kidnapping?" Too late he noticed Gonzalo had keyed off his excitement and watched him in the mirror.

"Quite the opposite," answered Morgan. "They didn't even know he was missing."

"That can't be right. Jasmine called the local police when it happened. Kidnappings might be commonplace, but they'd remember a privileged kid from an important family."

"That's what I thought so I pressed them. I asked around until a captain pulled me aside. At first I thought he was pumping me for more money, but he didn't seem the type. He said he knew Manuel Espinoza, but there was no record of an emergency call. It's his opinion that another department handled it at the state level, but I haven't had luck tracking it down. Police work in this country can be a little ad hoc at times."

"You're telling me."

"But the reason I find this particular officer credible is because, after some coaxing, he let slip that he had spoken to Manuel in that same police station a week ago. He was inquiring about drug enforcement."

Carver was stunned. That would have been days before he went missing. He eased back slowly, aware that Gonzalo was hanging on his every word. "Did he... explain what the request was in regards to?"

"Negative. Manuel was extremely vague, both about who he wanted to talk to and why. He ended up leaving the station without telling them specifics."

"He was scared."

"Maybe he wasn't scared enough."

That did stand to reason. Carver chewed his lip. Manuel had discovered something he wasn't supposed to know about. He was trying to reach somebody but didn't trust the Mexican police, likely because they were bought and paid for. And somebody had taken him to keep him quiet. For all Carver knew, this captain could have been involved in the abduction. Then again, anybody could have seen him at the police station.

"How much did you reveal about your inquiry?" Carver asked.

"Just that I was employed by Congressman Espinoza to locate his son," said Morgan. "I didn't compromise OPSEC by sharing unnecessary details. Money did most of the talking."

"Good."

"You think the trouble could spill over to us?"

A distant honk prodded Carver to check the mirror just in time to see Gonzalo's eyes dart back to the open market along the street. Clothes and trinkets hung from merchant booths lining the curb. The vendor stands expanded to fill a wide plaza between buildings. They slowed along the well-trafficked corridor as pedestrians crisscrossed in front of cars.

"Anything's a possibility at this point," he said. "We should continue playing our part."

"Copy that. I'll report when I finish my rounds."

Carver ended the call as the Lincoln stopped in a line of traffic behind a pickup with an industrial load attended by a dozing workman, sombrero shielding him from the sun. Gonzalo's eyes were fixed straight ahead as if that was the most interesting thing in the world. Carver wondered how much the driver had heard and if he could be mined for info. Gonzalo was acting cagey, though, which didn't offer a lot of confidence.

After a bout of honking, the passenger door of the stopped pickup opened to drop someone off. A determined man pushed through shoppers on the street. Carver's peripheral vision keyed on him as he was headed straight toward the Aviator.

"Gun!" he shouted.

Carver was already kissing the seat as the pistol rounds hit the ballistic glass. Gonzalo spun to locate the threat. In panic, his foot slipped the brake and the SUV lurched forward into the bumper of the pickup truck ahead of them. The gunman outside tried the door handle, but Carver had taken the precaution of locking it.

"Get out of here!" Carver ordered.

But there was nowhere to go. The gunman backed away a step and pointed the pistol, firing a few frustrated shots that spiderwebbed the window. Carver readied his weapon as he scanned for other threats.

The Aviator's door locks clicked in unison. Gonzalo

opened the driver door and dove outside. Carver watched stupefied as his security driver skittered away into the crowded plaza.

"Not what I meant."

Gonzalo fled right past a familiar man drawing a rifle and pointing it at the SUV's left side. Carver dove across the driver's seat, reached for the door, and shut it as the rifleman rushed him. He clicked the automatic locks and the rifle opened fire, causing Carver to hug the floor again.

He was officially boxed in and on his own. Judging by the state of the cracked glass, it wouldn't protect him for long. Carver waited for their mags to empty and sat up. Ahead, the man wearing the sombrero stood in the bed of the pickup truck and threw off the tarp covering his cargo. It revealed a no-shit .50 caliber machine gun on a swivel. The man pointed the antique M2 Browning at the windshield.

Carver unlocked his door and threw it open, catching the first assassin in the groin. Carver curled his Sig around the shielded glass and popped two rounds into his neck. He dove to the asphalt as the .50 cal boomed. The Aviator's windshield exploded and hot metal bit cantaloupe-sized chunks from the leather upholstery. The suspension bounced from the repeated impacts.

As the screaming machine gun swiveled toward his open door, Carver charged between textile booths and then turned up the sidewalk. Against a fixed turret and in the absence of cover, return fire from small arms was a pipe dream. Running parallel to the fire was his only option. The .50 cal tore through display tables as it tracked Carver.

The Service of Wolves

Gouts of blood burst from crouching civilians. It was wet work of the worst kind: out in the open and without regard for human collateral.

Fortunately, he only needed to outrun the Browning's onslaught for so long. Those ambushing him had intended to make a statement that even his ballistic armor couldn't stop them. It was overkill but also effective. But their mistake was getting too close. Since Carver had started only ten feet from the mounted weapon, charging along the sidewalk quickly bypassed the Browning's ability to track him. It was an old weapon jury-rigged to a recycled platform, kept low for easier concealment but with the downside of being unable to fire forward over the cab.

Carver jumped into the short clearing ahead of the Toyota technical as its driver readied to pull forward. The reports of the P320 paled in comparison to the booming machine gun, but they struck home through the glass. Half a mag tore the driver apart.

The vaguely familiar rifleman was at his three o'clock now. They pointed their weapons at each other and opened fire, but Carver did so on the run, retreating behind the wheel well of the pickup. He checked for additional threats on his side but couldn't spot anyone through screaming and fleeing pedestrians. He fired over the hood to suppress the rifleman, aiming high to purposely avoid hitting bystanders. He was in a bad spot and didn't have the luxury to dig in.

Carver inched toward the rear pickup bed, freezing as the barrel of the .50 cal banged against the corner of the cab. Another step and he'd be in the kill zone. Instead of proceeding, he punched his elbow through the passenger window. Staying as low as possible to avoid the rifle on the opposite side of the vehicle, he fired twice through the cab's rear window. As the guy manning the Browning dove to the bed, Carver surged past the M2's barrel and put a bullet into his head. The Sig clicked empty on the second pull of the trigger, but the job was done. He sat behind the rear wheel and changed mags as another barrage of bullets pounded the pickup's left fender.

After a moment without gunfire, Carver leaned down and searched under the truck. Feet scrambled in the distance but the street was empty. Motorcycle tires navigated between booths in the plaza.

Carver rolled out behind the pickup and caught the rifleman mounting behind a man with a helmet. Carver rested his arm on the truck panel and took controlled shots at his target. The first two missed but forced the men to cower. The third bullet hit the motorcyclist in the shoulder. The fourth in the chest just as he hit the throttle.

The bike lurched awkwardly as the rifleman hopped away, ruining Carver's next shot. The motorcycle and driver crashed through a booth and tumbled to the street. The stranded passenger returned fire, forcing Carver once again to take cover. While he could no longer see the rifleman, he had eyes on the motorcyclist in the street. He had been neutralized.

In a breath between bullets, Carver traversed the short opening between the pickup to the Aviator. Its entire right side was chewed up and in tatters, and all that remained of the windshield were chunks weakly clinging to the frame. He positioned where he could clock his target through the barely holding ballistic glass of the driver's seat. Five assassins had brazenly come for him in the middle of the day. There was only one left.

The rifleman was on his heels now, firing short bursts as he sprinted away from the failed assassination. Giving chase would be an enormous risk. The plaza was cluttered, but the obstacles were plywood and plastic, flimsy materials that would barely slow a bullet from punching through.

But then, perhaps he could use that to his advantage.

Carver pried open the eviscerated passenger door and slid across to Gonzalo's seat. He turned the wheel, and the Aviator kicked onto the curb and mowed through a stall of handmade piñatas. Small candy erupted like cluster munitions, and Carver gassed the engine.

The rifleman hurried toward an indoor arcade with many more now-abandoned stalls. His eyes widened when he realized he wasn't going to outrun the engine. Another burst of fire forced Carver to duck behind the dash. The missing windshield was a minor oversight, as he now blindly barreled through wood frames and flapping tarps. The SUV slammed through a beverage cooler. The fleeing assassin made a last-ditch attempt to dive from the vehicle's path, but Carver made a quick correction and hit him with three tons of modern engineering. The rifleman tripped under the hood, the suspension bumped, and Carver skidded to a stop.

He hopped out and pointed his weapon, but it was unnecessary. The man had been dragged ten feet without his rifle, leaving behind the same Galil ACE carbine he had encountered earlier. The assassin was the bodyguard from *La Cascada's* VIP section.

This was narco payback.

Punishment not just for Carver, but for the bodyguard as well. His punishment for his lapse in security last night was correcting his mistake, leading this attempted hit. He would not get the opportunity to be punished again.

Carver stood over the distressed man. His pained groans and the Aviator's idling engine were the only sounds in the plaza. The stampeding and the yelling, the firearm reports and errant car alarms—all had quieted. Scattered goods and debris littered the space between booths. Paper wrapping caught the breeze and tumbled past abandoned cars in the road. Aside from the two of them, the entire block was vacant.

"So New Generation wants me dead?" asked Carver, gun hanging unmentioned in his hand.

The narco wore a crazed grimace. "You're fucking dead, gringo."

"Positive thinker. I respect that. What were your orders after you killed me?"

The man stifled a high whine. Carver couldn't blame him. His leg was bent backward at the knee and the trail of smeared blood on the concrete indicated an agonizing case of road rash.

Carver lowered to a knee and pressed the Sig into the man's crotch. "You can enter the Great Beyond with grace and dignity, or you can do the opposite of that. Did the

The Service of Wolves

cartel kidnap Manuel Espinoza?"

The narco tried to lean away from the weapon as if there was some chance of escape. "I don't know nothing about that."

"Okay. Who gave the order to kill me? Pancho?"

The man bit down but Carver saw the recognition in his eyes. He heard a siren in the distance.

"He's the asshole, huh? What did he say?"

The bodyguard's eyes flared. "He said you're fucking dead for disrespecting him like that. If it's not me, it'll be somebody—"

Carver put two in his head. "You're repeating yourself."

He slipped the gun into his holster and considered the Aviator. It could get him out of here quickly but might just as easily die on him. Even worse, it was an eyesore that would attract undue attention and be impossible to sneak away in. Carver turned into the open-air arcade entrance and disappeared among the maze of booths.

It was hard to say if there was a deeper cause to this shoot-out than cartel vengeance. New Generation had brought out the big guns, quite literally in the case of the .50 cal, but Pancho was a hothead and narcos weren't known for their subtlety or forgiveness. After being embarrassed on their own turf, New Generation had been obligated to respond. Their reprisal was quick and it was ruthless, and there were more terrified citizens paying for the unfettered rule of merchants who trafficked in death.

12

A dirt-ridden police cruiser screamed down the street. Carver waited in a shuttered patio crowded with potted dwarf palms until it made the turn toward the market. As soon as he emerged, a large personnel carrier rumbled his way, and he recoiled back to his recess.

The extended open-air bed of the truck sat eight militarized police officers wearing white camouflage with black tactical gear and armed with automatic weapons. They were SWAT on steroids. A quick reaction force otherwise known as the National Guard. Though made up of special operations forces, they weren't a military institution. They were civilian led, the president's personal anti-narco task force.

This was no longer a localized Tijuana conflict, and the danger of getting caught or killed just increased tenfold. Carver wiped down the P320 and dumped it in a trash can with his spare mags. They would do more harm than good at this point.

The personnel carrier followed the path of the police car but lacked the same urgency, as if any problem would be solved by the mere sight of them. Carver wondered if it was more about a show of force than actual use of it. Either way, the crackdown had begun. He had no intention of testing their resolve.

Once the truck was out of sight, Carver bounded across the street in the opposite direction, cut down another alley, and ducked into a dark seafood restaurant. He called Shaw but reached voice mail. After conveying what had happened and that they were now targets, he tried Morgan. She was doing her rounds nearby so he gave her his location. Before long, she strolled to the back table and found Carver snacking on a shareable plate of ceviche.

"What the fuck happened out there?" she said under her breath as she slid beside him.

"I'm still piecing that together. My security driver left me in the lurch. I'm trying to decide if he set me up."

"You think he would?"

Carver shook his head. "He seemed genuinely surprised when the guns came out."

"Why would he want you dead?"

"The decision would have nothing to do with him. I just came from Christian Espinoza's house. I rattled him a little but didn't do anything to earn a death sentence."

She frowned at the thought. "Maybe it's not a conspiracy," she said. "You made a play against New Generation. They came back on you. Anybody could have been watching Christian's house and seen you leave."

"That's where I'm stuck. It's hard to say if this was even about Manuel, but I can't shake the feeling that it was."

She used a tortilla chip to spoon a large hunk of fish. "Should I stop making inquiries?"

"I think it's best. Shaw might be blown. You too if someone took note of you asking around. We need to buckle down until we know we're safe. That means switching hotels, not being seen together, and keeping out of the public eye."

The waitress came and asked if they needed anything else.

"I'm not hungry," said Morgan before stuffing another whole chip in her mouth. Carver shrugged and the waitress slipped the tab into a small glass on the table.

"Were you in the company car when it happened?" asked Morgan.

"The *Sólido* SUV. I wouldn't be here if it wasn't armored. It's scrap now."

"Might earn you a police interview."

"That angle of investigation would clear me of any wrongdoing. If it becomes a problem I'll tap Ignacio for legal help. But you might be onto something with the police interview."

She paused mid chip. "You intend to be detained?"

"I intend to be the one doing the interview. You mentioned that captain who seemed to know more than he let on."

"I didn't say he knew more."

"Fine, but he knew something. He's the only one who talked, at least."

She shrugged. "I can take you to him."

She grabbed another scoop for the road and they slid from the booth. Carver put some cash in the glass and they made for the door.

"Give me your keys," he said. "That way it doesn't look like you're giving me a ride." He put an arm around her waist as they hit the sidewalk. "I've got my car, I've got my girl at my side... I'm not the gringo they're looking for."

"In your dreams," she teased, slapping the keys into his palm.

As they circled the car, he retorted, "Believe me, if this *was* a fantasy, I wouldn't be unlocking a bright-blue Nissan Kick right now."

"It's cute and unassuming. And you better not have just compared me to a bargain crossover hatchback."

"No way, Jules," beamed Carver as he opened the door. "You're American made, all the way."

They drove past a pair of vigilant police officers. Even though Carver would have matched the description of anyone who talked, the combination of the car and the company removed him from suspicion. That and residents had a tendency not to notice anything around cartel activity. For once that secrecy worked in Carver's favor, and they arrived at the police station without incident.

At the front desk, Morgan asked for the captain she had spoken to before. She lied and said he was expecting her. When the man with dark, sunken eyes and a mustache peeked out from his office, he sighed and waved them in.

"Juliette..." he muttered, hands on hips and frowning at his multiplying guests.

"This is my boss, Vince," she introduced. "He was the one Congressman Espinoza hired directly."

The police officer shook Carver's hand but didn't introduce himself. The nameplate on his desk read *Capitán Mateo Gomez*. "And what brings you back here?"

"I understand you have some knowledge of my client's son," started Carver. "May we sit? We'll compensate you for your time."

The captain signaled to the chairs and rounded the desk for his. Carver regretted not having an envelope as he placed a stack of American currency on the desk.

"I already explained all I know," he said loudly, eyeing the cash carefully. "There is no open investigation. Cartel issues are handled on the federal level. Simple officers like us aren't trusted to protect the public interest."

He said it with a bitter sneer, as if his integrity were in question. Integrity or no, he discreetly slid the payment into the top drawer of his desk as coolly as if he'd checked the time.

"I've seen the special police around. Who watches the watchers?"

"They're accountable to *el presidente*."

"That doesn't really answer the question, does it?"

Gomez worked his jaw and hiked a shoulder. "It's not for me to ask such questions. I do what I'm told, and I help out *where I'm allowed to*."

More bitterness. If Carver was getting the right impression, this was a man with a moral compass. Whether or not he acted on it was a separate matter.

"Is it the government who tells you what lines to color in, or the cartel?"

The Service of Wolves

The captain's eyes went hard and Carver was worried he had pushed too far, too fast. Gomez leaned forward aggressively. "What are you accusing me of?"

"Nothing at all," assured Carver, "and I get it. I do. You keep your head down." He pointed at the desk drawer. "You take our money, but you take theirs too. Except they're the ones threatening violence against you and your family if you don't play ball."

"No threats from you, I suppose?"

"Not unless you're the one who took the kid."

Gomez leaned back and ground his teeth in a way that skewed his mustache. He was no longer angry at Carver but at the turn of the conversation. "What agency did you say you were with again?"

Carver gave a bureaucratic sigh. "I could tell you, but then we'd need to fill out *paperwork*, make the appropriate *phone calls*, and request *approval*. Who wants to go through all that?"

Gomez glared. He had no intention of doing any of those things.

"Captain," cut in Morgan diplomatically, "what we're saying is we're aware of the dangerous ground we're walking here. The last thing we want to do is create an official record and get you mixed up in this."

"I don't know anything about cartel business," he swore. "It's not my job."

"You don't need to worry about them," she assured. "We're Americans working through black channels. Military ops. We have no cartel ties and we won't sell you out."

Carver frowned. He had an idea of where the captain's hesitancy was coming from. The only way to address it was head on.

"Have you ever heard of *El Vaquero*?" he asked. Morgan eyed him quizzically.

The captain was less puzzled. "Never heard of him," he asserted. Then his eyes narrowed as he considered Carver anew. "Military, huh? You wouldn't happen to be the same man who shot up a street market on the other side of town? The special police are looking all over for him."

"Don't know what you're talking about. But I will say that I wouldn't take kindly to crazed gunmen shooting up a civilian corridor in broad daylight." Carver cocked his head and leaned forward. "Finding myself in that situation, I might even be the kind of man to do something about it."

The captain's face strained for a protracted moment. "I would too." He suddenly stood. "But I can't help you. I don't know anything." As he spoke, he walked to his office door and softly closed it.

Carver and Morgan turned to each other before twisting in their chairs to face the captain. His dark expression spoke of a man who had seen enough. "Manuel Espinoza is a good man. There aren't many like him, with his background, who want to help for purely selfless reasons."

"How well did you know him?"

"We crossed paths from time to time. That's it. I always thought it was strange that he came from that family. Doesn't seem the spoiled type."

"Did New Generation take him?"

Captain Gomez winced. "I don't know what happened to him, and that is the God's truth."

"But you know why he came to the police station last week. Manuel trusted you enough to go to you."

Gomez ground his teeth. "Yes and no. Manuel knows the local police can't touch cartel matters. He didn't ask that. All he requested was that I put him in touch with federal agents."

"Special police?"

"Americans."

Silence filled the office for a beat.

"I couldn't help him," said Gomez glumly. "I explained that we don't work with the Americans anymore. Our authority has been stripped. Yours was too. There was no way I could reach out without putting in an official request, and Manuel didn't want that."

Carver blinked as he processed the information. The captain's dark eyes spoke to a lack of sleep. He must have been living with the guilt of his inability to help. It had been impossible to accommodate Manuel's request last week, but now that the severity of the situation had fully blossomed, now that he had genuine Americans in his office, he could fulfill his professional and personal obligations. Better late than never.

"Which agency was Manuel trying to contact?"

"Border Security, DEA..." Gomez shrugged. "He said he didn't care as long as they could respond to drugs moving into your country."

"What drugs?" asked Morgan.

He shook his head. "He wouldn't say. Manuel was firm on the point. He understood the danger it would put me in."

"It hardly makes sense," said Carver. "A drug corridor into the US isn't anything special. What would cause Manuel to suddenly make a move now?"

"I asked him the same thing. He said something about a partnership, but he wouldn't explain further. I swear to you, he wouldn't tell me the details. He just wanted to talk to someone on your end." Gomez shook his head and sighed. "I thought I was protecting him."

Carver frowned. Before he could vocalize a follow-up question, Gomez said, "That's really everything I know." He opened his door. "I'm sorry I couldn't be of more assistance," he said for the benefit of anyone listening. "Please be sure to return if you wish to file a police report."

Rather than push him further, they filed out of the office and the police station. Carver started the car to get the AC working, but he didn't go anywhere just yet.

"If Manuel had wanted a federal agent," he said, "why not go through his father? We happen to know for a fact that Ignacio has an unofficial DEA contact."

Morgan pursed her lips. "Maybe Manuel really wasn't involved in the business and didn't know his father's contacts."

"Maybe he didn't trust his father."

"Maybe he didn't trust the DEA."

They were dark thoughts, all of them, and they would need looking into. Carver shifted into drive.

13

Carver considered commandeering Morgan's vehicle for the day since she would be lying low and wouldn't need it. He ultimately decided against it as he didn't want to engage in risky business with a rental that could be tracked to her. This was not a CIA operation and they were not shielded with cover identities.

That and he was looking for a little more legroom.

Morgan dropped him off at the car rental agency where he picked up one of the newfangled Ford Broncos that was an equal mix of retro and modern styling. The white truck provided a 4x4 drivetrain but fell short of ballistic armor. He silently resolved to abstain from further gun battles, but he ticked the box for the insurance option just in case.

While Morgan handled waking up Shaw and booking new rooms, Carver wanted to isolate them as far away from his business as possible. He returned to *Avenida Revolución* himself, checked into a new spot a block down, and recovered his belongings from his old room. He transferred them in a roundabout fashion, keeping a careful eye out to make sure nobody was covering him.

When it came to a course of action, he instructed his

team to take shifts watching Christian Espinoza's house. Carver didn't trust the businessman, and it was possible the hit was his idea. In any case, the priority was anonymity over access. They couldn't take chances. The cartel was hunting them.

As for Carver, he was a known variable working a job, and he couldn't hide forever. As evening fell, he passed by Manuel's clinic again but Jasmine was gone for the day. He found a quiet part of town and a restaurant with a view of the exits and ate a solemn dinner. Then there was nothing to do but face the music.

He took the Bronco out to the country, not quite knowing what to expect. At the dirt road to the ranch house, the police keeping watch flagged him down. He stopped the truck and greeted them through the open window.

"Mr. Espinoza's expecting me."

"Name please," said the officer.

"Vince Carver. I was here yesterday."

The officer frowned. "You're not on the list..."

"You're not even holding a list."

"The list is in my head."

"Then it should be easy to check it again."

The officer stared at Carver, unamused. "Nope," he said snidely, "you're still not on the list."

Carver hissed. "I'm employed by Mr. Espinoza about his son. I drove in and out yesterday with *Sólido* Security."

The man peeked into the back seat to check if anything was amiss. "You were instructed to stick with your escort."

"They forgot to instruct my escort to stick with me.

Listen, I respect that you have a job to do, but I'm obviously supposed to be here. If you could just check with Ignacio..."

The officer clicked his tongue a few times, trying to come up with a solution to this large problem. "How am I supposed to know you are who you say you are?"

"Are you serious?"

"I'm very serious."

Carver huffed and stared straight ahead. This conversation was agonizing. He opted to forgo it entirely and stepped on the gas. He maneuvered the Bronco around their cars before speeding down the dirt road leading to the house. They yelled and he'd hoped that would be the end of it, but they ran for a car.

The headlights erratically lit the grove of trees as he sped over gravel. Visibility was low, but the flashing lights and blaring siren behind him were clear enough. He sped up the driveway pounding the horn and skidded to a stop beside the water feature.

It was enough of a commotion that by the time he exited the truck with his hands up, the old guard dog was out the front door with his shotgun pointed. A *Sólido* guard jumped out of a parked Aviator and various lights went on in the previously dark house. Finally, the police car swerved behind him and two officers locked on him and shouted in Spanish. Floodlights from the ranch house lit the exterior and blinded him.

"Would you call them off?" Carver asked the gray-haired man with the gun.

The only reply was a steadfast glare.

"This is ridiculous," Carver muttered to himself.

He took a few careful steps toward the house, but the yelling at his back reached a fever pitch, and Carver was actually worried they might shoot him. Luckily, the shot caller finally arrived on the porch.

"What's going on out here?" he demanded, naturally accustomed to the tranquility of the country. Ignacio Espinoza wore an unflattering sweatsuit and appeared half asleep.

"I'm sorry," said Carver. "They wouldn't let me in."

"Maybe it's because you abandoned your driver."

"It wasn't like that." Carver turned to check the police still clocking him. "Can we do something about the guns? I have news."

Ignacio appeared troubled and hopeful and more than a little confused. He waved a hand at the officers. "What are you idiots doing? This man is my employee. Put down your guns."

The police were almost crestfallen as they complied. "You said no one but family and their security."

"He's part of my security team!" he berated. Ignacio cinched his temple with his fingers and took a calming breath. "Okay, it's done. I should have been clear. Don't worry about it. Just return to your post. From now on this man has in-and-out privileges. Got it?"

"Yes sir." They nodded respectfully, got in their car, and rolled slowly on their way, lights still flashing but thankfully absent the siren.

Alma converged at her father's back to see what the fuss

was about. The *Sólido* man by the SUV had already holstered his pistol but the CPO with the shotgun kept it trained.

"You mind?" added Carver.

The old man still wouldn't flinch.

"It's okay," instructed Ignacio softly.

It was clear the two friends had known each other for a long time. The bodyguard lowered his weapon without a change of expression, and Carver thought the dramatics were over.

"You're alive!"

Everyone turned to Gonzalo scrambling around the house from the backyard. Carver didn't know what he'd been doing other than that there was a guest house that way. The security driver excitedly hustled over to Carver. "I thought for sure you were—"

Carver took a commanding step toward him and planted a heavy fist into his cheek. Alma flinched and Ignacio scowled. Gonzalo tumbled to the ground.

"What the hell, man?" he cried.

"You left me there to die," Carver growled.

"No way." Gonzalo pushed to his feet. "You said to run. You said—"

Carver decked him again. This time the other security officer drew his pistol. Ignacio held up a hand to stop him.

"What happened to being there if something went down in the street?" spat Carver. "You call yourself a soldier?"

"I don't need to take this."

"You going to run away again?"

Gonzalo stood and reached for his gun.

Carver grabbed his arm and put his heel in the back of Gonzalo's knee. The driver collapsed, and Carver twisted his hand behind his back and stripped him of his weapon.

As he tossed it to the concrete, Gonzalo attempted to wheel around with a left-handed strike. Carver dipped back. The driver rushed and Carver batted his punch away, grabbed and lifted Gonzalo by the waist, and then slammed him hard into the driveway. The resounding splat had a satisfying echo that Gonzalo would feel for days. He groaned and rolled weakly on the ground.

Despite the other *Sólido* guard wearing a grimace, old Gray Hair seemed apathetic regarding the development. His eyes locked with Carver and his cheek twitched, which was probably about as respectful as the old man could get.

Ignacio groaned. "Now what was all that for, Vince?"

"He was behind the wheel when we were attacked. His job was to protect the car. Instead he cut bait first chance he got and left me on my own against five hit men."

Ignacio turned distastefully to the man on the floor. Alma's reaction to the violence was a little more surprising. While initially startled, she watched Carver more attentively now, one eyebrow raised in schoolyard fascination.

"What the hell?" fumed Ignacio. "I was being nice to you, you *puta*, rewarding you for surviving a gunfight, and I find out you didn't fight at all?" The patriarch's cheeks flushed. "Get out of here! Sleep in the barn for all I care. You'll be lucky if you still have a job in the morning. Go be lazy and cowardly on my son's watch."

Ignacio's commanding point was so unnerving that Gonzalo, as much pain as he was in, struggled to his feet to do as he was told. The other guard from his team helped him up and walked him toward the darkness. They shared no more friendly banter.

Ignacio beckoned Carver closer. "Are you okay, Vince?"

"I'm alive. I can't say the same for the narcos that came after me."

"You said five men?" He stared wide-eyed.

Carver pushed inside and they followed him. He could feel their eyes burning a hole in his back, like he was an investment that had just quadrupled.

14

Ignacio told his bodyguard he was fine and turned off the outdoor floodlights. Gray Hair retreated to his room down the rear hall, no doubt next to his principal's. Alma waited in the living room. For the first time Carver noticed she was wearing a nightgown. She picked up on his look and cinched the fancy material tighter around her neck.

Ignacio had the curtains and lights and locks all back in order and joined them standing beside the sofas.

"Did you find him yet?" he asked.

"No, unfortunately. I've been evading police most of the day. But I did reach out to the cartel."

"I heard. Christian tells me you recklessly shot up a nightclub."

"You hired me to make contact. I did that with a wad of cash and a smile. They came back at me hard."

"Twice, apparently."

Alma stared ardently, content to listen for now.

"There's something deeper going on here," continued Carver. "Manuel made inquiries at a police station. Were you aware he tried to contact a federal agent?"

Alma appeared surprised, but Ignacio's brow went slack.

"Oh, that. He asked me about it last week."

"And you didn't think to mention it?"

"What? It was nothing. Manuel himself said it wasn't important."

"What did he say, exactly?"

Ignacio crossed his arms as he recalled it. "Something about drugs being sold around his clinic. He was always like that, going on about safety corridors." Ignacio capped off the statement with finger quotes. "He just wanted the community to be safe."

"He takes after you that way, *Papá*," said Alma.

"Yes, well, Manuel has a kind soul. Some problems can be fixed, I told him, but usually shuffling them around is good enough."

"What was he dealing with?" Carver asked again.

Ignacio hiked his shoulders. "That was all he said, that he wished he could tip off American authorities, somebody who could do something about it. I told him that was crazy."

"You ignored him," accused Alma.

"I didn't ignore him. I asked what he was talking about. He swore it wasn't a big deal. He told me not to worry about it."

"Did you hook him up with your DEA contact?" asked Carver.

"What good would that have done? His clinic's street corner is not an American concern. Manuel didn't listen to reason at first. He's always been stubborn. He insisted on trying, but I wouldn't hear of it. In this country, you understand, you protect your family by keeping them out of that dirty business." He watched Alma as he said that. Then he sighed.

Carver had left out that he had a good idea what exactly that dirty business was, and that the Espinozas were neck deep in it. He sighed and wondered how much it mattered. Before him was a conflicted man. Carver believed he loved his children and wanted what was best for them, past mistakes aside.

"I guess you can't always control the choices your kids make," said Carver suggestively, hoping Ignacio's guilt would prod him to come clean.

The patriarch frowned. There was a momentary lapse in his facade, but he shook it off. "It's late. Let's forget about this bad business and resume the search in the morning. Good night."

He flipped off the overhead light and retreated. They waited in darkness as he shuffled down the rear hall and shut the door at the end. Carver worked his jaw and turned to Alma.

"You think Manolito got himself into trouble," she said softly.

"I do. I just wish I knew what information he had. It would be the best clue to who took him."

She nodded. "You need to talk to Jasmine again."

"I was on my way when I got attacked. I'll try again tomorrow."

"You're staying with us tonight then? Your room is still made up."

She took a step toward the front hallway to show him.

Carver let her lead the way. "Why would Manny go to the feds?"

She frowned. "He's smart, but he can be a little idealistic. If he went to that trouble, he had a good reason."

Alma seemed to be the only family member willing to strategize about Manuel's whereabouts instead of being evasive or brushing him off.

"He didn't mention anything to you?" he asked.

"I wish he did, but I'm afraid *Papá's* telling the truth. Manolito would have wanted to protect us, which would have meant keeping us out of it. This was the first I heard of him looking for an American agent." She huffed at the thought. "I wouldn't have let him drop it so easily. You can't leave something like that alone."

If Manuel had asked his father about contacting the DEA, that meant he trusted him that far. Based on everything else Carver had heard about the kid, it was consistent that he wouldn't fill them in with the details. Whatever it was Manny had discovered, he had kept it to himself.

Carver stopped when he realized he had followed Alma to the last door. It was open, with the light on, revealing a very feminine and almost juvenile bedroom, with fluffy pillows and throws. He turned around to see they had passed several closed doors.

"Come in," beckoned Alma over her shoulder.

Carver frowned at the empty house, but Alma's curves under the thin nightgown had a magnetic pull. "Why would I do that?"

With her back to him, she cinched the fabric at her waist, emphasizing an hourglass figure. "It's safer with me. After what happened with Gonzalo, do you really trust the security around here?"

"No. Then again I'm not entirely sure you've given me a reason to trust you either."

She spun around and alluringly approached. "Then come in and give me a chance to be convincing."

Alma pulled the satin belt from her gown. It fell slack and opened, revealing the soft skin of her stomach between her undergarments. She looped the belt around his back, tugged him past the threshold, and Carver quietly closed the door.

Her bra was a heavy-duty thing, not all pretty lace as if this were planned. She looked softer without the makeup and dress. More authentic, and definitely more inviting.

"Still don't trust me?" she said throatily.

"There's something to be said for a thorough investigation..."

She smirked. "It looks like I'll have to work for it."

"A beautiful rich girl like you... I don't believe you've put in a single hard day's work in your life."

"You have me all wrong, Vince. Just because I play hard doesn't mean I don't. Work. Harder." She emphasized the point with a squeeze of his crotch. Not one for nuance.

"I told you you'd remember my name."

He kissed her full lips and the robe fell to her feet.

Many women are turned on by powerful men. Alma was on another level. Already past excited, her skin thrummed with electricity and her body dripped with anticipation. She impatiently rebuffed every one of Carver's attempts at foreplay in a naked scramble for the main course. Their clothes flew to the floor and she pulled him atop the fluffy bed, embracing him with eager thighs.

"How many men did you kill today?" she breathed.

"Five."

She gasped, turned on by the violence. Watching him effortlessly put down Gonzalo had awoken something in her. She took all of him in, everything that he gave.

Alma wasn't a delicate flower, and she didn't lie about putting in the work. She wrapped him up and hung on his body, thrust with him, clawed his back, and sank her teeth into his bicep.

Carver welcomed it. After two days in Tijuana, an environment where he looked over his shoulder for both criminals and police, it was good to let his guard down, liberating to expend his pent-up energy, to share the thrill and vitality, the awareness that any day could be his last, by diving straight in and releasing it all in a climactic celebration of life.

It was only after they lay spent on the sheets, cool air soothing their sweaty bodies, that there was any time to reflect on what they'd done. They barely knew each other, yet her head was nestled under his arm and her finger traced up and down his side as if she'd done it a hundred times before. There was no quicker way to knowing someone than being intimate with them. It was a knife that cut both ways, and sometimes too deep.

"I know about the family business," said Carver to clear the air. "I know what you're involved in."

Her finger paused on his rib and her head swiveled to his. "And just what is it you think you know?"

"Cut the crap, Alma. I think you and me are a little past that now. Do you really want to find Manny or not?"

She stiffened. "Of course I do."

"I'd be a hell of a lot more effective at my job if I was playing with a full deck of cards."

Her pout was genuine. "You need to understand, we don't want your forgiveness, but we do want your help."

"Meaning if you'd been straight with me from the jump I would have turned down your money and walked back across the border."

She idly shook her head. "I can be a convincing woman, Vince, but not that convincing. And that's not what this was about, for the record."

"I didn't say that."

"I tried to warn you about my family."

He bit down. "You did. Everyone's telling me their own truths. The problem is everyone's keeping their own secrets too."

She sat up, enticing him with a view of her plump breasts over his chest, but she appraised him with an oddly curious expression. "Look at me, Vince. I'm laid bare for you."

He pulled her close so her face was an inch from his and he was bathed in swoops of brown hair. "Stop it and come clean. You do the books for *El Vaquero*. Is Christian starting a new partnership?"

Her hot breath quivered on his lips. "Why would you say that?"

"Something I heard. I need to know if your big brother's making moves."

"I see him less than you think."

"You must have overheard him or seen him acting strangely. He spent the last three days here."

She pulled back. "No he didn't."

"He told me he ignored business to support the family."

She stifled a laugh. "Christian? Support? That's a joke. He stopped by yesterday, and two days before, but that was it. It was hardly the whole day, and he spent more time with his horse than with us. He's been in Tijuana more than Tecate."

Carver watched the ceiling. "Interesting thing to lie about."

She released a long breath and relaxed beside him again. "Not if you consider his ego. Christian is self-important and self-absorbed. Everything he says paints him in a better light."

"He defended Manuel. Not much, but a little, when his wife went off."

"Like I said, it wouldn't do for him to appear petty."

"He certainly didn't hold back when it came to your father."

Alma's chin rubbed his shoulder for a thoughtful moment. "*Papá* turns a blind eye. He pretends, if the schism isn't mentioned, it isn't there." She stared a thousand miles away. "It's optimistic. Sometimes I think the act works.

Other times I worry my older brother is dangerous. He doesn't look forward to taking over just the family business, but the family as a whole."

Carver studied her expressive eyes. "Does he control all of you?"

"Dear, *nobody* controls me. And as impressionable as Manolito can be at times, he finds his own path too. But yes, Christian tries to dictate what we do. It's a power trip for him." She rested her head on its side. After a period of silence, her eyes shut.

Carver couldn't think about sleep just yet. The more he pondered the rivalries in this family, the more possible it seemed that Christian could kidnap his own brother.

That, of course, didn't explain New Generation's involvement. It was possible Esteban was telling the truth that they weren't a party to this particular crime. They were quick to retaliate, but that could just be how posturing was done down here.

He thought back to the shoot-out in the market. Gonzalo had sure raced out of there fast. Any decent close protection officer would have recognized what was going down at the first sign of danger, but it was possible there was more to it than awareness and cowardice. The assassins had needed to know where Carver was going to be. Christian and Gonzalo could have set him up. The entirety of his adventures with New Generation could be nothing more than a convenient dodge.

But then, it was Ignacio—not Christian—who had pointed him to the cartel. And Alma had happily obliged him with a location. They couldn't all be setting him up, otherwise why hire him in the first place?

There was a key facet Carver was missing, some knowledge caught in Manuel's head that he'd refused to let out. Some knowledge that might already be buried off the side of a desert highway, lost in the sands forever.

15

Raised voices, far and muffled, grew to enough of a nagging annoyance to draw Carver's lax attention. He tweaked awake beside Alma. Daylight through the curtains warmed the room. Ignacio was arguing with someone, and Carver couldn't believe he had slept so late.

He glanced at the sleeping beauty in bed and wished the sun would momentarily retreat, but interplanetary dynamics stubbornly adhered to forward motion. It was a concept that inspired him, really. Being careful not to wake her, he hurried into his clothes and slipped into the hallway without anyone noticing.

Another bedroom door was halfway open. It was his guest room, already checked, bed made and unused. He continued into the living room where the voices grew more crisp. Ignacio was in his office arguing with Christian.

"This isn't anyone's fault, *Papá!* How were we supposed to know?"

"We should have known!" spat Ignacio. "What good is this piece of shit security if they can't protect family?"

"You know Manolo. You know what he thinks of bodyguards."

They paused and turned to Carver as he entered the office.

"There you are," cried Ignacio with a wave of his hand. "Where have you been? Your room was empty."

Carver wondered how he had slept through them traipsing down the hallway and knocking two doors down. "Sorry," he said. "I went for some exercise."

The Espinoza men stood as mirror images of each other, beside the window with hands on hips. They were angry and exasperated and just a little desperate.

"What happened?" asked Carver.

Ignacio's hands flew to the air again. "A disaster is what happened! This isn't what I paid you for."

"Ignacio..."

"They made contact," explained Christian.

"Who did?"

"Nueva Generación."

"Here? Now?" Carver took a step and stopped when he saw the open padded envelope on the desk. Next to it was a handwritten note.

"Not here," answered Christian. "The cartel saw fit to contact me in Tijuana instead. It's their territory."

Ignacio smoldered at the message. Carver went to the desk and angled his head so he could read the letter without touching it. "Time to get out of the wine business."

He frowned. "Is that all? Is that the only demand?"

Alma rushed into the room, barefoot and wearing her nightgown again. It had been hastily thrown on without the belt, forcing her to hold it closed. She seemed distracted but concerned, and was careful not to make eye contact with Carver.

"Alma..." muttered Ignacio.

"What's with all the testosterone in this room?"

"We didn't want to wake you."

Her eyes rolled. "What's going on?"

Ignacio took a breath and brushed his mustache. "Go back to your room, *hija*."

"What am I, twelve?"

"You shouldn't be here," Christian said more assertively.

She converged and somehow stared them both down at once, but her vitriol was for her brother. "Screw you. This is my home, not yours. I'm more a part of this family than you are."

He reddened. "You always use that against me! You just can't handle the fact that I'm good at what I do."

"You're not half as good as you think, Christian."

"When you find enough dedication to earn a degree, then you can talk to me."

Her eyes flared.

"Guys!" boomed Carver. "Please!"

They stared hotly at him.

"Would everyone take it down a notch so we can discuss what's going on?"

Ignacio scowled. "What's going on, Vince, is that you failed." The patriarch reached into the padded envelope and produced a sandwich bag containing a bloody pinkie finger.

"Ahhh!" screamed Alma.

She grew faint and collapsed into Carver's arms. The

nightgown hung loosely. He held her waist to keep it closed, and Christian worked his jaw in distaste. Carver thought he might be less judgmental if he could see to it to help his sister himself. Alma's body was weak and shuddering. Carver led her to a chair where she buried her face in her hands.

"There's nothing else," said a crestfallen Ignacio. "There's no monetary demand, no promise to return him alive, no guarantee that he even is." His voice turned to a growl. "They're butchering my boy like an animal!"

Christian struggled to remain stoic. Alma was the opposite, whimpering and unconcerned with whoever saw her mourn. She leaned over the desk to chance a closer look at the finger before collapsing back into the chair and sobbing.

"You stirred the hornet's nest," accused her big brother. "Everything was peaceful until you walked into that club and attacked them."

Carver found it difficult to bite his tongue, but he did it, given the circumstances. "Do we know this was New Generation?"

"It was them," he asserted. "The deliveryman said as much when he dropped it off."

"And he couldn't be lying?"

"He wasn't lying!" he snapped.

Whereas a minute ago Christian was swearing to his father that no one was at fault, the look of displeasure on his face announced that he had finally found a scapegoat.

The worst part was, Carver wasn't entirely sure he was

wrong.

"I hate to be insensitive," he said, treading as tactfully as the question could allow, "but..."

Ignacio and Christian frowned at him.

"Are we absolutely positive this is Manuel's finger?"

Alma shot out of her seat and slapped him. "I know my Manolito's flesh and blood!" she screamed. Her watery eyes flared defiantly and she moved to slap him again. Carver didn't have the heart to stop her, and it was Christian who caught her hand.

"You're upset," he said. "It's understandable, but it's not what we need right now. Let's go."

It was a surprising sentiment from her rivalrous brother. Even more surprising was that Alma allowed herself to be led from the office.

Carver swallowed, now alone with his employer.

"It's my son's finger, Vince," he said solemnly. "I don't need a DNA test to tell me what I can see with my eyes. This isn't a trick."

"Got it."

Now that the office wasn't so crowded, Carver rounded the desk and peered into the envelope. He checked the reverse side of the note. Finally, he took a close look at the mutilated body part in the bag. It was just a finger, absent other signs of torture or struggle, cleanly severed with something like a cleaver. Out of respect for the family, he slid the bag back into the envelope.

"I know it's hard to see right now," started Carver, "but there's a bright side to this."

Christian filed back into the room as Ignacio snorted. "What possible bright side can there be to my son's finger?"

"This is proof Manuel's alive. That wasn't a certainty yesterday. And it's confirmation of who has him."

"I already knew they had him!" he yelled. "But why did they have to cut off his finger?"

"Let me handle this, *Papá*," urged Christian. "I *will* fix this. Don't bother relying on anybody else." He glared at Carver as he made the statement. "You can depend on me."

A moment of silence was all the agreement Christian needed, and he valiantly strode out of the office. From the window, Carver watched him link up with his security team outside. He passed around instructions to the guards stationed at the ranch house before heading to his vehicle. It was no longer the fancy sports car, but yet another black Lincoln Aviator. After this morning's surprise package and possibly yesterday's violence at the market, he wasn't taking chances. Carver noted with satisfaction that a disgraced and disheveled Gonzalo was returning to Tijuana with them.

"Is that it, Vince?" asked Ignacio, somewhat off-balance. "Is it time to cut our losses here?"

Carver studied him. It was a curious thing to say about his son, and more than a little odd. It was one thing to be dispirited, but if the old man thought Carver was giving up after a setback, he didn't know who he hired.

"This isn't over by a mile," he answered. "It may not look like it, but we're closer to your son than ever."

"But the note was vague."

"A little too vague, and that's the problem. None of this

makes sense. Unless there's been contact I don't know about?"

Ignacio shook his head. "Don't look at me."

While Carver could have called him out about the illicit drug empire, it seemed counter-productive at this time. But tact or not, he was fuming inside.

"Someone knows something they're not letting on," he swore, "and I'm not coming back until I find out who."

* * *

Carver waved snidely at the police as he passed their checkpoint and turned toward Tijuana. He was a few minutes behind Christian but figured that cushion would set him at ease. He turned on his phone's Bluetooth and paired it with the Bronco so he could put Shaw on speaker.

"It was another boring night," conveyed his friend, "but things picked up in the morning."

"Tell me about it," grumbled Carver.

"An older guy in a cowboy hat stopped by Christian's residence a little while ago to drop off a package. He was driving a beat-up Buick. Not exactly part of the post-office fleet if you get my drift. The envelope could have been a payoff."

"It was a threat. They cut Manuel's finger off and demanded the Espinozas get out of the wine business."

Shaw frowned over the line. "Damn. You gotta watch out for the old guys."

"Cowboy Hat was alone?"

"Yup. I couldn't get eyes on the handoff since he walked past the gate. He was in there maybe five minutes before leaving in a hurry. I'm betting he sped off before Christian could open the package."

"Christian was pretty upset. He came straight to Tecate to speak with his father."

"Did he now?"

Carver frowned. "I thought you were watching the house."

"Totally missed it," said Shaw. "This cowboy character seemed like a new lead so I covered him instead."

"Nick, you beautiful bastard! Where did you follow him to?"

"A warehouse space close to *La Cascada*. It's New Generation territory for sure."

"We just scored a direct link to the kid. Is it possible he's being held there?"

"That's a negative, boss. The space is wide open, with a lot of commerce, trucks moving in and out, third party loaders. Easy to snoop around but hard to hide somebody in. But the location's a lead. I'm putting Morgan on it. In fact, she's pulling up right now to relieve me. After I fill her in on the details, I'm gonna get some food and crash."

Carver smiled. "You're half right. Go get your food, but I want you back at Christian's house."

"Are you serious?"

"We're in a critical stage, Nick. Christian's on the road and should be back home in an hour. He's almost certain to make a move of his own. Watching him will tell us what he knows."

"Copy that." Shaw said it with a heavy grumble but, the truth was, he lived for this stuff.

* * *

Jasmine helped an old woman out of a wheelchair and into a van. She passed a bag of medication over to the elderly patient and conveyed final instructions with poise. Then she pulled the clinic wheelchair back to the sidewalk and watched the vehicle pull away.

"Service with a smile," said Carver, behind her.

Jasmine spun, mildly alarmed at his presence on the public thoroughfare. She pressed her lips together and straightened her scrubs. "You scared me."

"You didn't tell me Manuel's family was in the drug trade."

She toyed with a long curl of black hair and looked around. "What was I supposed to say?"

"You were supposed to tell me the truth so I could help him!"

Her dark eyes blinked back guilt. "You work for them! I can't trust you. I can't trust anyone except Manuel, and he's gone!"

Carver stepped close and lowered his voice. He'd meant to corner Jasmine, not cause a public scene. "He's not gone yet, but he might be if you don't come clean with me. Or maybe that's the problem."

She huffed defensively. "What does that mean?"

"That maybe Manuel isn't as clean as you let on."

"That's a lie! He knows what his family is involved in, but that doesn't mean he likes it. All he talked about was cutting them out, living on his own... giving instead of taking from the community." She sighed as if realizing how naive that sounded. "It was hard on him. He had so much love for them, but he never once condoned what they did."

"Did you know he went to the police?"

She locked eyes with him. "What?"

"You heard me."

She swallowed. "I don't... I..."

"Jasmine, I hate to do this to you, but this morning the cartel delivered his pinkie finger to the family." Her eyes widened. "Now, I know you're scared for your safety. I get why you didn't want to rat out his brother when I'm working for the family. But I'm not a narco. I don't threaten young girls. The only thing I want is to get Manny back home. You have my word."

She was almost afraid to blink. "You know about Christian?"

"That he's *El Vaquero?* I figured it out."

Her thick eyebrows bunched together. "Christian's not *El Vaquero*. Ignacio is."

Carver stared, dumbfounded. He was sure he'd revealed his suspicion about Christian to Alma. Had she purposely let him continue believing the wrong thing?

"Wait a minute," he said. "You're telling me Manuel was

going against his father?"

"Not against him, but not with him either. He couldn't destroy his family, Mr. Carver. Don't fault him for that. It was enough to urge Ignacio to do better. To keep the violence out of the streets. Manuel is why *El Vaquero* doesn't put fentanyl in his drugs. It's why he donates to communities in need. Manuel couldn't stop the trafficking, but he used his influence to curtail the damage."

There was an echo of truth to her words. Ignacio had mentioned moving problems as opposed to fixing them, and word on the street was that *El Vaquero* was different than the other, more ruthless, narcos. Ignacio was using his political power to enrich himself but, in a twisted way, also trying to serve the people he represented. At least, Manuel probably saw it that way.

"So why did he go to the police?" Carver asked.

Jasmine shook her head. "I didn't know he did. But Manuel was really stressed out the last two weeks. At first I thought it was the usual family stuff, but he couldn't stop thinking about it. He was more quiet than usual, until he had a big blowout with Christian. Honestly, I thought it was a good thing. I was hoping it meant he would stop visiting them."

"And Alma?"

Jasmine shrugged. "What about Alma? She practically raised him. Manuel loves her with all his heart."

"What about her intentions?"

She frowned. "What do you mean? She loves him back."

"It's genuine?"

The Service of Wolves

"She would do anything for him. Like me. There's no question in my mind."

Carver nodded. He had maybe missed the forest for the trees, but this conversation confirmed that his people instincts were more accurate than not. Jasmine's testimony was yet another indication that there was some sort of falling out between Christian and his little brother.

"I'm sorry you didn't know you were working for *El Vaquero*," said the girl sympathetically. "I assumed you did." And she had assumed any warning on her part could put her in the crosshairs.

"I should have known," he said bitterly.

"Believe it or not, a lot of people around here find themselves in the same situation. And once you're in, you can't always get out."

"That won't be a problem," he scoffed.

But she didn't notice his conviction. Her mind was in a different place as she stared at the hills on the horizon. "My mother used to always tell me something." She fought off a chuckle. "It was so stupid. She said, if you go out with wolves, they'll teach you to howl. Do you understand? The narcos, they are like wolves, and they are with us everywhere."

It wasn't just their proximity that rankled Carver. Between Christian and Ignacio, he found himself in the service of wolves.

Jasmine's forehead creased as she became distressed. She stepped to him, eyes locking onto his. "Please don't hold Manuel's family against him. He's nothing like them, even if he grew up looking the other way. You have to believe me."

Carver bit down. "You might be the only person I do believe, Jasmine."

Her eyes teared up. "Is he hurt bad?"

"I don't think so. Not yet."

She grabbed him and rested her head against his chest. "Will you save him, Mr. Carver? I'll give you everything I have. It's not much, but—"

He pushed her away, and she looked up at him, worried she did something wrong. "Kid, you just go back to work and keep helping people."

So the Espinoza family was rotten to the core. It wasn't like they didn't warn him. But Manuel was the apple that had fallen far from the tree. Somehow, instead of spoiling, he had tried starting his own orchard. For a kid of his age and upbringing, that took guts.

Jasmine watched him intently, imploring with deep, rich eyes. If she was a liar, she was the best Carver had ever seen.

Unfortunately, that meant Manuel Espinoza was a good kid, a man among wolves, and Carver had to save him, not only from New Generation, but from his own family as well.

16

After the heart-to-heart with Jasmine, Carver touched base with Morgan. Shaw had caught her up on the gory details so the conversation was brief. The man in the cowboy hat had returned to his beat-up Buick and was currently driving around town attending to chores. His stops included a small market, a restaurant, and a pair of liquor stores. They could be cartel properties or businesses being shaken down. Morgan logged the locations in case the information came in handy in the future.

In the meantime, Carver figured he would join her to get eyes on the mystery man. There wasn't much else to do, at least not until Shaw called.

"Christian's on the move," reported his friend. "He headed out with a full security team: two CPOs with him and four in the follow car."

Carver's eyebrows went up. "He only took one vehicle to Tecate so this must be something."

"Serious enough to leave his house undefended," agreed Shaw. "I'm tailing them."

"Don't let them see you. With that kind of manpower, they'll be on the alert."

"I'm giving them a big cushion. Those glossy wax jobs stick out from a mile away."

Carver chewed his lip. "My count is six *Sólido* operatives. I thought you reported eight men watching the property?"

"That was before the missus left earlier with the last two. She even took the butler, or whatever he is. I'm guessing she's going on a spending spree and needs someone to hold the shopping bags."

A completely empty house. This was a rare opportunity. "Okay, let me know if Christian loops back. It's time for a little snooping."

Carver flipped the truck around and sped for the mansion. He parked a block down, hopped the wall, and checked the windows on the way to the kitchen door on the perimeter. It was still unlocked, which didn't speak highly of narco security. He stepped inside.

The kitchen was empty. So was the living area and backyard. Carver cleared the hallway. The house was silent.

He peeked upstairs and quietly ascended. At the top of the steps, his phone buzzed. It was a text message from Morgan.

"Cowboy Hat made a stop at a residence. Picked up some guy bossing around a truck full of narcos. He looks important."

Carver bit down as he set the phone to silent. The upstairs hallway had several bedroom doors, most of which were open.

"Picture?" he texted.

A moment later: "Was too fast. Continuing to cover."

The Service of Wolves

After he cleared the floor, he tackled the next flight to the master bedroom at the top. It was a large space with windows spanning the walls and a large stone-framed fireplace. The bed was somewhat disheveled. The room, obviously lived in by the masters of the house. Two walk-in closets were like rooms unto themselves. One had a wall of high heels and a vanity with an open drawer. Several lace bras and panties were laid out.

The toilet in the master bath flushed. Carver dipped into the closet before changing his mind and attempting to rush out of the bedroom completely. Unfortunately, the bathroom door sprung open. Gonzalo stepped out and froze.

"What are you—"

Carver drew his Sig. "Don't move."

The onetime security driver threw his hands up, bright-red panties dangling around one thumb. Shaw's count of eight men had occurred before Gonzalo had disgraced himself and been reassigned back to Christian. It would have been easy to miss the extra face slipping in, especially without the house covered 24/7.

"What are you doing here?" breathed Gonzalo.

"I could ask you the same question."

He blinked.

"You're not going to wash your hands?" asked Carver.

Gonzalo turned to the sink, and then turned back to Carver. "You... want me to wash my hands?"

"I'll make you a deal, Gonzalo." He lowered his weapon, raised his phone, and snapped a picture. "You don't mention my unannounced visit to anyone, and I won't tell Christian what you like to do with his wife's underwear."

He nodded. "That's fair."

"Your fly's down."

Gonzalo looked. Carver stuffed the Sig into the holster and hurried down the stairs. Manuel wasn't here and he never was. He rushed outside before encountering any other surprises. After getting back to his Bronco, Carver had a backlog of messages on his phone.

Shaw texted about Christian doing laps around a string of warehouses skirting downtown. It was defensive driving, and he'd had to pull off to avoid being spotted. Morgan updated too. Her mark was also driving evasively. It was their bearing that tipped him off.

The parties were headed towards each other, and Carver had a general idea where they were going.

* * *

The Ford Bronco was parked along a sloped alley overlooking the yard of a seedy warehouse district. Carver, Morgan, and Shaw sat together in rapt attention of the plot unfolding before their eyes through three sets of binoculars. The Espinoza family's private lumberyard played host to several vehicles in a discreet midday meeting.

Gunmen for both sides secured the area. An older man with weathered boots and a cowboy hat strutted pompously from the driver's seat of a Buick.

"That's the guy who delivered the package this morning," divulged Shaw.

Sure enough, Christian hopped out of his Aviator and stomped toward him, ignoring the warnings of his *Sólido* team. The Espinoza brother was red-faced as he pounded the man in the chest.

"Here's the boss Cowboy Hat picked up," pointed Morgan. The new man exited the passenger seat in a relaxed fashion, punctuating the fact that everyone waited on him. He was thin, with slick hair and round glasses.

"Esteban Gallo," said Carver sourly. Morgan hadn't recognized him because she hadn't been with them at the club. "The Espinoza's are working with New Generation."

"This don't look like a healthy working relationship," muttered Shaw.

Christian shouted wildly at the man in the cowboy hat. The narcos tried to separate them until Esteban intervened. The commotion was too far to overhear, even the yelling, so they had no chance of catching Esteban's calm explanation. Whatever he said, it worked. Christian Espinoza was pacified.

"According to Captain Gomez," said Morgan, "Manuel had mentioned a partnership."

Carver pulled down the binocs. "This is the big secret he discovered. But why would he try to stop it? He knew what business the family was in."

"He was conflicted," she offered. "He wasn't a part of what they did."

"That's exactly my point. The kid looked the other way

his entire life. Why would he suddenly betray his family now?"

Shaw picked at his mahogany beard. "There needs to be something more. Esteban and his brother Pancho are real pieces of work. It could be as simple as Manuel not wanting his family in bed with the Gallos."

Something rang true about that, Carver had to admit. Some sense that Manuel only tolerated the meth business when it was handled the right way. But that wasn't the full story...

"You know," Carver opined, "the way Ignacio speaks about New Generation, he has genuine hatred for them. Inhuman, he called them. That's not just appeasement to Manuel, it's a foundational belief about their character."

He worked his jaw as he watched Esteban and Christian talk. The Bronco's elevated position was like the rise of a theater floor, and the framed lumberyard a distant stage.

"What if *El Vaquero* himself doesn't know about this partnership?"

Christian begrudgingly took Esteban's hand in a show of solidarity. The man in the cowboy hat offered his too but was ignored. That almost sparked another argument, and Esteban sent him back to the car.

"This is a power play," rejoined Morgan, taking his theory to the logical conclusion. "Christian Espinoza is pushing his father out."

Carver dipped his head in agreement. "It lines up with everything we know about him. He thinks he's the better businessman. He's making moves against the family... to control the family."

"Doing business with a notoriously cruel cartel," ticked Shaw. "Making a move against their patriarch. Those could be red lines Manny wasn't willing to cross."

The poor kid had been stuck between choosing the law or his family his entire life. Working the clinic, he'd doubtless encountered enough meth addicts and victims of cartel violence to despise what they plied, but even then he still hadn't been able to betray his father. Jasmine said Manuel loved his family despite their shortcomings. It was only when Christian made a play that threatened that delicate balance, when the family itself was in existential danger, that Manuel had decided to act. This time, he could do the right thing *and* save his family at the same time.

"So the kid goes to the police," posits Shaw. "Someone, somewhere tips Christian off. Why kidnap Manny instead of killing him?"

Carver shrugged. "My guess is he never intended to kill his brother. That's too far even for him. Christian just needed to lock him down until his takeover was complete. That's why there was no ransom demand. Once Christian secured power, he could let his brother go. Things would settle down."

"Then why the finger?" asked Morgan.

"Because New Generation's the one carrying out this operation. Christian's house is empty. He can't trust *Sólido* when it's Ignacio who pays them. The cartel's the one who took the kid and stashed him away." Carver assessed the situation with a grunt. "Christian Espinoza's in over his head. New Generation played nice until their exposure at the club. They struck back in panic at the street market. Failing that, they extracted their vengeance on Manuel."

"Which explains this meeting," concluded Shaw, "and why Christian is so livid."

Morgan frowned. "Except this partnership looks far from fracturing."

Perhaps it almost had, but she was right. With the prime offender stewing in the car, alone with his cowboy hat, Christian and Esteban wore smiles on their faces. The two were very nearly laughing away the previous day's bad business. Even the bodyguards looked relaxed.

"This was just a setback," agreed Carver. "With these guys, it's money that does the talking. Tomorrow will be business as usual. I wouldn't be surprised if the only genuine tears cried over this kidnapping are from Manuel's girlfriend and sister."

In a city where everyone was cynical and jaded, they had respected Manuel for daring to hope. Meanwhile, Esteban and Christian callously plotted their next moves.

"Okay," said Morgan, "let's run down what we know. *El Vaquero* has an illicit empire that is doing surprisingly well in a competitive field due to his government connections. He's successful enough that the DEA noticed a new player in the game."

"But when it comes down to it," countered Shaw, "the Espinoza operation is relatively small. They operate through Tijuana, but they hardly own the city. Which is where New Generation comes in. They're the dominant player in Baja since Sinaloa took some hits. They win the most wars. They're the most feared."

"Even among the police," added Morgan.

Carver took over. "That ferocity, that collateral damage, it's part of what Ignacio's fighting. He doesn't just want to control the drug trade, he wants to stop the violence in the streets. But that holds him back. Manuel's influence holds him back. And that doesn't sit well with Christian. Rather than let conscience dictate his decisions, he's worried about losing his fledgling empire before he inherits it."

They sat silently a minute to digest all the angles, to make sure there were no stray threads to the theory.

"How much of this does Ignacio know?" asked Morgan.

Carver leaned back in the seat. "He knew it was New Generation that took his kid. He told me from the start, even if he left out the dirty details."

"I mean, do you think Ignacio knows about Christian going against him?"

Carver frowned. "I don't see how he could. Ignacio has to be shrewd to have gotten as far as he did, but Alma said he has a blind spot for his family. This looks much bigger than even she suspected."

It had to be hard on a man, to learn of his children at each other's throats. At the same time, this was a problem of Ignacio's creation. He was in a cutthroat business. He raised a family into it. Carver was sure the old man knew that more than anyone.

The meeting in the lumberyard ended with a final handshake. The narcos and security team returned to their cars. There were too many guns in play to stop them. Carver ordered his team to switch targets so there was a lower chance they'd be noticed on the return trip. Morgan covered Christian while Carver and Shaw went after Esteban. The man in the cowboy hat dropped him off with his contingent and Carver continued after him alone.

They were closing in. He could feel it.

17

After the eye-opening revelations in the morning, the rest of the day proved to be a slog. The various actors in the plot all refrained from making immediate moves. They hunkered down in their residences, out of sight. Carver wished he had access to CIA capabilities, wished he could listen in on the enemy's communication channels, but he was out of the inner circle on this one.

It wasn't such a bad trade-off. The truth was, this was how he preferred to operate. Where he excelled. He was in the gray zone between official mandate and reckless vigilantism, where he didn't have access to the best toys but at least knew the job was honest.

The obvious irony was that he was currently on retainer to a drug cartel. But then, it was the arm of the DEA that had placed him here. Carver could leave anytime he decided it was the right move.

Unfortunately, the fate of Manuel Espinoza weighed on him. It was a burden made cumbersome precisely because Carver was calling the shots. Because it was the right thing.

Success or failure, it was on him.

He dropped the foil burrito wrapper into a brown paper

bag, added a few overly tiny napkins, and crumpled the whole thing into a ball that was tossed into the empty back seat. Shaw, beside him, still worked on his dinner as they took in the night scene of the quiet house.

The man in the cowboy hat was the weak link in the chain. No doubt about it. He was the rash underling who'd made the poor decision to cut Manuel's finger off. He was the one in direct contact with the kid. He'd threatened the stability of the fledgling partnership. The man in the cowboy hat was the one they had to keep an eye on.

So far, he'd only led them to a dive bar, a brothel, and an unassuming home.

After sunset, Carver had risked sneaking close enough to the house to see ants crawling into cracks in the stucco exterior. He had discovered only a domestic scene of a man drinking a beer and watching TV, belly hanging over stained sweat pants, while his wife stewed chicken on the stove.

Manuel wasn't in this house either so they had to watch Cowboy Hat until he moved. Hence the dinner in the truck. It was going to be a long night.

Carver's phone buzzed, and he was hoping it was Morgan with the information. Instead it was a message from Alma, a selfie at a diagonal from above. Her pursed lips were painted bright pink. Not accidentally, full cleavage tethered in matching pink lingerie dominated the bottom of the frame. Alma's nipple perked against the sheer fabric.

"You old dog," commended Shaw.

Carver blacked out the screen and pulled the phone

away. "It's nothing."

"That's definitely *something*, Vince. You didn't tell me the sister was a bombshell."

He bit down. "Alma's... a bit of a puzzle."

"She's the one who has you thinking this kid's a saint."

"No." Carver ground his teeth. "She does say that, and I believe her, but Jasmine's a more reliable source."

"Whatever you say, boss." He returned his eyes to the house as if the subject was over. Then, casually, "You gonna take her up on that?"

"Take her up on what?"

He nodded to the phone. "That looks like an invitation to me."

Carver checked the phone again, tilting the screen to obscure Shaw's view. Text came through under the image. "Missing u..."

He couldn't pretend the thought didn't stir his blood. A repeat of last night would be more than welcome. But what he wanted more was an end to this shady business. More and more, Carver wondered who he could trust. Getting distracted could get him killed.

He typed back, "Busy tonight. Won't make it back."

She replied, "Your loss. *Besitos*."

The message had its intended effect. Carver looked at the picture again. The truck's back door opened as Morgan returned, and he shoved the phone into his pocket.

"Captain Gomez was helpful," she said. She paused to wipe trash off the back seat. "It's a pigsty in here."

Shaw burped loudly as he crumpled up his bag and flung

it into Morgan's face. "Sorry, the pigs are done eating. None for you."

She returned a sardonic grin. "That's fine because I enjoyed paella prepared by Mateo's lovely wife."

Shaw spun around. "Mateo who?"

"Captain Gomez. Keep up. He looked up our address while we ate. The residents are Hector and Lydia Sanchez. Retired. Kids moved out."

Carver turned back to the old house. "So our kidnapper's name is Hector."

"Has he made any moves yet?" she asked.

"Do bowel movements count?" quipped Shaw.

"Nothing to report," said Carver, "except that Manuel's not in there."

She idly shook her head. "Well, it's getting late. I doubt he leaves the house tonight."

"I agree."

"It's not ideal with the wife there, but I say we take Hector now."

Carver worked his jaw. "We can do that, but if he doesn't talk, we blow the whole op. We already saw how New Generation treated Manuel. If they know we're onto him, they might just kill the kid and be done with the whole thing. I'd rather watch Hector from a distance until he leads us to our target."

Shaw reclined the passenger seat and released a long relaxed sigh. "Which means another night sleeping in the car. Good night, gentlefolk."

Morgan snorted. "Meanwhile Vince sleeps in the lap of

luxury."

"I believe he has another lap in mind."

Morgan's head swiveled to Carver for an explanation.

"I'm not going anywhere," he firmly answered. "I'm done playing spy. I want the kid and I want him yesterday."

She nodded and leaned back in the seat herself. "All this to save a drug kingpin's son."

"This has nothing to do with Ignacio anymore. For all I care, *El Vaquero* can rot with the rest of them. But Manuel tried to strike out on his own. He tried to do better. You know how hard that is in a place like this?" Carver turned back to the house, extreme focus becoming a kind of tunnel vision. "He doesn't deserve this."

Morgan solemnly followed his gaze. "It sounds to me like they don't deserve him."

* * *

Morgan said something, but it wasn't more than a mumble. Then she added, "We've got company."

Carver's eyes opened to slits. The neighborhood was asleep at this late hour. Brake lights from a black delivery van washed Hector's front yard in red. Its headlights were off. Somewhere among the dark twisty roads, a lone dog released a muffled bark.

"This isn't normal," remarked Shaw, wiping his eyes with a minimum of movement.

A man wearing a balaclava and black tactical gear hopped

out of the passenger seat and rounded to open the van's back doors. Five similarly dressed soldiers unloaded with trained precision.

Shaw sneered. "What is this?"

Carver checked his weapon, and the others followed suit. The men were armed with what looked to be short-barrel HK carbines. Without stopping to huddle, they broke into pairs and advanced around the left, right, and front of the house.

"Those aren't narcos," muttered Shaw. "They look military to me."

"Wearing all black?" countered Morgan.

"They're special police," said Carver. "And they know what they're doing."

Shaw nodded. "I think you might be right. Those rifles are FX-05s. Mexican special forces."

The soldiers flanking the house disappeared into the shadows. The pair at the front checked the door. Finding it locked, they spoke into the radio and backed away into the bushes.

"They're covering the exits," noted Morgan.

"They're gonna take Hector," Carver growled.

"You think this is how Manuel's kidnapping went down?"

Shaw checked up and down the sleepy street. "What are we gonna do about this?"

Carver sneered bitterly. "Counting the driver, there's at least seven of them. I hate to say it, but we're outclassed at the moment."

The Service of Wolves

"I'm glad you said that," breathed Morgan. "Even if we did take them down, our legal standing is questionable."

"There is no question. This is illegal," chuckled Shaw.

"You know what I mean. Shooting cops to protect a narco."

"It's no good," admitted Carver. "We don't know enough to make a move."

"So they take him, and we follow," suggested Shaw.

"That's risky too. If they're kidnapping someone, they'll be watching their six. A team like this would be more likely to shoot us than ask questions."

"Again, I'm with Vince," said Morgan. "This is black-book stuff. If they see us, we're as good as dead." Renewed movement in Hector's yard caused her to duck. "Stay down."

The front seats of the Bronco were still reclined, so Carver and Shaw just rested easy. The SWAT officers that had gone around back converged in the front with a hand signal. The one who had used the radio nodded and pointed to the van.

"They're leaving," whispered Morgan.

"That's... unexpected," frowned Shaw. "Did Hector run?"

"Not on my watch," she retorted.

"We don't have eyes on the back," said Carver, coolly slipping leather gloves over his fingers. "Anything's possible."

Morgan pointed as one of the soldiers handed a metal lockbox to the officer before loading into the back of the van. "What's in the box?"

"Money, maybe."

"A payoff?"

"Or a robbery," countered Shaw.

The van's back doors were secured and the officer climbed into the passenger seat. The vehicle quietly rolled onto the street at a steady pace as if it had just delivered a package. It turned the corner, still without headlights, and disappeared.

Carver leapt from the Bronco, Sig held low. He sprinted through three front yards before reaching Hector's house. Morgan and Shaw were right behind him. Carver signaled to the backyard and they followed onto the concrete patio. Under the overhang, the sliding glass door was partially ajar.

He peeked inside, eyes already accustomed to the dark. There was no activity inside. He slid the door wide and entered, leading with his gun. He took up position aiming at the rear hall as Shaw passed behind him to clear the kitchenette. Morgan advanced to the corner and signaled him on.

The house wasn't large. One bathroom and a bedroom that had been converted to a sewing room. Nothing appeared out of place. They entered the master bedroom to find a California king with the large sleeping masses of Hector and his wife. Carver had a bad feeling. He pulled his tac light and illuminated their bloody visages.

Hector and Lydia had been muzzled and held down and their throats brutally sliced open.

Carver flicked off his light and turned to his team. "Let's

go," he said. "Don't touch anything."

They filed out the way they had come with wordless discipline, leaving the door exactly as they had found it so there would be no trace they were ever in the zip code. Their disappointment wasn't evident until they returned to their vehicles, faces solemn as they drove off and left the sleepy neighborhood in the rearview.

They had just lost their best chance at finding Manuel.

18

The next morning, Carver returned to the Tecate ranch alone. His truck's suspension bounced as he turned off the paved street. The officers at the checkpoint didn't give him a problem this time. He nodded and headed down the private road.

He had played nice with the family yesterday given the incident with Manuel's finger. Carver now saw that had been a mistake. Everyone had their own stories, their own lies. It was a convoluted mess of personal interests competing for dominance. Like a title fight, there was no solving it without taking off the kid gloves and punching your opponent harder than they can hit back.

There was more to Carver's anger than the setback caused by Hector's fate. The narco hadn't just been killed, he'd been assassinated by an elite team of special police. The president's own. Pulling off something like that took political clout, and where else to look but the local congressman?

As he approached the house, a black Lincoln Aviator pulled ahead on the driveway and turned to a stop diagonally, blocking passage. A close protection officer

The Service of Wolves

exited with a hand signal to stop. Behind them, a Cadillac was parked ready by the front porch.

Carver hissed. He considered driving around them but didn't want a repeat of the scene from the other night. Instead, he pulled to the side of the road and hopped out. Without bothering to close the door, he advanced over the gravel on foot.

The *Sólido* driver and another guard also exited the SUV now. The trio of contractors fixed hardened glares on him as he stomped past. After dumping Gonzalo, they were proving to make competent decisions. This was no exception as they utilized the good sense to stay out of Carver's way.

He strode up the driveway pavers as Ignacio and his bodyguard exited the ranch house and came down the steps of the landing. They noticed his angry approach. Gray Hair held his shotgun in high ready position, pointing up from the hip.

Carver cut them off before they could make it to the Buick. "Did you have Hector killed?"

Ignacio pulled his head back. "Who? What are you talking about?"

"A New Generation narco. The special police broke into his house last night and murdered him and his wife."

Ignacio's face darkened. "Vince, I don't know who you're talking about, and I don't have time for this right now. I'm on my way to Mexicali for a special session of Congress."

"We had eyes on him," grated Carver. "The guy who was going to lead us to your son. Now he's dead."

"My son?"

"Hector!"

Ignacio took a second to process that. Then his expression deflated. "I had nothing to do with that. I'm a wine rancher."

"The family business," Carver spat. "You must think I'm an idiot."

"Vince..."

"Why didn't you tell me you were *El Vaquero*?"

Carver's accusation was loud and unabashed. Gray Hair blinked evenly. The *Sólido* team crept forward. It was a surprise to no one here.

Ignacio's jowls flapped as he released a breath. If it was a sign of defeat, it was the only one. "So what, Vince? I don't see how who I am changes our arrangement. I paid you an advance, and I paid you handsomely."

Carver nodded in contempt. "It's pretty ballsy for a drug dealer to reach out to the DEA for help, but then, they're mostly impotent in Mexico these days, aren't they? What little risk you exposed yourself to was worth recovering your son. I can't fault you for staying true to family, at least."

"The DEA isn't judge and jury, Vince. They're a political enforcement arm. Politics plays favorites. You know how the world works."

"Do they know who you are?"

"No one knows who I am, and I'd like to keep it that way as long as possible. That's why I didn't tell you. It's nothing personal."

It sure felt personal. Carver ground his teeth, angry that

someone could shrug off something so large. It pissed him off.

"Come now, don't act all righteous," admonished Ignacio. "I've been doing some digging on you too. It turns out that you're not employed by any government agency to speak of. No one knows who you are."

Gray Hair stared flatly, unfazed by the unfolding conversation. It was entirely possible he was the one who had done the digging for Ignacio.

"I'm supposed to be invisible," Carver countered.

"I understand that. And I understand why you have an army record that leads nowhere. I can read between the lines, Vince. But the latest word on your standing is that you're a washed up bodyguard." Ignacio stepped closer. "You almost got your client killed in Arizona last year. Your security company fell apart. Now it's just you in a dentist's office with two other employees. I'm no longer convinced you have the connections I need."

"You wanted a guy who could get things done."

"I can get things done myself. What I wanted was closer collaboration with the American government."

A snide smile spread on Carver's face. "You mean you want legitimate cover for your illegal operation. You want tacit approval of the US government so you can scare the cartel off."

"One step at a time, Vince. I would need to prove my value first. I understand that."

The jostle of the curtain in the living room caught his eye. Alma had noticed them and was now a spectator.

Behind him, *Sólido Seguridad* watched passively. Exactly who and what they were was out in the open now.

"What value?" asked Carver derisively. "You're a drug dealer."

Ignacio's mustache tweaked. "Don't judge me, Vince. I sell product because people buy product. I donate to charitable causes. I clean up the streets. I run my business far from the local community, and I settle disputes with law and diplomacy." Ignacio shook his head at the apparent misunderstanding. "*Nueva Generación*? They're terrorists. I'm a servant of the people."

"You're a greedy politician, the same as all the other greedy politicians before you. You only care about the public good when it benefits you."

"I'm sorry you feel that way, Vince. But like it or not, I'm the superior alternative. *Nueva Generación's* ranks are full of bloodthirsty psychopaths. Who would you rather have in power, them or *El Vaquero*? I can tell you for a fact, if you walk down any unaligned block in Tijuana and ask the hardworking fathers and mothers who they choose, it would be me."

Carver chortled at the binary proposition. "If only it were that simple, Ignacio. But it looks like I wasn't the only one operating under false pretenses here. You still don't realize you're in business with the very people you despise."

That got his attention. "What's that supposed to mean?"

"Christian's making a deal with New Generation. A power play to usurp his old man."

Ignacio's brow hardened. "Impossible."

But the words rang hollow. His expression had already revealed his doubt.

"Christian's the one who kidnapped Manuel," explained Carver. "Not directly. He outsourced the job to New Generation, and they had Hector take him off the street."

The man's face twisted. "But why?"

"Manuel must have found out what they were planning."

Ignacio stared blank-faced. "He would have said something."

Carver shrugged. "He didn't want to tear the family apart. As best I can tell, Manuel was reaching out to the DEA to shut down the partnership. If he could strike a blow to New Generation, he could scare off his big brother. Once Christian's new deal fell through, he'd have no choice but to stick by your side. Manuel was trying to save the family."

Stunned, Ignacio shook his head solemnly. "He should have told me..." was all he said.

"But he didn't. Christian lied to you, and Manuel lied to you about him, and you lied to me about it." Carver crossed his arms over his chest. "It's time to cut through all the bullshit, Ignacio. Just chuck it aside and deal with the hard facts. I'm here for your son. Hector was my way to find him. Did you have him killed or not?"

The politician's eyes were simple, pleading. "I swear, I don't even know who you're talking about." His eyes were also honest.

Carver paced to the edge of the driveway. His gaze ran over the bubbling water feature, the fountain spilling into a man-made stream that twisted past a grassy knoll overtaken by the roots of the sycamore tree. It was the same tree Gonzalo had taken shade under the first time he'd visited. Carver turned to the *Sólido* team. The three guards watched him rigidly from the end of the driveway, beside their Aviator. They were on high alert due to recent events, and who could blame them, but Carver didn't fool himself that they were on his side.

He returned to Ignacio. "If you truly didn't know about Hector, that means the kill team was sent by Christian. He might be able to use or fake your access, right?"

Ignacio's hands hooked on his hips. "It's possible, but—"

"New Generation's cruelty surprised him. He never meant for Manuel to get hurt. Hector was the one who delivered the finger. I'm guessing he was the one who cut it off too. Hector stepped out of line, and Christian killed him for it."

The politician appeared grief-stricken as his son's ruthlessness played out in so many words. But Ignacio was too shrewd to allow emotion to paralyze him for long. "Does this mean Christian blew up the deal with the cartel?"

"Not likely. Your son needed to save face. He needed to send a message that he's not one to be trifled with. But what does New Generation care? Hector was a nobody. A screwup. If keeping the peace means sacrificing their own guy, they might go along with it. The cartel knows the bigger prize is getting you out of the picture. Hector brought this on himself."

The patriarch of the ranch nodded along. He saw the

wisdom of such logic. He was comfortable with it, even.

"You need to operate under the assumption that Christian is still a threat. He's going after your business."

Ignacio's cheeks reddened. His demeanor was calm, but he must have been fuming inside. "That damn fool could never see past my affair."

"Forget about the family drama. You need to call him. Order Christian here right now. Act normal. Tell him you have new information."

"What would that gain me?"

Carver's face said the answer was obvious. "If Christian had Hector killed without being interrogated, if he's working with the same people who kidnapped his brother, then he knows exactly where Manuel is. Finding one brother is as simple as making the other brother talk. Get Christian here, away from his security team. I'll get him to tell us where Manuel is, and I'll go pick him up."

A frown had overtaken Ignacio. It was an ugly thing that contorted his mustache and wrinkled his face, making him appear ten years older. "It's not that easy."

"The hell it isn't," said Carver.

He sighed. "I have Congress to attend."

"You just need to make the call."

Ignacio clicked his tongue in frustration. "You're not fully appreciating my position here. The play Christian is making."

"Sure I am."

"I'm not going to kill Christian."

"I might."

Ignacio's eyes grew dark under his brow. "That would be unwise, Vince."

Carver upturned his hand in question, prompting the patriarch to proceed.

"I'm not going to wage a violent war against my son," decanted the politician. "We are at odds, but we're family."

"Manuel's your family too."

"He's leverage against me. Christian is using him in hopes that I stand down."

"Then stand down. If you won't fight, it's your only option."

Ignacio scoffed. "It's that simple for you?"

"It just needs to *sound* simple. The last thing I'll do is advise you how to run your empire. All I'm saying is, if you're not going to threaten Christian, then you should appease him. Tell him you'll do whatever it takes to get Manuel back. Even if you don't mean it. What's one more lie with this family?"

His cheek twitched in annoyance, but Ignacio moved past the jab. "I can't stand down."

"It's temporary. Give Christian what he wants, get what you want. Save your son and deal with the politics later."

He shook his head. "I would never recover from that. Power and loyalty are fickle things. It would be an extreme loss of face to capitulate to my son. If I give him that power, if he strengthens ties with *Nueva Generación*, I would never be able to wrest it back."

Carver hissed. "Would that be the most awful alternative? We're talking about your youngest son. The only good guy in all of this. When I first met you, you swore you'd do anything to get him back. You have a chance to return his life to him. He can go back to helping people. At worst, all you need to do is step back. Retire."

Ignacio shook his head again. "You mistake me, Vince. You see a grieving father and a political dealmaker, but you ignore the man who tilled this arid soil for years, who built this house with callused hands, who clawed his way into the limelight and the president's good graces. You ignore the man who architected an empire, and you ask me to simply give up everything I've worked for." He huffed. "I'm not willing to do that. Not even for Manuel."

Carver paced backward, away from the politician, surprised by his disbelief. He wasn't sure what he had expected, really. Appealing to a drug kingpin's sentiment was an act of desperation. Carver was a man who had taken out Libyan militants in a night shoot from three hundred meters, yet this was the bigger long shot.

He met Alma's inquisitive eyes in the window. She couldn't hear their conversation through the double glazing, but the body language and emotion on display were enough to convey the import of their confrontation. He wondered how she would feel about her dear *Papás* choice.

"You know," Carver mused, "all that stuff about *El Vaquero* cleaning up the streets is a fantasy. It's a nice sentiment, sure, but when was the last time you actually visited these so-called streets you want to save?" He turned to Ignacio as he lectured. "When was the last time you've seen, up close, what your product does to your citizens?

Some of them live in corrugated shacks that barely keep the wind out. They lack running water. But still they scrounge to buy up what you sell them. Manuel's the one who helps them, not you. He's the one that's on their side."

The indignant mention of his son caused Ignacio to hold his tongue. A part of him must have seen Manuel as his salvation.

"I can't say I ever bought that line, but I did see you as a family man. As a father who takes care of his own, even if you have your foibles." Carver stepped closer. "Now's your chance to stand by your principles. To do good for the streets. For the people. Now's your chance to *save your son.*" He took a breath. "You might not get another one."

Everyone stared at everyone for a cathartic moment. While the guards watched lazily, something softened in Ignacio.

"I admit, you have managed to surprise me," he remarked. "You have a good heart, and I don't mean that to be patronizing. But you are fixed on the ideal of a past, of a future that is not meant to exist. I must operate in the present." He mustered a breath. "These people, they want what's mine. They cut off my son's finger. They'll do worse. He's a cripple now, proof of my weakness. Don't you see? This isn't about Manuel, it's about me."

Carver was stunned. His feet nearly gave out beneath him. His face went icy. "So you're not just an asshole, you're a narcissist too."

"Fuck you, Vince. You wouldn't last one week in this business. You don't have what it takes."

The Service of Wolves

"And what's that?"

He set his jaw. "I need to sacrifice Manuel. This is a war. Don't you see that? Manuel's a weakness they'll exploit until they have what they want. If I give them an inch, they'll take a mile. The only way to beat them is to stand firm, to show them I have no weakness."

"Do you hear yourself?"

"I will not be bargained with. And if Manuel has to die for the greater good, so be it. But that doesn't mean our business relationship has to end. You've proven to be an indispensable asset. Stay by my side, Vince. I could use men like you."

Carver blinked coolly before stepping forward and leaning down so his face was inches from Ignacio's. "You know, I'm usually a pretty decent judge of character, but it took me all the way until this moment to realize what a piece of shit you are."

The dark look again. "I could have you killed right now, you know that?"

Gray Hair adjusted his hand to the grip of the shotgun. Carver's hand blinked to his holster. "Don't," he warned.

Amid the tension, Carver took a sideways backstep to include the *Sólido* crew in his view. They hadn't drawn their weapons yet, but they were standing ready. It wouldn't take much for them to make a move.

"Don't?" challenged Ignacio. "Or what, Vince? You're outgunned here. You can't fight everyone."

"The hell I can't."

Ignacio watched him carefully. There were a lot of guns

present. Though most of them were his, the standoff would set any normal man on edge. The fact that Ignacio didn't waver was a sign of exactly how familiar he was with the dark nature of his business. The man may have once been a wine seller, but now he was a merchant of death.

But that familiarity ran both ways. Carver was alone, surrounded by hostiles, yet his hand rested easily on the grip of the Sig holstered under his shoulder. Here also was a man ready for an explosion of action, a man acquainted with kinetics, one unbound by the rules of an official government agency. And he was a man who hadn't so much as blinked.

Ignacio's eyebrows twitched upward. Maybe Carver had surprised him again.

The front door swung open and Alma spilled onto the porch. "*Papá*, what do you think you're doing?"

"Leave it alone, *hija*."

"I will *not* leave it alone. This isn't how we do business."

There was a crack in Ignacio's steely facade. Then a grimace. There seemed to be a constant struggle within him between who he was and who he wanted to be. Carver had hoped to appeal to that idealistic side. He had lost.

Alma, however, had a different sway.

Ignacio scraped out a guttural decision to Carver. "Get out. For good. I no longer have need of your services." He withdrew his phone. "And let it not be said I am unreasonable. You performed your duties to a tee. Here's your final payment, for your time, as well as a generous termination fee."

As he swiped the screen, Gray Hair wiggled the fingers

of his trigger hand, getting Carver's attention. After confirming that *Sólido* had backed down, Carver nodded. Both men pulled their hands slowly away from their guns in perfect synchrony. Alma sighed in exhausted relief.

"There," announced Ignacio. "Our business is concluded. You will not repeat anything we discussed to anyone. Your discretion was part of the package."

He eyed Carver to check if the point would be challenged. Carver didn't have the energy.

"Good. I consider the matter closed. I have a government to run, and you are no longer allowed on my property."

He nodded toward the Buick and his bodyguard made for it. Gray Hair sneered at Carver one last time, disappointed they didn't get to dance but perhaps hoping for a rain check. He went for the driver's seat, and the *Sólido* team were all too relieved to load into the Aviator at the end of the driveway to take the lead.

"Is someone going to tell me what's going on?" Alma asked.

Ignacio put his arm around her. "Let's get you back inside." He guided her up the porch.

"Stop treating me like a child."

"Never," he said with a proud flair. "We will discuss this after—"

A flash of light pummeled Carver's side as the Buick exploded. Fire erupted upwards and he, Alma, and Ignacio hit the floor. The living room windows shattered inward. Carver's ears rang. He turned to see the butt end of

Ignacio's car bounce on the back axle, back door still open and swinging. The trunk flap had blown into the air and followed a downward trajectory into the large sycamore, where it hit several branches before settling in the yard. The back seat of the Buick was a jumble of debris and smoke.

Carver sprang to his feet but failed to maintain his balance and fell to a knee. He shook it off and tried again, this time yanking Alma and Ignacio off the porch and shoving them into the house.

"*Qué diablos!*" whined Alma.

Carver didn't know if she was complaining about the bomb or his gruff treatment. She was in shock.

Ignacio was a little more put together. He planted a callused hand on Carver's shoulder and shoved back outside. His Buick was on fire. The patriarch stared at the car, visualizing an alternate timeline with his death only seconds gone.

One of the *Sólido* guys emerged from the Aviator's back seat, pistol in hand. Carver pulled the Sig. The guard fired a couple of times, and they ducked. Carver returned fire in frenzied succession, emptying his magazine as the guard scrambled back into the bulletproof vehicle. Carver dropped his mag and slid a new one into place, but the SUV's tires kicked up gravel and peeled away. The *Sólido* team was cutting bait.

"Who did this?" barked Ignacio, not yet thinking clearly. He spun to his side, searching for his trusty bodyguard before realizing he had perished in the car. Ignacio turned to Carver, fuming. "Who did this?"

The Service of Wolves

"Isn't it obvious?" he muttered.

The maid rushed over and attended to Alma, who was sitting up on the floor, breathing deeply to calm her nerves.

"Who?" snapped Ignacio, face nearly violet. "Bring them to me!"

Carver checked to make sure the security team was not returning, and then calmly slid his pistol into its holster. "You fired me, remember?"

He turned down the porch steps.

Ignacio followed across the driveway like a yapping dog. "Where are you going?"

"I'm no longer welcome on this property."

"I paid you a lot of money!" he screamed.

"A termination fee, if I recall."

"YOU HAVE A JOB TO DO!" he bellowed.

Carver kept walking, answering the old man without giving him another look. "My job is to find your son, and that's exactly what I intend to do."

Ignacio sputtered out as Carver's boots left the pavers and hit the gravel. Maybe the old man suddenly realized how big and scary the world was outside the confines of his carefully landscaped life. Building a house was not the same as building an empire. Carver loaded into the Bronco and drove away.

That was twice now that *Sólido* Security had cut and run. Two gave you twenty they had known about the car bomb. Perhaps they had even planted it. A faulty trigger must have killed the bodyguard early. Carver's unplanned confrontation had unhinged Ignacio from his routine just enough that he had barely escaped the attempt on his life.

It wouldn't be the last one.

Carver didn't bother waving at the officers on the way out. He didn't alert them about the rogue security team or the car bomb. Whether they knew or not was no longer his problem. Likewise, he didn't go heavy on the gas or otherwise attempt to interdict the fleeing security team.

Christian's security team.

Ignacio would see that soon enough. Once his nerves were calm, the picture would clear. They may have been taking the father's money, but the team was loyal to the son.

Christian Espinoza wanted operational control of the family business, and he had just shown how far he was willing to go to get it.

19

After Hector's assassination, Carver's team had been left in the lurch. The situation wasn't entirely without benefit. Instead of taking it as a setback, they had used the night to rest and shower. For ex-soldiers trained to survive harsh jungle and desert environments, it was practically the spa treatment. They were now rejuvenated, energized, and ready to go.

The question that remained, naturally, was where to go?

Without direct leads to Manuel, their best option was to watch the known players, Christian Espinoza and Esteban Gallo. Both men were well protected, which didn't entirely rule out the option of going in by force and getting them to talk, but it limited their opportunities.

Christian was locked down in his *Cumbres de Juárez* compound. It was the safest strongpoint in case of retaliation for hitting Hector. Counting the original residential security team, Gonzalo, plus reinforcements from the Tecate ranch, there were sixteen trained guns in a highly defensible base. Juicy as he was, Christian was a hard target.

The math on Esteban worked out more or less the same.

While he didn't travel with quite so many men on hand, he had a much deeper pool of soldiers at his ultimate disposal. It came with the territory of being a cartel boss. Esteban Gallo was secure in his estate home, and he had enlisted extra protection at *La Cascada* after Carver and Shaw's visit.

Both men would be most susceptible on the road, which wasn't to say they'd be vulnerable. Christian traveled in armored Aviators, Esteban might have some measure of ballistic protection, and Carver's team manned private rentals.

Just about any way he attacked the problem didn't make for a fair fight. Not from a numbers standpoint. But then, that was the purpose of special operators. Their team was small but agile, able to direct itself and make intelligent decisions to strike when an opportunity presented itself.

For the time being, none did.

Carver vigilantly made the rounds throughout the day, passing by the Espinoza lumberyard and warehouse complex Gonzalo had taken him to earlier. In contrast to the previous day's illicit meeting, workers filled the loading docks and shuffled around inventory. Business hummed, the world moved on, and Manuel Espinoza was nowhere to be seen, a footnote missing a finger and still in the capricious custody of a ruthless cartel.

The day went like that, more or less uneventful, with the team of three operating in shifts of two in order to stay fresh.

"These guys are good," grumbled Shaw over the phone. "With Hector out of the picture, I don't foresee more sloppy mistakes. No one's compromised OPSEC by visiting Manny."

Carver hiked up the service stairwell of his hotel at a brisk pace. His butt had been glued to his car seat for more hours than he could count, and it felt nice to get the blood humming in his muscles. It was now late at night, and he shared Shaw's frustration.

"We watch and we wait," he said.

"We watch and we wait," repeated Shaw with a sigh. It had become the day's mantra.

Carver slipped his phone into his pocket as he entered the hall and approached his room only two doors down. He froze when he noticed the seam of darkness beneath the door. He had left the light on, and the *No Moleste* placard hanging on the doorknob precluded maid service.

He drew his pistol and advanced down the hall, tactical boots easing lightly over the durable nylon carpet. He checked around the corner to the elevator well and didn't find anyone. There was nobody watching this level. Carver hadn't noticed anyone on the way into the building either but, as he had avoided the elevators, he could have missed something.

Nobody should know about this location. They had just changed hotels two days prior, after Gonzalo had stopped escorting him around. The only explanation was that he'd been followed at some point.

Carver returned to his door and frowned. If it was the afternoon, he would have requested that a maid freshen up his room. At this late hour, it wasn't an option. He considered others.

He could go in hard, but that put him most at risk. An assassin inside would hear the door unlock, lie in darkness while Carver's silhouette blotted the doorway, and have the quicker shot.

Or Carver could simply abandon the room. It had been compromised. Losing it wasn't a big loss as the room didn't contain anything important. His kinetic gear was in the truck.

Instead of the black-and-white options, Carver chose to operate in the gray. He twisted the bulbs of the closest wall sconces until their lights cut out. Then he stood a full body's span away from the door frame, on the side opposite the handle, and waited a minute for his eyes to adjust to the darkness. He leaned over, knocked, and returned to position, gun ready.

After a moment someone inside shuffled. Carver pointed the weapon, the door clicked, and Alma peeked out. Her eyes widened at the barrel of the Sig.

Carver cursed. He first made sure her hands were empty. Then he grabbed her by the throat and shoved her inside.

"Vin—" she choked in surprise.

He controlled her position but didn't squeeze as he cleared the room. The door shut and he moved to the empty bathroom. Only then did he release Alma's neck.

"I'm alone!" she hissed. "It's just me!"

He turned on a table lamp as she rubbed her throat. Alma wore a loose-fitting green blouse, something that didn't stand out as much as her usual outfits.

The Service of Wolves

"I wanted to surprise you."

"Congratulations, you did. How did you find me?"

He held the pistol pointed at the floor while he ran a hand up and down her legs, checking for weapons. She rolled her eyes. "Why would I need protection from you? I feel safe when we're together."

As his hand passed over her inner thigh, she grabbed it and pulled it in with a provocative smile.

"You still didn't say how you found out where I was staying."

"Come now, Vince. I know the area. I have contacts. It wasn't hard."

"You're having me watched?"

"Is that so bad? You know you could use a little protection yourself sometimes."

"I'd settle for a little privacy."

She huffed. "Privacy is overrated." Alma released his hand and unbuttoned the top of her blouse, spreading it open to show off a black lace bra. "Don't say I'm not welcome. I'm not used to rejection. I may be used to being alone, but you're making me a lonely woman, Vince."

She slipped one strap of the bra down her shoulder. She was good at going hot and heavy, but Carver knew something was up. As she reached for the coup de grace, he pulled her hand away.

"Stop it," he said. "It's always an act with you, isn't it?"

She pouted with thick painted lips. "It isn't an act. I need you right now."

"You need something else or you wouldn't be here."

Her chest rose and fell in excited defiance. "Sharp, as always. I don't know where *Papá* found you."

"It's good to know I still have some secrets."

She let out air. "There are too many secrets, Vince. No one will tell me what's going on." She pressed into him, squeezing cleavage against his chest. "Is it so wrong to seek out a physical connection?"

Carver's face didn't budge. "Business before pleasure."

Her lips twisted wryly and she backed off. "I was trying to get to that." She slipped dainty fingers into her bra and plucked out a thumb drive. "There's something you should listen to."

Vince took it to his laptop on the table and plugged it in. There was a short wait as the partitioned drive it booted to scanned for hidden executables. While the countermeasure could only do so much against sophisticated spyware, Morgan insisted it would be extremely effective against non-state actors. The drive passed the security check, and Carver found a single audio file on it.

"It's a recording of *Papá* setting up a meeting with Esteban Gallo," she explained.

Carver watched her carefully. "What are you doing with a recording of your father's phone call?"

She smirked and casually hiked a strapless shoulder. "Do you not think recent events call for caution? I'm starting to wonder who is worthy of my trust, and who isn't."

"So you come to me."

A glint in her eyes. "You are *very* worthy, Vince."

"And this call's a big enough deal to secret away into my

hotel room in the middle of the night?"

"Do you and I need a reason to meet like this?"

His fixed stare was unamused.

She sighed. "*Papá* never talks to the narcos directly. He's too careful for that. *El Vaquero* is an urban myth. A story the people spread. He's not supposed to make appearances in person."

Carver chewed his lip. This was a different level of involvement for Alma, and he didn't like the implications. But she was here and offering information. He double-clicked the file and scratchy audio came through the tinny speakers.

"You tried to kill me?" growled Ignacio in Spanish.

Esteban's voice came back with the utmost calm. "I've never killed anyone in my life, Congressman. But I can kill careers."

"Don't play games with me! There's supposed to be peace between us. You know the agreement."

"The agreement is outdated, *Vaquero*. We're dealers. It's time to deal."

"Don't presume that I'm the same as you," swore Ignacio with venom. "You shoot people in the *mercado*."

"More baseless accusations. But I do fight for what's mine—same as you, Ignacio. Let us then call each other businessmen. You're dreaming if you think you can expand on your own. Enough is enough. You have the infrastructure and I have more product than I can move. It is high time we talked."

Ignacio didn't shoot back with an immediate rejoinder.

His breath was heavy. "There's a lot we need to talk about," he conceded.

"Not over the phone," cautioned Esteban. "We meet in person."

"Tomorrow?"

"I can make that happen. *La Cascada*, 10 am?"

Ignacio grumbled over the phone. After a moment's hesitation he said, "I'll be there."

The line clicked dead and the recording ended.

Carver had been studying Alma's face the entire time. It hadn't revealed much, but she was right about this recording being a big deal. Although Esteban was careful to dance around the subject without explicitly incriminating himself, the subject matter was obvious. For a politician like Ignacio, one with a carefully cultivated public image, the implications were damaging.

"Why give me this?" asked Carver. "This is enough evidence to burn your father's empire to the ground."

"I am not interested in empire, Vince. I want my brother rescued from this mess, the sooner the better. I'm imploring *Papá* as well."

"Yeah, well I'm not sure Ignacio sees the situation clearly."

"And why is that?"

"Based on that recording, he still thinks New Generation is responsible for the car bomb."

Her lips perked. "Who else?"

"Your older brother, Alma, that's who."

Her brow creased. "Family killing family? It cannot be."

The Service of Wolves

"It's a story as old as time."

"Blood is too thick for that."

"They call it drunk with power because it thins the blood."

She frowned. It created a cute dimple in the center of her chin. "Okay," she conceded. "After a certain line is crossed, perhaps family can turn on itself."

"After a certain line is crossed?"

"Yes, Vince. And you cannot convince me we're there yet. Christian is maneuvering for control, is he not? All this secrecy—the deals, the kidnapping—why would he go through all that just to kill *Papá* now? Nothing has changed."

"No lines crossed," repeated Carver.

Granted, the severed finger was an escalation, but that had been on Christian's side. There was no evidence that Ignacio had stepped out of line yet, no reason to kill him, and Alma was best positioned to know that much.

Carver privately wondered if the finger was enough. Ignacio had coldly written Manuel off as a cripple. What if Christian was doing the same? Maybe, by his calculus, his father was more dangerous now. Maybe he feared retribution and, after making a move with Hector, inertia dictated that he continue.

Maybe, now, there would never be peace until one of them was out of the picture for good.

As indecision crept into his thoughts, Carver found his attention more and more drawn to Alma's open blouse. "Are you just going to stand there like that? It's distracting."

"You're right," she said. "I must look ridiculous."

Carver was about to say her conclusion was in the wrong ballpark, but stopped when Alma, instead of rebuttoning the blouse, took it off completely. She was left in a knee-high skirt and lace bra. Her heels already rested on the floor beside the bed, having come off before he was in the room.

This seduction was entirely intentional, and he entirely didn't mind.

"You don't want to see it," pressed Carver.

She took a playful step toward him. "*Nueva Generación* wants *Papá* out of the way."

"*Sólido Seguridad* took shots at us on your porch."

Another step. "They could have been shooting at you."

"How is that better?"

"Think about it from their point of view. You show up out of nowhere, yelling like a lunatic, and then *Papá's* car explodes."

His lips twisted. The security team had run after that. Though that wasn't overly suspicious. Self interest seemed to be what they were best at.

"It's a reach," he decided. "The cartel's partnering with Christian. He would know if they went after his father."

"My brother's in over his head," she countered. "He's not in control of this. You have to see that."

"Why do you insist on defending him?" he asked hotly.

"I'm not. I'm..." Her confidence suddenly withered. "I don't know what I'm doing. I don't know what to think of anything anymore." She pressed into him and hugged him tight. Her body was cold and shivering, and she said nothing more.

"Alma..." started Carver, but he honestly didn't know where to go from there. He didn't even know what he was doing with her. She did the books for a corrupt drug lord. Carver was disciplined enough to not allow feelings to interfere with his work, and he wasn't here to convince her of her family's worth. He was just supposed to do a simple job.

"Are we done talking now?" she asked. Her voice was small, a million miles away.

"We're done," he said, relieved.

Alma drew away bearing a meek expression. This time, as she unhooked her bra, she was almost embarrassed. She covered her naked breasts with one arm as she zipped the back of her skirt. She sat on the bed and wiggled back toward the pillows, trying and failing to be modest. It was maddeningly cute.

Once at the head of the bed, she pulled the blanket up to her neck, slipped out of her panties, and tossed them on top of her heels on the floor.

"I missed you last night," she said quietly. "It's not often a man... keeps up with me."

Carver admired the image of her hiding under his blanket. "Is that a challenge?"

"Take it however you like."

He had every intention of doing so.

Despite Alma's tough talk, she was a more gentle lover this go around. She kept slowing herself down to stare deeply into his eyes, cultivating a connection on a deeper level than he cared to think about. Carver wasn't sure she couldn't see through his gray irises and into his soul.

Later, as they lay on the bed staring at the lackadaisical rotation of the ceiling fan, she said, "Don't let me fall asleep, okay? I can't spend the night. I just... I just want to lie here a little while."

Carver didn't say anything. Their silence was part of the chemistry. The unspoken comfort of mutual need. But it didn't last long. Eventually, the carefree feeling in the room turned. They were, in a very real sense, on the clock.

"I'm worried about Manolito," she whispered. "*Papá* says he's doing what he can, but—"

"He's doing what he can to control the business," cut in Carver. "I don't know how much you overheard or suspect, and I hate to be the one to break it to you, but your father has already given up on Manuel."

The flick of her lashes caught in his peripheral vision. He turned to find conflicted eyes, perhaps more open than they were a moment before.

"I'm sorry," said Carver, "but you have a right to know."

"You need to find him," she pleaded. She rolled to her side and leaned over him. "I control the finances. I can pay you myself."

"Ignacio already compensated me."

"But he fired you."

"I'm not abandoning your brother without a fight."

She watched him for a long moment. She tried to appear judgmental, but the edge of her lip folded, and her eyes smiled. "You're a good man, Vince Carver." She gave him a long, heartfelt kiss.

Alma crawled over him to get off the bed, and all he wanted was to grab on and hold her tight. But he didn't. She put her underwear on. In businesslike fashion, she affixed her skirt and slipped on the heels while topless, aware that Carver watched her.

"You can keep the audio file," she said offhand. "It might give you clues about the deal between *Nueva Generación* and my brother. Whatever it is."

"It's in the recording," he said. "The cartel wants the legal infrastructure. It legitimizes and expands their operation."

"Sure, but what are the specifics?" Alma searched the floor for her bra. "When is the partnership starting? You haven't discovered that?"

She walked away and plucked her bra from the floor with an extreme bend at the waist. Topless and in heels, it was something to see. Carver watched her innocently slip it over her shoulders, facing away but angling to the side just enough to give him something to remember. Her question about the deal had been asked casually, as if the answer didn't matter at all. That made Carver wonder if the answer was everything.

"I was trying to find Manuel," he said plainly.

She recovered her blouse. "I know." She came over and kissed him again before starting on her buttons. "You've been worth every penny *Papá* paid you. I'm sorry things ended the way they did with him. But maybe it's for the best."

"What does that mean?"

She shrugged. "It's obvious you don't like him, Vince. What he does."

Carver sat up on the bed. They didn't mention that she was in the same dirty business.

Alma made for the door. "Manolito will like you. I'm sure of it." Then she let herself out.

As soon as the lock clicked, Carver slipped on his underwear and recovered his gun. It was just a precaution as he didn't plan on giving chase. Instead he moved to the window and peeked outside to *Avenida Revolución*.

After their encounter was said and done, Carver couldn't be sure which of them had squeezed more information out of the other.

A minute passed and then Alma exited the building. She looked both ways, crossed the wide boulevard, and entered the back seat of a Baja California state police car. The driver finished his cigarette and threw it out the window. As he did, Carver caught a glimpse of his face. It was the cop who had given him a hard time at the ranch house.

Friends of the family. What a mess corruption made down here. Carver wasn't sure he could ever share Shaw's romantic views of the city, but his friend had a point when it came to the women.

20

Carver shifted in the seat of the Bronco, two blocks from *La Cascada*. It was a warm morning with a clear sky, blue slightly marred by a relentless and all-consuming sunny haze. The visual manifestation of the heat made it impossible to eradicate from the mind.

The nightclub's parking lot was empty save for a few vehicles flush with the building. It was normally locked up at this early hour, but a security team was in and out making preparations. Esteban and Pancho were both around, the latter stomping back and forth in cowboy boots giving terse orders. Most of the activity occurred inside where Carver couldn't see, but it was clear there were more guns than necessary for a friendly meeting. Carver wondered if Ignacio was walking into a trap.

Either way, some instinct or sixth sense told him something was happening today. If not here then elsewhere. Given Alma's new intelligence, Carver had everyone on deck. Shaw was covering Christian's residence, and Morgan was watching the heightened activity at the warehouses.

"What we have here is a flurry of business," she reported over the phone. "Tractor-trailers are filling the yard, so many that most are waiting in line."

"All at once?" he asked.

"Seems like a logistical failure to me. It's not even a single large order. They're loading pallets of wine, hardware, paint, lumber, drywall, and other merchandise from warehouses you didn't point out to me."

"It's not a surprise Gonzalo avoided showing me the more illicit areas of the operation."

"The problem is it's impossible to see what's legitimate and what isn't from the outside. What do I do when the trucks hit the road? Stay here? Follow them? I can't track them all."

Carver chewed his lip. That impending feeling of his was getting stronger. "I think it's finally time I got on the horn with our keeper. This is wandering into the DEA's domain."

"Glad to hear it because I'm going crazy. At least in Special Reconnaissance I could call in an airstrike."

Carver wanted to smile as he hung up, but the empty parking lot prevented any premature mirth. Two narcos posted outside the door while the rest waited inside. The clock read 10:14 and Ignacio still hadn't made an appearance. Carver swiped through his contacts and set his phone against his ear.

Special Agent Albert Pineda picked up right away. "Long time, bro. I was getting worried."

"I'm sure you were. Are you in Mexico right now?"

"San Diego Division Office. Believe it or not, even I have desk work. How's the vacation?"

Carver breathed hotly into the mic. "Things were a lot

more complicated than I was led to believe."

"How so? I remember being quite clear on how fubar the situation was in TJ."

"Does that extend to Tecate?"

"What's that supposed to mean? Look, we're a week out. Have you found the kid?"

Carver groaned. "Almost. I think we're close."

"I can't tell if that's supposed to be reassuring."

"I'm not calling about that."

"Gotcha," said Pineda. "Tell me what you need."

Carver was hit with sudden indecision and ground his teeth. "You mentioned new shipments crossing the border. What kind of capabilities do you have to track them?"

"That's a big part of what we do. Between us and Border Patrol, we have access to cameras, drones, and local enforcement. Are you talking trucks or tunnels?"

"Multiple semis. There's a lot of weight so we can't tell what's legitimate and what's not."

"That's the way it goes," he assured. "If you're tracking trucks, we use internal BOLOs. A vehicle description and plate number are all we need. We flag them at the border and trace as far as we need. You wouldn't believe how wired up San Diego is."

Carver was silent a moment. That solved Morgan's problem easily enough, and it passed the ball to the DEA so he didn't have to worry about it. On the face of it he couldn't complain, except...

"I need to know if you knew about the old man," said Carver gruffly.

"Old man," mumbled Pineda. "You talking Congressman Espinoza?"

"Yes."

"Okay. Did I know what?"

Carver bristled. "Did you know he was *El Vaquero*?"

"What?"

"You heard me."

"Wait, wait, wait. Slow down here." Pineda took a moment to marinate. "You're saying Ignacio Espinoza is *El Vaquero*. Are you high?"

"I'm quite serious."

The line was dead a few more seconds. Pineda hissed, and it sounded like the phone had been drawn away from his face before he came back. "This is fucked, bro. If Ignacio is the new player entering the meth trade..."

"Then a drug boss is working with the DEA to topple his competition. I need to know if you knew."

"I understand the implications, Vince. And hell no, I didn't know. Are you kidding me?" He pulled the phone away again and cursed. His distress sounded genuine. "Look, man, I live and breathe taking guys like this down. I have nothing but disdain for them. *Especially* the ones who infiltrate the government. I'm telling you, I had no idea."

"Well it's true. Ignacio admitted as much. I have audio of him suing for peace with Esteban Gallo. His son, Christian, arranged for the cartel to swipe the kid as leverage, only I don't think Ignacio's going for it."

"Nice family," Pineda croaked. "This is the modern DEA. I keep telling the brass we can't fuck with our dicks in our hands. Now everything is so backwards we're the ones getting fucked."

"Colorful."

"Dude played me," he bemoaned. "And that doesn't happen a lot. I'm not young and bright-eyed, if you catch my meaning."

"Don't take it personally," said Carver. "Ignacio's a savvy politician. He's not your average punk narco with a gun."

Just as the statement was made, a pair of black vans turned down the block and into *La Cascada's* parking lot. Carver's nerves tightened like guitar strings. The vans were just like the one that had visited Hector's place.

"Hold up," he said, "we have a developing situation."

The vehicles skidded to a stop in front of the nightclub. The back doors opened and police in tac gear filed out. They wore white-and-gray camouflage with patches on their arms, with black gloves, boots, kneepads, belts, and helmets. On the side of each helmet was the Mexican flag.

The two narcos at the door glanced nervously at each other. One stepped forward with a hand up. The other raised his gun.

The National Guard opened fire. The nightclub's concrete wall spattered with dust and paint chips as the narcos succumbed to overwhelming fire.

"Is that a gunfight?" asked Pineda.

A SWAT crew rushed the front door with a stun grenade. After a three-count, the officer moved to toss it in, but automatic fire ripped through the closed door. The officer with the grenade went down and the flash-bang went off outside, dispersing the police.

Pancho Gallo kicked the door open, rushed outside, and swept his rifle over the entryway. He hit three more officers, at least one mortally. The second unit of officers dropped to their knees and plugged him with precise return fire. Pancho dropped to the concrete with holes all over his body.

The police pulled back their wounded and covered the entrance while another breaching crew advanced. A second grenade went into the door, successfully this time. When it blew they barged inside. Chaotic gunfire echoed through the interior.

"Scratch what I said about Ignacio suing for peace," said Carver. "The special police are gunning down the cartel."

"Wait, really? They pulled back from that in Tijuana."

"It's happening."

Pineda blew air. "That's a government order. This comes from Ignacio, and the National Guard doesn't play around. Are you under fire?"

"I'm not involved and I don't plan on changing that. This isn't my fight."

"Right on. Shit, this is a major development. Combined with your intel, it's safe to say you unmasked the new drug ring. I have ten things I need to do right now. I'm suiting up and contacting my team. Call me with developments. And don't get shot."

As the call ended, Carver reserved a wry smile for his own benefit. There was a sick satisfaction to watching the cartel get the same treatment they'd been dishing out to innocent civilians. But this was far from true justice. This was gamesmanship. It was business.

Ignacio had said he had no intention of fighting Christian. Maybe that was true and the best way to strike back was to strike New Generation directly. Hitting one of the cartel bosses might be enough to blow up the whole deal and force the son to come crawling back under the father's wing.

Pineda was right. This was some family.

After a few minutes of silence, the National Guard marched out with a scowling Esteban Gallo, hands cuffed behind his back. He went red-faced at the sight of his dead brother. He spit toward the officers before being shoved into the police truck.

Esteban was defiant now, but he was in custody. If he played ball, maybe it meant Ignacio could recover Manuel from the cartel. But Carver's gut feeling wasn't so rosy. Esteban would deny, deny, ask for his lawyer, and deny some more. Admitting to holding a hostage ransom was the last thing he would do. And implicating the rest of his cartel would be a death sentence. These guys didn't fold under pressure, they doubled down.

"They should have killed you," grumbled Carver as he started the truck. With a discreet U-turn, he left the neighborhood before it flooded with additional authorities.

As he sped away, Shaw checked in. Carver set his phone to speaker on the center console.

"Single SUV leaving Christian's compound," his friend reported.

Carver bit down. "Everything's coming to a head. Ignacio just declared war on the cartel. Esteban's in the custody of the special police. Pancho's dead."

"Couldn't have happened to a nicer fella."

"You think Christian's on the move?"

"It's impossible to say one way or the other, but he could be attempting to secure Manny. I'm tailing them."

Carver nodded. "Esteban's out of the picture now, so Christian might be our only lead left."

"Copy that."

Carver didn't bother calling Morgan next. He was almost at her location and would tell her in person. In the meantime, the drive allowed him to digest what was playing out.

Either Christian or the cartel had taken their shot with the car bomb. Ignacio responded with a brazen strike against New Generation. That removed cartel leadership from the immediate picture, but they couldn't be ignored entirely. They still had Manuel somewhere, which was a problem. There were going to be more fireworks, and this time they would blow off more than a finger.

Tijuana was becoming a brutal battlefield, and Manuel was caught in the crossfire.

Carver parked next to Morgan's Nissan. She transferred to his passenger seat and he caught her up on events.

"A war makes things harder for us," she bemoaned. "It puts their soldiers on alert and lowers the chances of a successful exfil."

"I know it," grated Carver. "Shaw's running down a lead

The Service of Wolves

now. With any luck, we can pick up Manuel before the cartel finds out what happened to their bosses.

His eyes were fixed on the line of semi-trailer trucks. Most were locked up, running, and ready on the side of the road. Eight big rigs total.

"You weren't kidding about the convoy," he muttered. "They're just about ready to go." He grabbed his phone. "Read me the plate numbers. I'm sending them to the DEA so nobody gets lost."

They recorded the plates as the last two trucks were loaded and took their places in line. The whole thing took five minutes, prodded along by workers trying to pick up the pace.

A black Lincoln Aviator turned down the street and honked as it passed the loading yard. Shaw's SUV followed a block behind them. The Aviator stopped and opened up. There were four PPOs inside, personal protection operatives from *Sólido* Security. After they shook some hands, they loaded back into the Aviator and joined the end of the convoy.

Shaw noticed them, pulled up, and joined them from the back seat of the Bronco. "Looks like a regular hoedown."

"Christian's still at his house," relayed Carver. "This is just one *Sólido* team."

"They're running security on the shipment," said Morgan. "That didn't happen yesterday."

"Now why would a wine delivery need an armed escort?" snickered Shaw.

"This is it," said Carver. "New Generation tapping into

the Espinoza's legal infrastructure."

Morgan nodded. "Has to be. The drugs can be liquefied, hidden, reconstituted. It could be the wine."

"It's somewhere," agreed Shaw.

"And it's leaving now," said Carver.

The first tractor-trailer rumbled forward, its wide berth pivoting north. One by one, the other trucks followed, creating a large shipping caravan.

"So what's our move?" asked Shaw. "I could go back to keeping tabs on Christian."

"Maybe. But it looks like his priority is getting the drugs out clean."

"Is that our problem?" asked Morgan.

"Not directly. It *is* the cartel's problem, though, and they're already hurting. They need this to go off without a hitch."

Shaw chuckled. "You're talking leverage."

"We already tried asking nicely."

"Last truck is away," pressed Morgan. "It's now or never. What are we doing?"

"You two have your gear in your trunks?" Carver asked.

They both gave affirmatives.

"Then the plan is simple. We're going after this convoy. We're intercepting their drugs. And we're making the cartel an offer they can't refuse."

21

The primary access point between Baja California and San Diego is the San Ysidro Port of Entry. It's the busiest border crossing in the Western Hemisphere, continually upgraded over the years to the point it supports thirty-four northbound lanes of traffic leaving Mexico, with a separate smaller roadway and inspection facility for those driving south to enter. This border crossing, while well known, is closed to commercial traffic.

Nine miles east, in Otay Mesa, is the largest commercial port of entry in California. It handles over fifty billion dollars of freight annually and is vital to West Coast commerce, yet its designed expansions have encountered numerous delays. Between ten and sixteen Frankensteined lanes of northbound truck traffic lead into the US, depending on the current state of construction, and handle both commercial and private vehicles, as well as pedestrian traffic.

This particular hour found the team tied up at the checkpoint for forty-five minutes. Morgan sat in the passenger seat beside Carver. While he busily attempted to get in touch with the DEA, Morgan had Shaw on speaker. The ex-SEAL drove a separate truck so they would have more assault options. They were equipped with ballistic vests, sidearms, and rifles in the trunks.

"Pineda's not picking up the phone," hissed Carver, terminating another connection with voice mail.

"He's mobilizing a team," allayed Morgan. "The man is preoccupied."

A Customs and Border Protection officer wearing a blue police uniform waved Carver into the adjoining lane, funneling the passenger vehicle away from the tractor-trailer he was following. He pretended not to notice but the officer was insistent.

"All right, all right," he grumbled with a half-hearted wave.

Carver's white Bronco pulled ahead into the next lane, now only two cars from the checkpoint and immediately behind the *Sólido* team in the black Aviator. Shaw's silver Ford Ranger advanced ahead of them, two lanes over.

The Espinoza big rigs were white and generic, without identifying brand names or labels. Anonymity by design. Protection in a herd. They fanned into separate lanes, with some of the semis already at the checkpoint and others lagging behind.

Shaw sighed over the speaker. "Any idea when we're making our move?"

"I'm working on it," said Carver.

The situation was developing quickly, and the team had already debated interdiction options. Not many were ideal. It was more about waiting for an opening that was least horrible.

"How far are we going with this?" posed Morgan.

It was a question on each of their minds.

Carver eyed the various targets surrounding them. If they were a herd then Carver and Shaw were the wolves among them. He thought about the warning Jasmine's mother had given her about the cartels, and he wondered which wolves would win. Surprise may very well be on their side, but that was a far cry from operational supremacy.

"Manny's a good kid who deserves to be saved," was all he said aloud, but Morgan and Shaw knew him enough to read between the lines. Carver had accepted a job, it was the right thing to do, and he would burn everything else to the ground if that's what it took.

"Hell," mustered Shaw after a few seconds of silence. "These boys took shots at us. I wouldn't mind sticking it to them where it hurts."

Morgan set her jaw and nodded. "I'm good with saving the kid. This is our best chance of getting him out."

Carver's cheek twitched in satisfaction. They would do what needed doing. It was why he preferred a small team of dependable operators over an army.

"Gotta disconnect," chimed Shaw as the car ahead of him cleared the checkpoint. His was the first passenger truck among them to reach the border officers.

Carver's lane advanced as well, leaving the Aviator ahead of him second in line. He wondered if the security team was allowed to pass with their weapons or if they were moving incognito.

"I should have taken my own car too," grumbled

Morgan. Her eyes were on the fleet of eighteen-wheelers, many now behind them.

"We're all going to the same place," pacified Carver, trying his phone again. "We're not interdicting the entire convoy. We need to be smart and surgical. But we need more hands." He waited with the phone at his ear until he hung it up in frustration. "Damn it. Why won't Pineda pick up?"

Carver was growing increasingly agitated. There were too many guns and hands for them to track alone, yet the DEA was MIA. Christian was trying to kill Ignacio, Ignacio was shooting cartel heads, and Manuel's possible good outcomes were dwindling by the hour. Carver's normal cool was strained to the limit.

"How much can we rely on Pineda?" asked Morgan.

He hiked a shoulder. "Seems stand-up enough."

"I'm just saying, you didn't meet him through official channels. This whole thing might turn into a liability for him."

"You think he's going to sell me out?"

"Or worse."

"Worse as in expendable. You think we're in danger from the DEA?"

"It's not what I think. I'm just talking out loud, Vince." After recognizing Carver's skepticism, she huffed. "Look, I doubt Albert Pineda wakes up in the morning and wonders which American citizens he's going to murder that day, but if he's dirty and you're in a legitimate position to expose him..."

The Service of Wolves

Carver's expression tightened. He didn't think it was likely. Then again, caution was thorough, and if you're not thorough, you're careless.

"That's why I have you to watch my back," he grumbled darkly.

The *Sólido* team cleared the checkpoint quickly and without drama. Carver slid down his window as he rolled ahead. The Border Protection officer was a skinny guy with pink skin and dark sunglasses.

"US citizen?" he asked.

"Yes, sir."

"ID?"

Carver already had it in his fingers. He passed it over and glanced to the distance. The Aviator drove on. Shaw was ahead of them by now, somewhere out of sight. A couple of the tractor-trailers had already cleared the checkpoint, with the rest of them either being checked now or next in line.

"You on business?" asked the officer.

"I wish," answered Carver. "We're in private security, but we're not on the clock."

The man leaned down to get a look at Morgan too and check if any contraband was lying in plain sight. "ID, miss?"

"Sure." Morgan dug into her pocket and handed it over.

The border officer eyed it sideways. He bent the ID and peered inside the car again before saying, "One moment." Then he walked away and entered his booth.

Morgan hissed in annoyance. "We're in private security?" she mocked.

He smiled. "I'm stalling. Look." He nodded to the lane

beyond her window. Two border officers checked the perimeter of a white tractor-trailer before having the driver pop the back doors. "This is our prime candidate, right?"

"It's the truck loaded with Espinoza wine."

A handler led a canine unit around the trailer. The vested German shepherd trotted forward with boundless energy and a wagging tail. It hopped inside the rear.

Still unattended at the checkpoint, Morgan whispered, "What if they're caught?"

"I'm wondering if that works for us. There are too many trucks for us to interdict. Maybe we can tie them up at the border."

"And give our only bargaining chip to Border Protection?"

"You and I would know what happened to the meth, but the cartel wouldn't."

The skinny border officer exited his booth and returned to the Bronco. "Did either of you purchase any goods that you're transporting into the United States?"

"Nothing," said Carver. Morgan agreed.

The man handed their IDs back. "Have a nice day."

As he stepped away from the Bronco, Carver checked the wine trailer. It was still being searched. More and more, he figured stopping the drugs here was their best shot.

"Move along, sir," instructed the officer.

"Yup. Thanks."

Carver pulled ahead slowly, watching the search progress in his mirrors. It was impossible to see what was happening behind the trailer. He veered a lane over to get a better

The Service of Wolves

angle and rode the brakes. A border officer wearing a vest whistled sharply and called out for them to keep moving.

"Shit," said Carver. "No luck."

The driver of the wine truck thanked the officers and circled back to his cab. They had given him the okay to cross.

"Then we keep following," said Morgan.

Putting his team at risk and getting in a gunfight in San Diego were high on his list of things to avoid. He knew it was reckless but this was his best, least horrible chance.

"I have a better idea."

Carver pulled to the side of the lanes and shifted to park. He removed the Sig from his shoulder holster and stuffed it under the seat. Then he hopped out and marched toward the checkpoint where the truck driver was climbing into his seat. Two border officers turned as he approached. A guard with a rifle yelled, "Get back in the car!"

"Just a minute," said Carver. "I have information." He spotted the canine handler and pivoted to him. "Hey, what was in that truck?"

"Excuse me?"

The guard with the rifle advanced. "You. Stop moving."

Carver stopped by the handler. "Inside that truck. I have reason to believe there are drugs incorporated into the wine."

"What reason is that?"

"I saw some sketchy stuff when I was in Mexico."

The handler's face remained defensive. "Who are you?"

Before Carver could answer, the guard with the rifle

converged. "I said what the hell are you doing?"

The driver of the semi slammed the cab door and started the engine.

"He says he thinks there are drugs in that truck," explained the handler, "but he doesn't say why."

"Are there?" asked the guard.

"We didn't get any hits."

"It's in the wine," urged Carver.

"They tested the wine," said the handler. "Two bottles. They were clean."

Carver's tongue caught for a second. "Then one of the other big rigs."

They turned incredulously to the twelve lanes of commercial vehicles waiting their turn forty deep.

"Get the fuck out of here," hissed the handler.

The truck driver gazed at their commotion as he pulled away, face smug.

"Hey!" yelled Carver. He stomped aside to flag down the semi.

Carver was grabbed from behind. He spun reflexively, but stopped short of fighting back. The modicum of resistance earned him a shove to the pavement. The dog lunged, bound by its leash and barking aggressively inches from Carver's face. The border officers did a fair bit of barking themselves.

"All right, all right," he yelled. The guard with the rifle pulled his hands behind his back. Carver shook his head and sighed. "No need to make a scene," he grumbled, and wondered why he hadn't followed the same advice.

22

Despite Carver's urgent pleas, border enforcement resumed unimpeded. All he could do was scowl as the entire fleet of Espinoza rigs were cleared to enter the United States. He sat with his hands behind his back cuffed to a metal bench wondering what went wrong.

Border Protection hadn't been sure what to make of him, but they sure took him seriously enough after finding his pistol in the Bronco. While illegal in Mexico, they were properly registered and legal in the US. That said, Carver had failed to declare them. Combined with his antics, they weren't taking any chances with him.

Morgan either, for that matter. She sat cuffed beside him, glowering.

"One would think that glare would wear off after an hour," he said.

"One would," she tersely returned, sharp eyes not softening in the least.

The border officers had also confiscated their cell phones so they couldn't say what Shaw had gotten up to, except that Morgan had given him a heads up as Carver was being detained. They now waited without word for another half hour before Morgan's glare broke. Her eyes snapped to the bald army grunt marching down the hall towards them wearing a grand smile and black Ray Bans even though they were indoors.

"Brother, I took you for having more finesse than this!"

Carver gave Pineda the side eye. "What would give you that idea?"

He snorted. The DEA agent wore an olive-green tactical vest over a similarly colored T-shirt. He shook his head at the pair of them. "They said some crazy cowboy came to tell them how to do their jobs, and then, on top of it all, pick a fight."

"If I had started a fight they wouldn't be telling anything."

A full set of perfect teeth pivoted to Morgan. "Nice to make your acquaintance. And you are?"

"Jules to my friends, Juliette to you."

Pineda chuckled. He liked her already.

"What are we doing about Espinoza?" prompted Carver.

"I got you, bro. While your butt has been planted on that bench, we scored hits on all the plates you sent over."

"So what are we waiting for?"

"Who said anything about waiting? One of the trucks was tracked to a supplier in Chula Vista with suspected gang ties. They unloaded quick but we swarmed them. Caught them flush with deconstituted methamphetamines."

"Was it in the wine?" asked Morgan.

"Liquefied into paint, if you can believe it. Better that way as nobody would attempt to drink it. They did such a good job with the solvent, I bet you could trim your house and it would hold up better than what you get at Home Depot. One hang-up though."

"What's that?"

"This isn't *El Vaquero's* meth. We tested the drugs on-site and there's fentanyl present. It's not the new strain of pure product we've been seeing."

"That makes sense," said Carver. "This is New Generation's deal. Their drugs with Ignacio's infrastructure. Either way, we've got our leverage."

Special Agent Pineda crossed his arms over his chest and waited on their shared look. When they didn't volunteer anything, he said, "This is the part where I ask: leverage for what?"

"I want to trade the drugs for Manuel Espinoza."

His brow furrowed and he lowered the shades to look Carver eye to eye. "You still plan on saving the kid?"

Carver unabashedly met his gaze. "If anybody deserves to get out of this mess, it's him."

Pineda took a step away and scratched the back of his head. "I don't think you're following how this works. Cameras tracked the drugs from the highway to the drop-off where they're processed and distributed, but we didn't have an eye in the sky. There were too many trucks to get on top of all of them. It's like what's going on in Ukraine right now. You wanna get past air defenses, what do you do?"

"Overwhelm it with numbers," answered Carver, getting his point. "What does it matter if you sent boots in?"

"Because these South Bay gangs run professional

operations. The truck was mostly unloaded in record time. The product had already been checked. And most importantly, by the time we rolled in, the payment was already away. One of the bangers claimed they paid out two duffel bags of cash."

"To who?"

"They didn't know."

"Doesn't Espinoza care what happens to his drugs?" asked Morgan.

Pineda shook his head. "The Chula Vista operation is run by a gang affiliated with the Mexican Mafia. They buy in bulk where they can and distribute, making them part of the same ecosystem. But they're an American institution, not cartel members."

Carver's face soured. "You're saying once Christian Espinoza makes his money, he doesn't care what happens stateside."

"You got it. Espinoza might take a temporary hit in eligible buyers, but the drugs are no longer his problem."

"Is the cash gone for good then?" asked Morgan.

"It can't be," insisted Carver. "What about the *Sólido* team? Are they talking?"

An eyebrow popped up behind Pineda's sunglasses. "*Sólido Seguridad?* How do they play into this?"

"They were the ones protecting the convoy. If they followed one truck to its final destination, it would be the one shipping meth."

The DEA agent frowned. "You never relayed plate numbers of security vehicles."

Carver grimaced as he realized their mistake. The SUV had arrived at the warehouses at the last second, after the eighteen-wheelers were loaded and logged.

"If someone got away with the cash," reasoned Carver, "it would be them. Black Lincoln Aviator. Four guns."

"I can review the security feeds at the site," offered Pineda. "See if it's them."

"It's them. What about us? Can we get out of here?"

Pineda spread his arms. "Lucky for you, this is America, and the DEA still has a little pull." He whistled to get the attention of a guard down the hall and waved him over. "I appreciate this," he said as the officer arrived and put his key to their cuffs.

"Our weapons?" asked Carver.

"Being held at the front," said Pineda.

Carver suddenly felt awkward about the misunderstanding. His anxiety over Manuel had pushed him into a tactical error. He nodded thanks to the guard who strolled away with two pairs of handcuffs.

"We trade favors with CBP all the time," explained Pineda. "None of this is on the books, so there's nothing for any of us to explain. The best way to cut through bureaucracy is to sidestep it entirely."

Carver stretched his legs and shook Pineda's hand. "I owe you one."

"Not at all, bro. You're helping me out, remember? Follow me."

They went to the front desk where the same guard was setting out their personal belongings. There were no formal procedures or documents to sign.

"This is a real score for my team," continued Pineda. "We intercepted a shipment, disrupted a new partnership, and the best part? We've isolated the source. This kind of work can take months when we're lucky. And on top of everything else, we snagged ourselves a big fish. Cooperation or not, the Mexican government won't appreciate the impropriety of a dirty congressman amongst the anti-corruption party."

"A wolf in sheep's clothing," remarked Carver. "Speaking of which, you should probably take the evidence."

Carver slid the waiting thumb drive with the audio incriminating Ignacio across the counter. The DEA happily accepted custody.

Carver and Morgan holstered their pistols, and he asked, "Did you get our rifles too?"

"What rifles?" asked the Border Protection officer.

Carver stopped himself, realizing they hadn't yet searched his trunk.

"I don't even want to know," stressed the guard, ending the conversation with a swipe of his hand through the air.

Pineda laughed. "My friend's just playing. He's funnier than he looks." He put an arm around Carver's shoulder and pulled him to the door, barely giving him enough time to scoop up his phone.

The sun was powerful outside as Pineda led them back to the Bronco. It was parked away from the traffic lanes and didn't appear to have been tampered with. The border

The Service of Wolves

officers must have exercised caution once he had asked them to contact Pineda on his behalf.

"So you're not quitting on the kid," stated the DEA agent.

Carver shook his head. "I'm not quitting on the kid. But if I'm honest, part of my motivation is sticking it to these narcos too."

"Stick it to them how?"

Carver returned an enigmatic shrug. "These cartels are importing ruin to our country. You can play whack-a-mole up here at the various processing centers, but there'll always be more heads popping out of more holes. Maybe this one time we're in a position to do something with a little more gravitas."

"Gravitas," Pineda muttered with his trademark grin. "I knew there was a reason I liked you."

Carver's phone buzzed, still in his hand. It was Shaw, and he had left a couple of messages while they'd been detained. Carver listened to his friend's report and called him a beautiful bastard.

"He's on the security car," Carver relayed to the others.

"Who is?" asked Pineda before realization hit his eyes. He shot a finger up to beat Carver to the punch. "Your boy drinking expensive espresso across the street."

"The one and only. The *Sólido* team is on their own. No more herd immunity. We know exactly where the money is."

The DEA agent raised his palms like it was raining gold. "I can scramble a team to intercept them."

"Where are you now?" asked Carver into the phone. "Already at the border?"

"Shit." Pineda pulled his phone now. "I can have them detained."

"Wait," instructed Carver. He listened to Shaw another minute, nodded, and said, "Keep on them." When he hung up, everyone waited on him.

"Well," pressed Pineda, "you going to tell us or what?"

"It's too late," reported Carver. "They cleared the port of entry at San Ysidro. They're in Mexico."

"Damn it to hell." Pineda punched the air and stomped away in frustration. "I can't pull anything together in time to stop them. Not the way things are south of the border these days."

They watched each other, hands on hips, thinking how to salvage the situation.

"Maybe it's a good thing," suggested Carver, voice taking a familiar edge.

Morgan recognized it. She glanced to him for confirmation, and then she went to the trunk to check their rifles. "Everything's here."

Pineda crossed his arms over his chest. "You still want your leverage."

Carver dipped his head. "A DEA raid in the US has too much oversight. An exchange of gunfire would be impossible to hide. Once any recovered money is officially on the books, we can't offer it in exchange for Manuel."

"Not without a whole lot of bureaucracy," agreed Pineda.

Carver grinned. "I figured we'd sidestep it entirely."

The special agent took off his sunglasses to wipe his eyes. "So you're going to stumble on the security team in Mexico, independent of any federal agency, take the money, trade it for the kid, and no one's the wiser. Do you have any idea how illegal that is?"

Carver wordlessly clenched his jaw.

"I'm a federal agent, Vince." Pineda slipped his shades back on and snorted in amusement. "Lucky for you, I'm DEA. Half our ops are black, and the other half are gray enough you need night vision to tell the difference. It was nice knowing you." He gave him a fist bump and winked at Morgan. "Jules." His smile held for a moment before he turned to go.

Carver blinked. "Did you just give us your blessing? You're going along with this?"

"Going along with what?" answered Pineda, back to them as he walked away. "The Drug Enforcement Agency is no longer sanctioned for operational oversight in Mexico."

23

"You have a way with people," remarked Morgan from the passenger seat. "You know that, Vince?"

The southbound crossing was easy to get through, and they made good time converging on Shaw's location. The Aviator drove through the Tijuana outskirts. Shaw's silver Ford Ranger was behind and they were next.

"Where is this coming from?" Carver asked.

"Special Agent Pineda bailing you out and all but sanctioning this op. You're a real charmer."

"Tell that to the border officers who detained us for an hour and a half."

"Not your finest moment, but you're not in jail so there's that. They may have called you a cowboy, but we're trailing behind a money car in Mexico. This feels more like outlaw work to me."

He grinned. "Just think of us like a posse. This is a simple recovery operation."

"I'll tell you what's simple. Their vehicle is armored and ours isn't."

Carver conceded the point with a nod. "We need to get them out of the car. We don't have the hardware to break into it."

"Have we tested those windows against the Mk 11? Shaw could ready his in a minute."

"A single rifle wouldn't be enough to get them to abandon their cover. It would be too slow and we'd attract the local police. Or worse."

Morgan frowned. They were both Army, which meant they were used to having technical superiority over the enemy. "What else can we do?"

Carver ground his teeth as he mulled it over, ticking each strategic category as it came to him. "They have more guns and armor, but we have an advantage: two vehicles to their one. We need to outmaneuver them."

He wasn't sure where they were driving to. The money didn't appear to be going straight to Christian's house. Perhaps it was owed to the cartel. They drove away from the busy city center, away from the warehouses and nightclubs. He wondered if the police raid on *La Cascada* was shaking things up.

"We might be able to contain them," agreed Morgan, "but maneuvering alone doesn't help if we're concerned with time."

"No, it does not," he agreed.

Their strike only worked if the security team panicked. If they were smart, well trained, they would stay in the vehicle and wait for backup. Short of a truck-mounted machine gun, armor was armor.

The Lincoln Aviator took an unexpected turn into a spacious gas station. Carver slowed as Shaw rounded the next street to park beside the building. For a minute he thought this could be a safe house, but the *Sólido Seguridad* vehicle parked at a gas pump.

"You've got to be shitting me," croaked Morgan.

Not one to shirk an opportunity, Carver pulled the Bronco up to the pump immediately behind the Aviator. Shaw was already calling Morgan's phone to strategize.

"Tell him to stay close," Carver said, "and be ready to block them in on my signal." He lowered his window and grabbed a baseball cap from the back seat, positioning it low over his brown aviator glasses.

Gassing up a secure vehicle was not an ideal contingency. It was, in fact, a careless oversight that risked the operation. That said, the security team was otherwise smart about the execution. With two duffel bags of illegal cash under their care, only one of them exited the vehicle. The door immediately shut behind him and the locks clicked, three guns waiting inside.

Carver didn't recognize any faces on their team, but that didn't mean they wouldn't be on the lookout for him. As the single guard outside the SUV glanced their way, he turned to obscure his face. He opened his door and moved to the pump, showing only his back. The *Sólido* contractor lost interest and turned to his machine.

After the gas was going, Carver set it to pump hands-free and shuffled to his open door.

"This is our chance," Morgan whispered, fingering her Glock below the dash.

He kept his gaze on her, not drawing the attention of

their targets by looking directly at them. "If we make a move, we get one guy. The rest are protected with the money. The driver's ready at the wheel."

She rubbed her chin to disguise a growing frown.

Rushing the SUV might work out. He might manage to catch the guard entering the vehicle. Then again, he could just as easily be walking into three gun barrels. With the Aviator's tints, he couldn't say for sure if the guards were keeping an eye on them or not. At any rate, the driver could gas it at the first sign of trouble. The team could be away whether or not they left one of their own behind. They would have lost the element of surprise to neutralize one person.

Risk was an inseparable part of kinetic action, just like gravity was to falling. No matter the level of planning, it was impossible to guess every outcome, every reaction, every time. It was simple physics, really, which was anything but.

Planning, preparation, and training mitigated these risks. So too did the ability to objectively assess opportunities. Sometimes you had to call a duck a duck. In this instance, the risk was unacceptable.

"Stand down," ordered Carver.

His tank had already been nearly full so he manually clicked off the gas pump. Unlike the lax security team, he had filled up in the morning, but he kept the nozzle in the truck hoping the *Sólido* crew wouldn't notice. Then he headed into the store to buy a few things. Carver returned to the truck and dropped a plastic bag on his seat. It was showing two packs of smokes, two lighters, and two bottles of malt liquor.

Morgan arched an eyebrow. "You planning on partying them to death?"

The *Sólido* operative finished at the pump and returned to his back seat. The SUV door shut and locked immediately, reassuring Carver that he'd made the correct decision. As the Aviator started its engine, he surreptitiously emptied the new bottles onto the concrete.

"There goes our chance," hissed Morgan.

"It's fine," he told her.

Carver pulled the pump from the Bronco and filled the bottles with gasoline. By the time he returned to his seat, Morgan had found the two rags at the bottom of the bag. Carver used them to wipe his hands.

Shaw was already back on the road covering the Aviator. Carver handed the bottles to Morgan and followed.

"I haven't seen a Molotov cocktail in a while," she admitted. "You want to smoke them out."

He hiked a shoulder. "We need them to panic."

"A fire at a gas station would have been cause for panic."

"Even I'm not that crazy."

They went over their options, Shaw still on the phone. As they closed on a decision, the Aviator slowed. There were few buildings around, and everything was run-down, and it didn't look like the SUV was stopping anywhere.

"They might be onto you," Morgan said into the phone on speaker.

"Copy that," returned Shaw.

Instead of acting furtive, Shaw suddenly laid on his horn.

The Service of Wolves

After a few honks, he pulled into the opposing lane of traffic to pass the Aviator. He stuck a middle finger out his window and yelled, "Asshole!" before speeding off.

Carver smiled. "Can't say the man doesn't have style."

The Aviator waited a second before inching ahead at a lower speed, allowing Shaw to disappear in the distance. The *Sólido* crew didn't seem to notice the Bronco further behind the action, and everyone resumed cruising speed.

After a few minutes of driving through slums, Shaw had scouted the path ahead. It reminded Carver of their days working close protection when Shaw ran the point car. He gave them the location and told them to get ready.

"I think that's it," said Morgan.

Ahead, on the right, was an old building missing a roof. Across the street on the left was a partial length of wall that once attached to a structure that was now long gone. Carver had been following at a distance, but now he pressed his boot into the gas. The truck gained on their target.

Shaw's pickup peeked out from behind the wall on the left, slowly at first, as if he were pulling out. Except the Aviator was bearing his way. The *Sólido* team tapped the brakes, and Shaw continued to move into the street, oblivious, encroaching into their lane.

This next part could have gone a few ways that entirely depended on the security team. Perhaps *Sólido* recognized Shaw's truck. Either way, they weren't taking chances.

Instead of slowing or stopping, they swerved to the right of the pickup, right tires leaving the asphalt, and attempted to blow past the obstacle. The maneuver would have worked if Shaw didn't accelerate into their front fender, shoving them further into the dirt where they skipped and collided into the concrete wall of the abandoned market.

The impact was sudden and kicked up a cloud of dust. The Aviator's white reverse lights came on as Carver's Bronco rammed into their back bumper. *Sólido* was now boxed in. Carver and Morgan hopped out of the vehicle, lit the Molotovs, and shattered them beneath both sides of the Aviator. Flames ripped upward and licked at the windows.

The SUV slammed backward into the Bronco, still attempting to break out. Carver jumped back in the truck and stepped on the gas, applying opposite pressure. Their wheels spun in the dirt, kicking up debris.

Shaw posted behind the Ranger's hood with his M4 carbine. He fired into the air twice in warning before aiming at their windshield. Morgan moved flush to the market exterior. The building's windows were blown out and the barricaded door had collapsed, giving her a pocket to take cover in.

Finally, the Aviator's engine stopped revving. It was going nowhere and the flames were spreading across its undercarriage. Smoke collected in the cabin. The passengers were coming to grips with their predicament.

"We just want the money!" called Carver, stepping outside the Bronco again and aiming his X95 bullpup. Though the door was positioned between him and the enemy, he was acutely aware that it wouldn't stop a bullet.

The back door of the Aviator opened and a rifle barrel peeked out. Carver exchanged fire as he retreated behind the Bronco's tailgate.

Morgan's rifle barked as the other doors opened. Behind their armor, *Sólido* had the advantage in laying suppressive fire. Both Morgan and Shaw had to duck behind cover too.

Carver pivoted to the right side of his truck. Thickening smoke wafted from the Aviator's open doors. Two gunmen blasted the wall of the market, pinning Morgan inside. They advanced on her. The closer operative had a duffel bag over his shoulder, creating a large blind spot in which Carver hid. He fired two short bursts, cutting him down. The other operative spun and opened fire, forcing Carver back. With bullets no longer pounding against the market wall, Morgan popped out to suppress him.

"Cross fire!" yelled Shaw.

This was another inherent risk, otherwise known as simple physics. There was no way to predict beforehand exactly how the vehicle grouping would line up. There was no way to know the best cover opportunities at a site they hadn't scouted, especially given thirty second's notice. The way this scenario had unfolded, with Shaw on the left and Morgan on the right, they were pointing their guns at each other.

To mitigate this, Shaw retreated to the rear of his pickup, moving to a similar position as Carver. The angle was advantageous, as the *Sólido* guards couldn't use the Aviator's doors as rear cover. Shaw fired a burst at the crew on his side. Bullets popped into another long duffel slung on the gunman's back. He yelped in pain and dropped his rifle, but Shaw's mag ran dry. By the time Carver flipped back to his side to support, both operatives that had exited the left of the Aviator successfully retreated to its front.

Because Shaw had been forced to reposition, they were losing containment. The two operatives rounded the corner of the market exterior. Carver and Shaw ducked as automatic fire ripped into their rental trucks.

Morgan's M4 fired a measured barrage at the gunman she was still engaged with on the right. He returned fire as he backed toward the corner where the rest of his team had retreated. Shaw and Carver simultaneously took advantage of the distraction, stepping out from their trucks and pulling their triggers. Blood painted the dusty concrete as the *Sólido* operative collapsed.

"Clear!" called Shaw.

Carver rounded back to check the man he'd originally shot. "Clear!"

Morgan peeked out to assess the battlefield.

"Two around the corner," notified Carver, pointing twice. "One wounded."

She nodded and changed mags. They advanced past the burning Aviator, interior now engulfed in flames. They would need to move their rental trucks in a few minutes but that wasn't a priority. Neither was the duffel bag on the ground. Carver stepped past the dropped rifle. There was at least one more out there. Shaw blind fired a burst around the corner wall.

"Don't shoot!" cried a man, out of sight. "Don't kill us!"

Shaw turned to Carver before again facing the corner. "Throw your guns down!" he called.

Something bounced in the dirt. Shaw ducked down and did a quick poke and retreat of his head. He nodded, raised his M4, and turned the corner. Carver and Morgan were immediately behind him, fanning out so they all had firing lanes on the two men. They sat with their backs against the wall, hiding behind a measly metal garbage can. There was no other cover in the barren landscape. As they converged, Morgan kicked the surrendered rifle away. Carver pulled their sidearms. One of the men was grimacing in pain.

Carver slung his rifle over his shoulder and pulled the money bag away. "You're hurt." He turned the man's shoulder, not especially gently, and checked his side and back. Then he examined the duffel bag at his feet. "It's just your hand." He turned to Shaw. "You shot the money."

Shaw's beard twisted with his scowl. "I disarmed him, didn't I?"

"You expect me to believe that was intentional?"

"We needed one alive," he said defensively.

Carver turned to the two men. The one was clutching his bloody hand and squirming. Granted, it was a nice hit. The other sat beside him with a clenched jaw and staring bloody murder.

"What about that guy?" asked Carver.

Shaw shrugged. "I don't like that guy. I like this guy better."

"Gentlemen," chided Morgan. "Please."

Carver shook his head and sighed at the sorry security crew. He hadn't expected them to surrender. With any luck, this could turn out better than he'd planned.

Shaw said, "I'd better get the other bag before it burns up. And move the trucks while I'm at it." He lugged the one bag away as he went.

"Okay," announced Carver, taking a knee before the two captives while Morgan covered them. "What you have here is an opportunity."

"We don't know anything," insisted the scowling man.

"Come on now, let's not mess up a good thing."

"Good?" he challenged. "You killed half my team."

"But not you. That's good, isn't it?" Carver offered a prodding, quizzical expression. "You don't want to die, do you?"

The bleeding man widened his eyes and shook his head urgently. "No! No! Please don't kill us."

His disagreeable friend wasn't so wide-eyed. "It doesn't matter," he muttered. "*Nueva Generación* will kill us anyway if you take that money."

This, Carver figured, was progress.

"Then it's your lucky day," he announced with chivalrous generosity. "Because I don't want the money. I want Manuel Espinoza. We'll trade. The cartel gives us the kid, and we return the money."

They eyed each other, clearly skeptical. The man clutching his hand wanted to believe though. Carver could see it in his eyes. The other was a pessimist. He said, "We don't have nothing to do with that."

"I get it. The cartel has him. But you mean to tell me you don't know where he is? Christian never visited?"

"Of course not," answered the pessimist, but he didn't

extrapolate.

Carver turned to the wounded man. The sudden attention prompted him to speak.

"He didn't want his brother to know he was behind the whole thing," he confessed. "Christian didn't even tell us about it until—"

"Paco!" snapped the pessimist.

Carver glared at him hard, and then sighed like a teacher willing to listen but quickly losing his patience. "Paco, Christian didn't tell you about Manny until when? Until he lost his finger?"

Paco blinked. He lowered his eyes to his bleeding hand, and then glanced at his friend. Slowly, he met Carver's eyes and gave an apprehensive nod.

"You need to be quiet," warned the other man.

Carver shook his head. "I think you're confused. Being quiet is the opposite of what we're doing today." Carver drew the Sig Sauer P320 from its holster and draped it over one knee. "I thought I made myself clear. If you talk, you live. You know how opposites work, right?"

The pessimist gulped.

Carver went back to building a rapport. "Manny's a prisoner of the cartel. He's not part of the business, but he knows about it, knows who his family is. Maybe he figures if they hadn't killed him yet, he was protected. Maybe he runs his mouth, talks back one too many times..."

He didn't mention that his advances against the cartel were the likely cause of what happened next. Shaw wandered back to them with his rifle slung across his chest, duties complete.

Carver continued. "Long story short, the cartel was angry with Manuel. They punished him by taking his finger. Except that wasn't part of the plan, so maybe Christian needed a backup plan. He apprises his security team of the situation, *just in case*. Am I in the ballpark?"

Both captives were silent.

"Look, I have the money now. Ask yourself what Christian needs more, to hold on to his brother, or to get his money back. Heck, you'd be doing him a favor by telling me, if you think about it. Two birds with one stone."

Paco nodded. Any logic where he lived was fine by him. "We know where he is."

"Paco, you idiot, shut the fu—"

Carver put a bullet between the pessimist's eyes. Paco jumped as his friend's head bounced against the wall and left an ugly smear.

"That takes care of our problem," said Carver matter-of-factly.

"Told you I didn't like that guy," gloated Shaw.

"When you're right, you're right."

"Please don't kill me!" begged Paco, tears welling in his eyes.

"Hey," tempered Carver. "Hey now. The bad part's over. I think we can put this away." He flashed the pistol and then holstered it.

"You're gonna kill me too," Paco whined.

Carver shook his head. "No. That was nothing personal, Paco. Neither was anything you did. You were paid to protect the money, you took shots at us when we made a move on it. I get it."

He sniffled, taking shallow breaths. "You're not going to kill me?"

"We don't need to kill you. Lead us to Manuel and the only other people eating bullets work for New Generation. I'll let you go. You have my word."

Paco's breathing slowed. He stared at Carver, unnerved by his captor but intentionally avoiding sight of the splattered brains two feet away. He swallowed and mustered the willpower to nod.

24

"That's it?" asked Paco. "I can go?"

They were outside the stash house. It was an unremarkable single-story home in a poor neighborhood that likely was ignored by police. Paco had upheld his end of the bargain.

Carver nodded. "Run that way. Don't stop. Don't look back. You got it?"

The man nodded nervously. Carver had destroyed his phone so he wasn't an immediate worry. He hesitated. Carver glared and he got the point. Paco bolted down the street. A block away and he was still running. Carver turned to the operation at hand.

There were no visible lookouts covering the street, but they had observed one narco leave the property with a gun in his belt. Ideally, an op like this would wait till nightfall, but it would only be so long until New Generation realized their money was missing. The time to move was now. It didn't hurt that one of the narcos had temporarily stepped out.

Carver led Morgan and Shaw in a huddled line, staying low and jogging forward. The tight grouping lowered the visibility of their approach. Failure only took one stray glance out the window. As they advanced, a woman in the house next door opened up and stepped onto the porch. Shaw waved her inside and she wordlessly retreated.

They hit the property line and banked along the hedges to the side of the house. The front door would be most heavily guarded. It was best to go in hot and heavy, all at once with overwhelming force, and from a direction intruders were least expected.

The three of them ducked lower as they passed the windows, their steady advance bringing them to the back patio. It was a small space with a barren vegetable garden and a cracked outer step. Smoke rolled off meat sizzling on a charcoal grill. A narco with his back to them busily flipped chicken drumsticks. His pistol was on the table beside a bottle of Corona.

Carver gave Shaw a hand signal that ended with a horizontal slash. Shaw touched Carver's shoulder and advanced. As Carver covered the narco, Shaw drew a knife and came up behind him. He smothered his mouth and buried the blade into the side of his neck. Then he punched forward, ripping the trachea apart. Arterial spray hissed on the hot grill as Shaw lowered his victim to the ground.

The medium-sized back window had its curtains half drawn. The glare of the sun prevented deep inspection so they had to hurry. Carver opened the back door and stepped inside.

A narco shut the fridge and stared, dumbfounded, with a beer in his hand. Carver put two bullets in his heart and pressed forward. Morgan, following, popped his skull.

Two doorways led out of the kitchen. Carver took the first on the right, spinning to an empty dining room. Morgan and Shaw advanced to the larger living room, and all hell broke loose.

They dropped low and opened fire as a shotgun blast went high. A pistol joined the chorus, putting a hole through the wall next to Carver. He ducked and ran perpendicular across the vacant dining room, hitting the central hallway with the front door at the end. As he swiveled, a narco retreated from the living room, holding his pistol sideways and firing blindly. He ran right into Carver's line of fire and was summarily dispatched.

Carver advanced to the living room entry opposite Morgan and Shaw. A man filled with holes was sprawled backward across the couch, shotgun in his grip. Another narco had attempted to take cover behind a bookcase but hadn't made it.

"Bedrooms," said Carver.

He turned the corner in the hallway. The bathroom was empty. An open closet housed washing machines. At the end of the passage, two opposing doors were shut. Shaw came up beside Carver and they breached at the same time.

Manuel Espinoza was alone in the room at the back of the house, bound to a heavy bedpost and propped up on two pillows. The bedroom was dim, with cardboard taped over the windows. The unmistakable scent of urine was overpowering.

"Clear," called Shaw from the opposite room.

Carver checked the closet. "Clear." He let his rifle go slack and drew his foldable police blade, springing open the belt-cutter and putting it to the thick nylon bindings. "Manuel? My name's Vince. I'm taking you home."

The boy was groggy. He didn't at all look like the beaming optimistic kid from the pictures, but it was him. He blinked warily as Carver freed his wrists, taking special care to check the meager bandaging on his hand. Aside from that and a black eye, the kid didn't appear to have further injuries.

"Is this real?" he asked sheepishly.

"It's real. Your father hired me. Let's get you out of here."

Carver hefted the young man to his feet.

There was no reason to wait around. They made a beeline to the front door and hit sunlight. Halfway across the yard, a car slowed in the road. It was the beat-up junker that belonged to the narco who had left the house. One look at them and he peeled out. Shaw raised his M4 and fired three times, shattering the rear windshield of the speeding car.

"Forget it," said Carver, hustling to the truck.

Engine screaming down the block, the narco was too far to recklessly shoot at now. He didn't matter anyway. They had what they'd come for.

* * *

"You tried to escape?" asked Carver incredulously.

They were driving back toward the city center, Morgan riding with Shaw in the Ranger and Manuel in Carver's passenger seat recounting his exploits. His energy was increasing by the minute.

"I almost did. I was on the front step when they dragged me back. They knocked me around a little, but I fought back. That's when they went crazy." He presented his bandaged hand in explanation.

Carver couldn't hide his relief.

"What is it?" asked Manny.

So he was not only brave, but observant too.

"It's nothing. I just thought maybe they did that to send me a message. I was looking for you and..."

"Don't worry about it," hurried Manny. "Everything that happened, it was my fault. You're the one who saved me. Those guys were animals. They were going to kill me. I know it."

Carver cocked his head, unsure what to do with the enthusiastic compliment.

"Come on," urged Manny, flashing a wide smile that creased his eyes. "Lighten up. That was amazing back there."

Carver allowed himself a grin. "You got it, kid."

He had seen that look of elation before on freed prisoners. Carver wasn't a stranger to hostage situations, and similar feelings affected rescue teams too. It was an explosion of satisfaction once everything you've worked for served a purpose, once that purpose was fulfilled. Watching

The Service of Wolves

how quickly Manny regained his composure was encouraging.

Carver dialed Alma and put her on speaker.

"Good news," he reported.

"Did you find out what happened to Manolito?" she asked tentatively.

"Did better than that..."

"What? What do you mean?" A sliver of apprehension edged into her voice.

Carver prodded Manny's shoulder. "He rescued me!" he exclaimed.

"Dios mío!" she cried.

Alma went into a rampage of fast-flowing Spanish that was impossible to keep up with. After exchanging their immediate sentiments, she switched back to English.

"I'm sure you're on your way to see Jasmine. She'll be so excited."

"*I'm* so excited," he corrected. "I don't even know what to say to her. I screwed everything up."

"Don't think that way. And don't worry about what to say to that girl. She'll have enough to say for both of you. You hear me? You spend some quality time with her. She suffered without you. We all did. But promise I'll see you tonight?"

"Of course, Alma... But just you. I don't want to see Christian just yet."

She waited a beat, and her voice came back sober. "Is it true then, Mr. Carver?" she asked, switching to formalities. "Did my brother kidnap Manolito?"

"I'm afraid so," he answered. "A plot with the cartel. The *Sólido* crew confirmed it."

"But I'm okay now," tempered Manny.

Her tongue clicked. "But your finger..."

"Don't worry, Alma. I learned my lesson. I'll get over this."

"You'll do more than that. You'll thrive. I guarantee it."

After the call ended and they neared their destination, Manny's smile widened. Despite his nerves, his optimism was creeping in and he was on his way to a full recovery.

"Your sister had a point," broached Carver. "And so did you. You should spend a little more time on your life and a little less on your family's."

The kid set his jaw. He was bright and had a promising future, but his advantages also encumbered him.

"You might think it's stupid," he explained, "but I really do believe that my father's better than *Nueva Generación* and the other cartels. He does an ugly thing, but I'm a good influence on him. It was me that made him promise not to use fentanyl. The lives saved by that alone make this worth it." He nodded to his missing finger. "My words can make things better, just like my hands do at the clinic."

"That's noble."

"And it's stupid."

Carver snickered. There wasn't much to say to the truth.

"Jasmine thinks like you," said Manny.

"She cares about you."

"I wonder if she'll forgive me." He stared out the window sullenly.

The Service of Wolves

It seemed out of character to lose faith in her, but Manny had been through a traumatic experience. These things took time. After a moment of silence, Carver said, "Jasmine told me about something her mother used to say. If you go out with wolves, they'll teach you to howl."

He'd expected the kid to laugh it off as an innocent memory, but he stared at his bandaged hand solemnly, taking the words at face value. Maybe this was the first time he really heard them.

"I know I'm playing with fire," he confessed, "but the streets of Tijuana are a hellscape. We're surrounded by fire no matter what we do."

"That's a little nihilistic, isn't it?"

"Actually, it's what motivates me to do something. The wolves are closing in, Vince. Is it better to let them run wild or train them into dogs?"

The sentiment wasn't new to Carver, but it was surprising coming from the boy. Manny was clearly conflicted about his place in the world, about his family, but he spoke about it cogently, with open eyes. He wasn't as naive as Carver had initially imagined.

His phone buzzed. It was Christian, of all people. Carver frowned and let it buzz again. "You're not a kid anymore, Manny," he said, "so I won't treat you like one. You want open eyes, you want to barter with wolves, then you should hear this."

He clicked his phone to speaker.

"You have my money?" seethed the oldest Espinoza son.

"I have a little more than that, Christian. I raided the

New Generation stash house. I recovered your little brother. He's safe, by the way."

"*Puta madre*, are you trying to get me killed? That money belongs to Esteban Gallo. So did the men you must have killed."

Carver bristled. "And what about Manny? Just a casualty in all this?"

"I didn't want that," he swore. "Like it or not, he's family."

Manny pressed his lips tight as he listened.

"Right," continued Carver with skepticism. "Just like you didn't want Ignacio to get hurt by his car exploding."

"*Pendejo!* I suppose everything's my fault now. You blame me for the economy too? For all the citizens of your country who would buy drugs no matter who sells them?"

"Don't give me the innocent act."

"I want my money, Mr. Carver. Don't presume that I have nothing left to trade. I know you've been talking to that bitch speaking into my brother's ear, speaking against the family. What's her name? Jasmine? You want me to pick her up?"

"*Hermano!*" yelled Manny.

Christian panted over the line. "Manolo. How long have you been listening?"

"What are you saying?" lamented the young man. "You would hurt Jasmine now?"

"*Hermano*, I... This is business."

"Jasmine has nothing to do with your business!" he screamed, red-faced. "Neither do I. You know that."

Christian's voice was icy. "You were going against the family."

"YOU were going against the family!"

The elder brother snarled. "I'm working for all of us, you ingrate. Watch and learn, little brother. This is how business is done. This is how respect is earned."

They were almost at the clinic and Manny was getting worked up. Before the shouting match got worse, Carver took the phone off speaker and put it to his ear.

"No more abductions, Christian," he warned. "I went through all this to save Manny, and I'll do it for Jasmine too. You don't want me hanging over your head."

He grumbled. "You have my money."

"I don't care about the drug money. The only reason I took it was to get Manny back. I'll hand it over if you leave them alone."

The line was dead a moment. "Just like that?"

"Just like that," said Carver. "I'll drop the bags off at your place. But I don't want to see any guns, do you hear me? If I see a single weapon, I bail."

Christian cleared his throat. "Fine."

"You take a shot at me, your money's gone forever."

"I don't care about you, Mr. Carver. My father hired you to do a job, and I must say you excelled at it. Give me my money, get out of my city, and we have no further quarrel."

"And you'll leave Manny and Jasmine out of this for good."

"I would like nothing more. You have my word."

"Then it's a deal."

"Good. I'll expect you within the hour." He hung up.

The next minute was filled with silence until Carver pulled to the curb outside the clinic and shifted to park. Manny's optimism had faded again.

"You sure you're gonna do this?" he asked hesitantly. "I don't mean any disrespect, but that must be a lot of money."

"I already made a lot of money. I'm doing this because it needs to be done. Your brother's only allegiance is to himself. You heard proof of that."

His head fell. "I know. He'll never stop. I thought I was saving him from the cartel, but he's just as bad as they are."

It was a hell of a thing. Even when it came to endless disappointment, family could surprise you.

"Hey," said Carver, giving the kid an upbeat nudge. "This is no time to be down. Look." He pointed past Manny's window.

Jasmine wandered the sidewalk wearing scrubs, spinning slowly as she scanned the area. Her gaze locked onto Manny through the open window and she froze, overcome by sudden emotion. A huge smile sprouted on her face and she broke into a sprint toward the Bronco.

Carver smiled inwardly as Manny vacated his seat. The kid made it ten feet before they collided and embraced. He spun her around, they kissed, and they both excitedly talked over each other. So much for not knowing what to say.

Carver took his time getting out of the truck and circling to Manny's door so he could close it. He leaned against the hood and felt the sun on his face. For the first time today, the warmth was invigorating.

Manny and Jasmine traded promises while staring deeply into each other's eyes. They laughed a lot and cried a little. Mostly they held on to each other so tight that Carver believed even the cartels would have trouble prying them apart. It was a nice thought, but he realized such sentiments required action behind the scenes.

Jasmine and Manny seemed to notice him, finally. She rubbed Manny's chest and split away to meet Carver at his truck. Her smile was shy now, with dimples that beat her man's by a mile, and she twirled her thick black hair in her fingers.

"I can't thank you enough, Mr. Carver."

"Forget about me."

She grinned. "It's not so easy to forget. Remembering the bad times helps us appreciate the good."

"I can't argue with that."

Her lips twisted and she looked down.

"Go on," he said. "Get out of here."

Her eyes met his and he noticed the mischief too late. Jasmine lunged onto him, her short figure climbing up to plant a proper kiss on his cheek. When he set her back on her feet, she said, "Take my love with you, and give it to someone who deserves it."

Carver bit down and nodded. "You keep that young man out of trouble. He needs your advice just like his dad needs his."

Manny stepped beside her and offered Carver his hand. It was a confident shake that came from the type of guy who had a plan.

"I guess I won't see you again," he said.

"Not if you're lucky."

He broke off the handshake and grabbed Carver in a hug.

"Good luck with her, kid. It looks like you'll need it."

Manny laughed, and Carver returned to his truck and left them behind.

It had been a successful op, all things considered. There were a few hours of daylight left. Maybe they could make it to that pool in San Diego again. This time Carver might even get in.

His phone broke him from his thoughts. It was Christian again. One last nagging item. Carver rolled his eyes and answered the phone.

"If I said I'm on my way, I'm on my way. I'm not going to stiff you."

In stark contrast to his previous anger, Christian laughed, heartily and deeply. "That is good to hear, Mr. Carver. But... just in case you start letting the whispers get to you, that it would be easier to leave with my money... I wanted to give you extra motivation to return what is mine."

"What are you talking about?" Carver asked, annoyed.

"Alma is just arriving in my driveway as we speak. She must be in town for some reason... Any guesses why?"

Carver was silent.

Christian laughed again, this time with more menace. "I know you're fucking her, *gringo*. You think you can come into our family home and have your way with us? Take our money, bed my sister, disrespect me?"

The Service of Wolves

"Christian..."

"I know your type," he spat. "You're a bleeding heart. It's like you said, look how hard you fought for Manuel. And you have a thing for my sister. How far would you go for her?"

"You wouldn't like the surprise."

"I'll make this simple for you. If you don't show up, soon, she dies."

"This isn't necessary."

"I totally agree. Return my money and she can fuck whoever she wants."

Carver ground his teeth to hold back what he really wanted to say. "No guns," he warned.

"Oh, I know—"

Carver ended the call. He snarled and tried Alma's phone. There was no answer. He sped up and called again.

"Vince, I'm busy right— Hey!"

There were sounds of a struggle. Men gave clipped orders.

"What are you do— That's mine! HEY!"

The call went dead. Carver tried calling back, but it went straight to voicemail. *Sólido Seguridad* had Alma.

Carver slammed his fist into the dashboard.

25

Slow is smooth and smooth is fast. Carver didn't arrive at Christian's house as immediately as he would have liked, but having a tactical plan trumped unbridled speed nine days out of ten. The Bronco climbed the gentle slope of the *Cumbres de Juárez* road until he arrived alone at the end of the cul-de-sac.

As he neared the imposing ten-foot wall and iron gate of Christian's property, two personnel vehicles pulled across the street behind him. Carver passed the gate and looped his truck around, but troops in gray camo and black tactical gear took up positions in his path. The National Guard was in the neighborhood, and they had sealed off his only escape route.

So much for not bringing guns. Carver reached for the Sig under his seat and placed it in his shoulder holster. His bullpup was on the floor in the back, but he decided against going for it.

The automatic gate spurred to life, its solid black mass sliding to reveal Tijuana police in the yard. Local squad cars joined state police and a black transport van. Officers watched him like hawks, each of them armed. Instead of

The Service of Wolves

advancing on him, they waved him in.

Carver worked his jaw. There was nothing to do but stick to the plan. Going against every survival instinct he had, he pulled the Bronco into the driveway and parked. He grabbed the thick loop of rope from the passenger seat, hooked it over a shoulder, and stepped out of the truck, relieved to see the iron gate remained open.

Special police closed in. They spun him against the truck and patted him down, quickly finding and confiscating his pistol. They took both of his knives and, noting the metal hook hanging over his shoulder, took the rope too.

"I need that," he said.

They ignored him while they searched the Bronco, taking the X95 out of the picture as well.

Carver sighed and glanced over the scene. The special police busily moved around the property. A few police officers chatted. One took notes into his phone.

"No está aquí," reported one guard after failing to locate the money bags.

"They're not there," announced Carver somewhat redundantly.

They sneered and spat and double-checked the truck to make sure.

"Christian's expecting me," he continued. "If he wants his money, he needs to talk to me first."

They engaged in a clipped conversation that ended just as quickly as it had started. They grabbed Carver by the shoulder and said, "Let's go." Then they led him toward the house.

A pair of special police exited onto the porch leading a member of the residential security team outside in handcuffs. They passed wordlessly, and Carver craned his neck as he followed the increasingly confusing scene. The contractor was loaded into the prisoner transport along with other members of *Sólido Seguridad*.

"What's going on here?" he asked.

They shoved him into the house. Carver didn't appreciate being manhandled so he continued the brisk pace, opting for a looser escort in case he needed to attempt an escape. He reminded himself that he was here to do business. That was the language of these people. They marched past the curious eyes of local cops. The living room was empty, but the sliding glass door on its far wall was open wide. Alma was outside, surrounded by police. Carver was glad to see her and picked up his pace, walking along the concrete patio, down the steps onto the lush span of grass, and rounding the stonework that edged the pool.

The hardscaped backyard platform that cantilevered over the edge of the hill was nicer than most resorts. Shaded palms and other potted greenery lined the glass balcony wall. An oval hot tub was built as the central feature within the large pool, with a stepstone bridge leading to its crystalline blue water, but all the stonework in the world couldn't draw the eye away from the facedown floating body of Christian Espinoza. He was in the half of the pool near Alma where the crimson water looked decidedly less refreshing.

Carver stopped in his tracks. Uniformed guardsmen

watched on. Gonzalo, weirdly, was standing around too.

"What is this?" Carver asked.

Alma shrugged her shoulders. "The new reality, Vince."

It seemed significant that none of the local city or state officers were in the backyard. "These are your father's special police."

"They're mine," she returned.

"How'd you manage that?"

Her lips folded into a coy grin. "I happen to have a recording of *Papá* discussing terms with a known cartel leader who is in custody and will soon confess to his many crimes."

"What about the crimes the special police have committed?"

He received a few glares from the guardsmen as well as a waning smile from Alma. "It's in their interest to keep this quiet. They understand who's running things now."

"You pushed your father out."

"That's right, Vince. I now have the full authority of the family."

Damn it all. He'd come here to save her. Now his life was at risk for what? Family politics?

He nodded toward Gonzalo. "Why isn't he in cuffs in the back of the van too?"

The bodyguard chortled. "What can I say? Alma and I got close over the last week I was assigned to the ranch house."

Carver blinked calmly. "You mean she used you for information."

"Screw you." Gonzalo's eyes flicked to Alma before returning to Carver. "We kept things professional until after this mess was over."

Carver snorted in amusement. "In other words, she wouldn't sleep with you, but your groveling dumbass went along with it like a donkey chasing a carrot."

His face reddened. "You piece of shit. I should—"

"You should what? Come at me again?"

Gonzalo froze mid step. He scowled and reached for the gun at his waist.

"Leave it alone, Gonzalo," said Alma.

His hand stopped over the weapon. "You saw him disrespect me," he whined. "And back at the house—"

"I said leave it alone."

Gonzalo gave Carver a deadly stare before relaxing his hand.

"Thank you." Alma took a breath and clapped her hands together. "You too, Vince. I know you came here to save me."

"I guess you had that covered, huh?"

"But I will need my money now."

He swallowed down his distaste. "Are you doing deals with New Generation too?"

"*Dios*, no. They lost their income fair and square. I am under no obligation to pay back any spoils of war. I wasn't even the one who stole it. But I do need it to pay the commissioner and his National Guard. The family's blessing gives me access to their services, but I would like more than loyalty. I want devotion."

Carver eyed the commissioner. The guardsmen were equipped with matte-black helmets; he was the only one with a flat-topped patrol cap, white and gray splotches matching the uniform. He was a stern man with a pointed mustache. All around the yard were elite troops outfitted with tac vests and FX-05 Mexican assault rifles, men who followed his orders. Every one, bought and paid for.

Carver scoffed. "How do you think New Generation will respond to this?"

Alma uncaringly hiked a shoulder. "They took a hit, but the cartels are resilient. They'll fight amongst themselves for a while before figuring out that I'm a force to be reckoned with." She spoke as their equal, as accustomed to the push and pull of power as the most hardened drug lord.

"You can't beat them," said Carver.

"I don't intend to. We'll learn to coexist." Alma stepped close to him, some of her past warmth returning. "And I will continue to strive toward the ideals of my little Manolito. You'll never understand how much I thank you for saving him. I will forever say, without a shred of irony or deceit, that he is truly the best of us."

Carver studied Christian's body in the water. He was face down with no visible exit wounds. The cuffs of his white shirt were soaked with crimson water.

"This was your way of ensuring that Manny thrived," he said grimly.

"Is there any better guarantee?"

Carver shook his head. The kid no longer had wolves at his heels, but their howling was louder than ever. Alma had asserted that Christian was in over his head, but Carver hadn't for a second figured his biggest threat was from her. In that moment, he wondered at the depths of Alma's plotting.

"Ignacio was cool and careful," he realized, "until the car bomb almost got him."

Christian had denied attempting to kill his father, and Carver's eyes now focused on Alma.

"You were watching from the window. You never intended to kill him. You were going to call him back with some last-second business and blow it up. Not only did you take his trusted longtime bodyguard out of play, you scared him into overreacting. Ignacio talked to Esteban on a call you recorded. You needed your father out of the way so you set him up."

The woman was as shrewd as advertised. Alma was definitely cut from a politician's cloth.

"I did what I had to do, Vince."

"Was this the plan from the start?"

She chewed her painted lip and stepped close. "I was always going to take over one day, but it wasn't supposed to happen like this. I was forced into action when *Papá* cut and run on family."

He gave a single nod. "Once he abandoned Manny, he was fair game."

"Look on the bright side, my love. You may have been working for a drug dealer, but you saved a good person. I never lied about him being the only light in my life. Or that he was a light in Tijuana. Christian never saw that. *Papá* did, of course, but he didn't know how to protect him. You know I speak the truth when I say I will *never* allow Manolito to be involved in this part of the family. That's my promise to you, for what you did."

Even now, with all the cards on the table, Alma knew how to express her value. She knew how to deal. If not to make an arrangement happy, then to at least make it tolerable.

"But enough talk," she said, her tone dropping to match the severity of the subject. "I'll say again, Vince. I need my money."

Carver considered the yard and figured a deal was a deal. "I'm going to need my rope back."

She arched an eyebrow. "Your rope?"

"Obviously you didn't expect me to walk in alone with two duffel bags of cash."

She pressed her lips together, amused. "Not your style."

He gave her a pleasing smile. "My rope?"

She called out in Spanish and one of the guardsman went into the house. He returned with the grappling hook. Alma nodded and he handed it to Carver. His possession of it set the nearby soldiers on edge, like he just might swing it around and gash some of them open. Instead he casually strode to the balcony and lowered the hook over the edge. At the bottom of the steep slope was a residential street. The distance was dotted with several other hills like this one. The commissioner converged on Carver and peeked over.

"I have a contact with the money on the side of the hill,"

he explained. Carver had always known this confrontation would lead outside because this was where the money was. It was what protected him.

The commissioner barked some orders. Two guardsman approached the wall and aimed rifles downward. Another pair rushed back to the house.

"Stop!" snapped Carver, jarring the men enough that they momentarily paused. "If my associate is threatened, the money goes up in flames. If you send anyone around to get it, same thing." He looked at Alma. "The deal was no guns. Nobody leaves this patio."

She frowned, one hand crossed over her chest, propping up her elbow as her red nails tapped her chin. She told the police to stand down. The commissioner repeated the order. The men at the wall stepped back and held their guns low, and the others returned to the pool.

Satisfied, Carver resumed lowering the rope. Once it touched down on dried brush at the base of a concrete support column, he whistled. Still high up the hillside, Morgan appeared from under the house and looked up. He flashed the OK signal and she hooked up a duffel bag and tugged twice. Carver heaved it up and set the bag on the floor.

The commissioner knelt down and unzipped it, eyes widening at the riches.

"Christian said there were two," noted Alma.

"Coming right up."

Carver and Morgan repeated the process and handed over the second bag. While the money was being counted,

The Service of Wolves

Carver moved toward the house, meeting Alma's eyes as he passed her. Everyone was distracted enough with the payday that they didn't notice him retreating until he hit the grass between the porch and the pool, everybody outside at his back.

"He's leaving," warned Gonzalo.

Shuffling footsteps began to follow and Carver spun around.

"Are you going to kill me now?"

Alma snorted as she tried not to laugh. It would have been cute in other circumstances. "Vince, I know *Papá* threatened to have you killed. I would never be so crass." She made a show of glancing at the soldiers in the yard. "Isn't it enough for us to look around and understand what could have happened?"

Gonzalo moved aggressively to Carver's flank. "Maybe I should kill him for you." He wisely didn't close the last ten feet between them.

Carver scoffed. "Do you really think that's your call, tough guy?"

The bodyguard sneered, hand inching to his pistol. "You think you can stop me?"

Alma watched Carver's reaction carefully, pleased when his attention turned back to her. "I'm happy to see you recognize power," she said. "*I* am the arbiter of what happens here." She put her pinkie to her lips. "But... you are a good person, Vince. I was sincere about that too. You came through for us in a big way." Her eyes flashed. "Came through for me. In fact, you went above and beyond. If you check the bank account you gave *Papá*, you'll find I paid out a bonus."

He chortled. "You can't buy me off, Alma."

"No?"

"No. But lucky for you, I'm not DEA. I have no intention of taking you down."

She returned an amused smile. "So I'm the lucky one?"

He didn't know what to say to that.

"It's not a bribe," she explained, "it's the recovery fee you were promised. It's not a fraction of what's in those bags, but it's honest money, just like you."

"You're not gonna kill him?" seethed Gonzalo.

"He did nothing to deserve it," she told him. "Commissioner, make sure Mr. Carver leaves Tijuana."

Carver took a step into her, knowing it was dumb to press but unable to help himself all the same. "Sending me away without one last dance, then?"

As Gonzalo grumbled, she gave Carver a genuine grin and tapped his chest. "You are very sure of yourself, Vince. And, to your credit, you are a very good dancer." Her eyes twinkled. "But I am a businesswoman, and our business is concluded."

She stood on her tiptoes and kissed his lips. Gonzalo glowered at the sign of affection. He had seen a taste of what he couldn't have.

The commissioner put his hand on Carver's shoulder to hurry him along. Carver brushed him away and stared knives at him. "Touch me again and neither that badge nor that gun will protect you."

The Service of Wolves

The commissioner's face hardened. He turned to Alma, and she shrugged it off with an eye roll. Her contractor was dramatic, she seemed to say. But her money was good and the commissioner took a step back and avoided further eye contact.

Carver backed away. He had to hand it to Alma. For all her scheming, she had been straight with him. That was an attractive quality, and she had many. But it was still a shame to see her so consumed by power. He figured there was nothing to do except to let wolves be wolves.

"With this gringo?" spewed a red-faced Gonzalo. He'd seen the kiss, he'd realized they'd slept together, and it was freaking him out. "Are you kidding me?"

"Leave it alone, Gonzalo," said Alma.

"Fuck that! Ain't no way he's getting away with this!"

Before the police could react, Gonzalo drew his pistol and stepped toward Carver. He raised the gun and his head exploded. Everybody but Carver collapsed to the ground. Gore chunked to the concrete. Gonzalo toppled over. Heads swiveled to the distance as the crack of a rifle cut through the sky and a red mist faded on the breeze.

Carver stood over a team of cowering special police. Alma was shaking on her knees, eyes wide as she rubbed blood spatter from her cheek.

"You still feel like the arbiter of what happens here?" he asked.

"Please, Vince," she pleaded, harried. "Gonzalo was an idiot. He acted on his own. I wasn't going to kill you."

The sight of her cowering at his feet was a little too

much, even for him. He took a knee beside her, leaned close, and softened his voice. "I know that, but isn't it enough for us to look around and understand what could have happened?"

She blinked repeatedly, still in shock. Which was just as well. Shaw was a crack shot with the Mk 11 Sniper Weapon System, even from a distant hill. Carver was surrounded by an army of sorts, yet nobody dared move. He glanced over the team of special police, gaze lingering on the commissioner who had no further fight in his eyes. Carver looked one last time at Alma and decided he had nothing else to say. A single 7.62mm NATO round traveling at three thousand feet per second had said enough.

On his way through the house, he played out fantasies of taking out every narco and cartel in Mexico. If he could do it, he would. He and his team would get pretty far too, he'd wager. But abolishing human nature was a losing proposition from conception.

There would always be wolves.

Everything considered, Alma Espinoza was a known quantity. She blessed the noble goals of her little brother, she had kept her end of their deal, and she didn't want him dead. As far as devils he knew, Tijuana could do a hell of a lot worse than her.

The front gate was still open. Carver climbed into his bullet-ridden Bronco, drove past the police perimeter without an escort, and sent his team the all clear.

Afterword

Another Vince Carver thriller on the books!

This go around I aimed to write a more grounded story where, instead of focusing on the cruelty of anonymous cartels, much of the intrigue centers on a single powerful-but-relatable family, their secrets, and Carver's slow peeling of that onion.

The Service of Wolves is just one take of many on a very serious problem in America's backyard. The situation is almost unfixable, and I tried to get that across while also giving Carver a solid win we can be proud of. If nothing else, this book is a spotlight on the evolving realities of a country constantly at war with itself.

So let's talk about that evolution...

Mexico is and has always been a gateway into the United States. Pablo Escobar and other cartels took advantage of that gateway until the criminals in Mexico realized they were in possession of the higher-worth asset. Product is only valuable given ready consumers. It turned out that Mexico could create their own product but Colombia couldn't make their own consumers.

But agriculture is, ultimately, an intensive pursuit. Just as cocaine changed the marijuana game, chemistry further ushered in the third and fourth waves of the opioid era: synthetics.

No longer are fields of cocas or poppies necessary. Cheap chemical precursors are bought from China, shipped to South American ports that are less regulated than their Mexican counterparts, and then smuggled north to be processed, packaged, and made ready for consumers.

Of course, the gateways like San Ysidro are valuable, and everybody wants a piece.

The cartel wars put a heavy strain on the rule of law. Police funding and training through the Merida Initiative failed to tackle corruption. In 2006, the military was deployed for civilian policing, and the next decade and a half were characterized by widespread human rights violations, including extrajudicial killing, kidnapping, and torture.

Imagine being detained, taken to a military base, and possibly never being seen again. Imagine the futile struggle for justice against a faceless military machine.

President Andrés Manuel López Obrador, aka AMLO, instituted a new National Guard in 2019. A new federal police force in the civilian sector, an army against corruption and the abuses of the military.

While this book was being written, just a few short months

ago, the National Guard has been transferred to military control. And their record of abuses thus far outpaces the army they replaced.

Force alone is a questionable strategic framework for long-term security. Unsurprisingly, everything comes down to economics. Enter the Bicentennial Framework for Security and the High Level Security Dialogue, efforts at bilateral solutions in the hope of improving US-Mexico collaboration. A recent review by cabinet members concluded that the talks were bearing fruit but thus far resulted in little investigative or judicial improvement.

Meanwhile, the transnational criminal organizations in Mexico are perhaps more powerful than they've ever been in history.

So goes the spin cycle of reform and corruption. Of violence and crackdown. The mad scramble for a solution that leads to further dangers, such as the rise of private security and an alarming lack of accountability among personal armies.

It's a war with constantly changing tactics attacking an intractable problem, and one that may be impossible to solve. Just like the Gallo brothers going after Ignacio Espinoza's legitimate infrastructure, the real world cartels evolve along with enforcement. They hide their drugs in ceramic tiles and household paint. They control water distribution with a heavy hand. They even dig their fingers into legitimate non-drug sectors. As if profiting from America's appetite for drugs wasn't enough, *they have also gone after our avocados.*

I've rambled enough, but I'd like to personally thank you for reading this and other Vince Carver adventures. I'm the one who records his journey, but you're the one who gives him life. It sounds backwards but it's true. Without you, Carver would be nothing more than a pointless figment.

If you enjoyed the read and have anything at all to say, including setting me straight about an error, feel free to email at matt@matt-sloane.com. Input is always welcome.

-Matt

Read Next:

Project Sundown
Vince Carver Book Four

Continue the Vince Carver series
where Matt Sloane books are sold.

Matt-Sloane.com

Be notified when new Vince Carver
thrillers are released, right to your inbox.
Sign up at the website and never miss another book.